KISSING COUSINS

MARCIA LYNN McCLURE

Published by Distractions Ink
P.O. Box 15971
Rio Rancho, NM 87174

©Copyright 2008, 20011, 2013 by M. Meyers
A.K.A. Marcia Lynn McClure
Cover Photography by ©Keith Wheatley/Dreamstime.com
Cover Design and Interior Graphics by Sandy Ann Allred/Timeless Allure

First Printed Edition: February 2011
Second Printed Edition: April 2013

McClure, Marcia Lynn, 1965—
Kissing Cousins: a novella/by Marcia Lynn McClure.

ISBN: 978-0-9827826-8-2

Library of Congress Control Number: 2011923278

Printed in the United States of America

To...
AJ, Aimes, Kay, Sandy the Elder, and Sandy the Younger...

Encouragement is the greatest motivator!
Thank you, thank you, thank you for being my little engines
that always think I can!
I love you!

CHAPTER ONE

"You've got a party of four at table five, Poppy," Whitney said. "And you're gonna need the ring."

"Oh, no! Not the ring," Poppy Amore whined. If Whitney thought Poppy was going to need the ring, then Poppy was certainly going to need the ring.

Reaching into the hostess podium, Whitney withdrew the ring and handed it to Poppy. "Sorry, girl," Whitney said, tucking a strand of blonde hair behind one ear. "But at least it looks like it will be a good tip."

Slipping the wide gold band on her left ring finger, Poppy sighed. "It better be," she said, rolling her eyes.

Poppy hated the tables requiring "the wearing of the ring," as the staff of Good Ol' Days called it. Wearing the wide wedding band usually only settled the flirtatious male customers a little. If they were going to be flirty—or downright lewd—they were going to be flirty or downright lewd whether or not their waitress was wearing a wedding band—at least in Poppy Amore's experience as a waitress.

Still, as Dean Martin crooned "On an Evening in Roma" over the restaurant sound system, Poppy drew in a deep breath and headed for table five. Sure enough, four older businessmen sat at table five, talking and laughing as they perused their menus.

Pasting on a smile, Poppy approached the table. "Good evening, gentlemen. Welcome to Good Ol' Days! I'm Poppy, and I'll be your server this evening," she said.

1

"Nice!" one of the men said, smiling and studying her from head to toe. He looked to be near fifty with thinning brown hair. Poppy had seen some very handsome forty-something men in her lifetime—this man wasn't one of them.

Poppy held her order tablet in her left hand, making certain the thick gold band on her ring finger was well on display. "May I start you out with something to drink?" Poppy asked.

"I'll take one *you*, right here next to me, honey," another man said, patting the empty chair next to him. This man had dark hair, graying at the temples, and could've been quite a handsome fifty-something if it hadn't been for his apparent cretin's personality.

Poppy smiled and shook her head as she said, "We're a bit too busy for me to sit even for a minute tonight, sir."

"I'll take a Coke," the third man said. "With lime, if you have it." This man smiled at her with understanding. He seemed a bit older than the others with a rather grandfatherly smile.

"Of course, sir," Poppy said, jotting the drink code down on her order tablet.

"Me too," the fourth man said. "Only with lemon. No lime." This man was also older, and paternal looking.

"Yes, sir," Poppy said, jotting again. "And for you gentlemen?" she asked the two men who had squandered her time in flirting instead of giving her their drink orders.

"Coke here, too. No citrus," the balding man said. "Though I'm with him—I'd rather have you," he added, pointing to the man next to him.

Poppy simply forced a false smile in his direction.

"Just give me water," the worst flirt said. "You married, honey?" he asked.

Smiling, Poppy held up her left hand and wiggled her fingers as she showed the wedding band to him.

"Well, I'm willing to work around that, if you are," he said, winking at her.

Forcing a smile and tipping her head to one side, Poppy said, "I'm not."

"Your loss," the man said, shrugging his shoulders.

"Or not," one of the other men mumbled. All four men chuckled at the obvious verbal slam.

"Any appetizers this evening, gentlemen?" Poppy asked. Inwardly she was quite rattled, as she always was whenever a table was difficult to work. Outwardly, however, she hid it well, forcing a smile and appearing as calm and accommodating as possible.

"We want an order of the fried cheese and some chips and salsa," the grandfatherly man said. "And maybe a couple more minutes."

"You bet," Poppy said. "I'll get those appetizers started for you and be right back to take your order." Nodding, she stepped sideways away from the table. Too many bad experiences had taught her what could happen if a waitress turned her back on a table, so she side-stepped away from tables instead. Especially ones with men like these sitting at them.

"I need an order of fried cheese and one of chips and salsa for table five," Poppy called to the kitchen over the order counter.

"You got it, Poppy," the head cook said.

Swaggart Moretti was, hands down, the best cook at Good Ol' Days. He was also the restaurant owner's grandson, and drop-dead gorgeous! Poppy smiled at him as he winked at her, delighted by the mussed condition of his dark hair. As always, her stomach did a little loop-the-loop as she looked at him.

Poppy had secreted a crush on Swaggart Moretti ever since she first met him her freshman year in high school. He had already graduated and was far too old for her back then—and far beyond her now. Her smile faded a bit as she thought of his girlfriend, Jennifer— a tall, gorgeous brunette—the perfect physical match to Swaggart's tall, dark, and incredibly handsome. Although Poppy had determined to give up her crush on Swaggart long ago, she still couldn't stop the giddy nervousness that always washed over her in his presence.

"Thanks," she said, adjusting her apron.

"Heard you've had to invoke the power of the ring already tonight," Swaggart said, smiling his dazzling smile.

Poppy rolled her dark brown eyes and said, "What power? Still, I guess it's working about fifty-fifty so far, and that's better than nothing."

Swaggart chuckled, his dark eyes twinkling with amusement as he said, "I'll call you for those appetizers."

"Thanks," Poppy said, brushing a stray strand of cocoa-brown hair from her cheek. She shoved her order tablet in her apron pocket and turned to the beverage fountain. Swaggart was so handsome! His presence was definitely an amenity of working at Good Ol' Days.

Poppy filled three glasses with Cokes—one with lime, one with lemon, one without either—and one glass with ice water.

"Table seven's ready, Poppy," Swaggart called. Bobby, Swaggart's cousin and one of the other cooks at Good Ol' Days, placed two heaping plates on the order counter.

"Got it, Poppy?" Bobby asked.

"Got it," Poppy said, putting the four drinks she'd just poured on a black serving tray. She would deliver table five's drinks first and then come back for seven's dinners. She smiled, thinking how much she liked the chaos of working at Good Ol' Days.

"Here you go, gentlemen," Poppy said, distributing the drinks among the four businessmen. "Your appetizers will be right out. Are you ready to order?"

"Yes," the oldest man said. "I'll have the sirloin, medium-well."

Poppy tucked the black tray under one arm. Retrieving her order tablet from her apron, she scribbled an order notation. "Would you like the loaded baked potato or the garlic mashed potato with that, sir?"

"Loaded baked," the man said. "And can I get the squash as the other vegetable?"

"You bet," Poppy said. "And what kind of dressing would you like on your salad?"

"Is your house dressing good?" he asked.

"Yes, sir. It's my personal favorite," Poppy assured him with a smile.

"Then I'll have that," the man said, folding his menu.

"And for you, sir?" Poppy said, turning to the other older man.

As he began to recite his order, Poppy glanced up to see three or four large groups of people entering by way of the restaurant's front door. Several other couples and two large groups of people were lined up outside the restaurant entrance doors. Whitney was madly taking names for seating. It looked as if the four businessmen at table five were just the beginning of a very busy evening. Still, Poppy sighed, pleased. It was always preferable to be too busy than not busy at all.

She finished taking table five's order and hurried to the order counter to pick up table seven's plates. Busy! That's what she preferred. Bing Crosby was asking "Did You Ever See a Dream Walking?" by way of the sound system, and Poppy smiled as she hummed along. She loved the atmosphere in the restaurant—the walls adorned with antiques and memorabilia from the 1940s and 1950s, the good music from the same eras. Good Ol' Days was a fun place to work—great food, great friends, great atmosphere, and great music. It was a good job, and Poppy was thankful for it.

"It's crazy tonight!" Poppy said as she returned the wedding ring to Whitney. Whitney quickly put the ring back in its hiding place in the hostess podium.

"I know! What's the deal?" Whitney said. "Richard? Party of five?" she called, marking one name off the very long list of names on the eraser board in the crook of her arm. "Did those guys tip you good?" she asked. "Was it worth the agony?"

"Twenty-five bucks," Poppy said.

"Not bad," Whitney said. Brittany appeared then, and Whitney handed her five menus just as a man, a women, and three children stepped forward.

"I'm Richard," the man said.

"Will you seat Richard and his party at table ten?" Whitney asked Brittany.

"Sure," Brittany, a cute little high-school blonde, said. "If you'll follow me," Brittany said to Richard and his party.

"I hope you're not taking a break," Whitney said to Poppy then.

"Right!" Poppy giggled, looking around at the mob of people still waiting for tables.

"Good!" Whitney said. "Because wait until you see what I had seated for you at table eight!"

Poppy rolled her eyes and held out her hand. "Give it back to me then," she said, wiggling her fingers. "But I'm not sure I should hog the ring for two tables tonight."

"Oh, you won't want the ring for this table," Whitney said, smiling. "Kathy? Party of two?"

"Really?" Poppy asked, smiling. "How hot is he?" If Whitney said Poppy didn't want the ring, then Poppy knew she didn't want the ring. The last time Whitney's eyes had twinkled like this after seating someone at one of Poppy's tables, the guy had turned out to be extremely good looking!

"Hot enough you're gonna owe me big time!" Whitney said.

"For real?" Poppy asked, giggling.

"Oh, yeah!" Whitney said. "He's got a date…but I can tell its business or something like that. So just enjoy the view. Think of it as my apology for giving you those four jerks earlier."

"Well, only two of them were real jerks," Poppy said. "But thanks for the bonus anyhow."

"You're welcome," Whitney said.

"Hi," a brunette woman asked as she approached Whitney. "I'm Kathy."

Poppy smiled at Whitney and left her to her mad seating charts. Table eight and some handsome guy was waiting, but Poppy felt the need to take a breath first.

Stepping into the restroom, Poppy studied herself in the mirror. She was a wreck! The hectic pace of a busy Friday night was beginning to show. Quickly, she tucked her white shirt more snugly into her black slacks and readjusted the rolled up sleeves. Taking the small quarter-sized jar of lip gloss out of her apron pocket, she used her right ring finger to smooth a quick application of shine on her lips and used her pinky to wipe away the small dot of old makeup at the corner of her eye. Running her fingers through her hair, she washed her hands and forced a smile. She hoped she looked presentable enough. Waiting on handsome guys was a double-edged sword—it was exhilarating and nerve-wracking at the same time. Still, it added some excitement to the job.

With a heavy sigh, Poppy left the Good Ol' Days women's room and headed for table eight.

"Oh my heck!" Brittany exclaimed in a whisper as Poppy made her way past the kitchen. "Have you been to table eight yet, Poppy?"

"No," Poppy said.

"Oh my heck!" Brittany said, clasping both hands over heart. "Take a deep breath now, 'cause after you see him…oh my heck…he is gorgeous! I wish the hostess was *my* best friend! I would've given anything to wait on this guy!"

"Okay," Poppy giggled. Brittany was so dramatic. Her theatrical reactions to things always made Poppy smile.

"No, seriously!" Brittany said. "Even you will be impressed, Poppy!"

"Okay! I'm going then," Poppy giggled. She shook her head, amused at Brittany's dramatics as she headed for table eight.

Approaching table eight from the kitchen side of the restaurant, she could see a woman facing her and a man with his back to her. The woman looked really well put together, with perfect hair and perfect makeup and wearing a white blouse and black jacket. Poppy sneered at the woman's appearance. Rings and bracelets fairly dripped from her fingers and wrists. Poppy was all too familiar with this sort of woman—a woman with the "serve me because I'm better than you" arrogance that drove her crazy. Still, from the back, the guy looked good. With dark, short hair and broad shoulders and wearing a white business shirt, he certainly seemed handsome from the back. If he was as gorgeous as Whitney and Brittany said, maybe dealing with his high and mighty companion would be worth it. Poppy determined she would address the woman first—start off on the right foot with her, before looking to see if the guy were really as hot as Whitney said.

Approaching table eight, order tablet in hand, Poppy said, "Good evening. Welcome to Good Ol' Days. My name is Poppy and…and…"

She'd messed up big time! The woman smiled and nodded at her, and then habit caused Poppy to look to the man seated to her left. The sight of him caused her thoughts to hesitate for a moment. "And

I'll be your server this evening," she managed. The man was stunning! "May I start you out with something to drink?" Poppy asked, returning her attention to the woman.

Good grief! She was a mess! Her hands were trembling, and she honestly felt a bit light-headed. The man seated across from the snooty woman at table eight was incredibly attractive! Whitney and Brittany had not overstated his appearance. As she struggled to jot down the woman's order for a Diet Coke with lime, Poppy tried to calm herself. In the next moment, she would have to face the man, and she had to regain her composure.

"And could you keep my drink fresh?" the woman was saying. "I abhor watered-down beverages."

"Sure," Poppy said, turning to face the man.

"Hi," he said, smiling at her. White teeth and well-shaped lips gave his smile a true movie-star quality. A square jaw boasting just enough five o'clock shadow to give him a male-model appeal and his dark, dark, dark eyes complemented everything else about him perfectly!

"H-hi," Poppy breathed. "And what can I get for you, sir?"

"Is your name really Poppy?" the woman asked.

"Um…yes," Poppy said, tearing her attention from the handsome male customer. "Poppy."

"Like the flower?" the woman asked.

"Yes, ma'am," Poppy said.

"How sweet," the woman said. And there it was—that all too familiar "he's with me" look in her eyes. "Are you new here?"

"No, ma'am," Poppy said, sensing the slam about to come.

"Oh," the woman said. "You seem like you're new."

"No, ma'am," Poppy said. "It's just been a really busy night and…"

"Oh, I'm sorry," the woman said to the man then. "She still needs to take your beverage order, Mark."

"Oh, yes," Poppy said, blushing and returning her attention the man. "What can I get for you, sir?"

The handsome man smiled at her again, and she had to consciously fight the urge to sigh with delight.

"I'll just have water," he said. "Thanks."

His voice was so deep, so clear and smooth. Poppy was near to giggling with nervous delight!

"Would you like to start with an appetizer?" she asked. She gasped and felt her eyes widen as it began then. "Oh, no!" she mumbled. *Not now!* she thought.

She heard Dean Martin begin to croon "That's Amore" via the restaurant's sound system. A moment later, every employee at Good Ol' Days joined every regular customer present in singing.

Poppy felt the blood rush to her head, felt her cheeks begin to burn with the heat of a deep blush.

"What's this all about?" the woman at table eight asked. It was obvious she was irritated.

As Dean continued to sing a song whose very title included Poppy's name—the patrons and employees gleefully accentuating the word *amore* each time it should be sung—Poppy said, "Oh, it's nothing."

Too late! Josh, who was bussing a table nearby, danced up to Poppy, putting an arm around her shoulders and singing in unison with seemingly everyone else.

The handsome man seated at table eight chuckled as he watched several other employees surround Poppy and join Dean Martin in singing the famous Italian love song.

The woman seated before her continued to express irritation with the sour expression on her face, while the man only leaned back in his seat and seemed to enjoy the spectacle. As for Poppy, she could've melted into puddle of humiliation. Every other day or so, when the looped music piping through the restaurant made it around to Dean Martin's rendition of "That's Amore," every employee joined the regular customers who might happen to be dining in singing to Poppy. The owner of Good Ol' Days, Mr. Dexter, had started the tradition when he'd first discovered Poppy's last name—Amore.

Most of the time Poppy just laughed and sang along too, but this time was different. She already sensed the woman sitting before her was not only possessive of her handsome date but arrogant, self-centered, and wanting every smidgen of his attention.

At last, the song ended, and everyone familiar with the tradition clapped and whistled. Poppy forced a smile and nodded as people smiled at her.

"Is it your birthday?" the handsome man at table eight asked.

"Um…no. It's my last name…Amore," Poppy explained. "It's become kind of a silly little tradition here. Every time the song plays everyone just—"

"Well, that's ridiculous," the woman mumbled. "It completely disrupted everything."

"I'm sorry," Poppy stammered. "Would you like an appetizer?"

"It's up to you," the woman said, smiling at the handsome man sitting across from her.

"I'm good," the man said. He smiled at Poppy, and she felt her knees literally weaken for a moment.

"Are you ready to order then?" Poppy asked, feeling overly hot and a little unsteady.

"Well, with all the interruptions, we haven't really had time to look at the menu," the woman said. "Come back in a few minutes. But I'd like my Diet Coke now."

"Of course," Poppy said. "I'll be right back."

As she turned to go, she heard the woman say, "I've heard this is a great place, but I'm a bit skeptical after all that."

"I thought it was fun," the handsome man said.

Poppy tried to will away her blush as she headed for the beverage area.

"Bad timing?" Swaggart chuckled as he winked at her over the order counter. Bobby chuckled with amusement.

"You have no idea," Poppy said, shaking her head.

Swaggart flashed his own bewitching, dazzling smile at her, and Poppy was somewhat recovered. If she could look a gorgeous guy like Swaggart Moretti in the eye, she could look the man at table eight in the eye—wench of a date with him or not.

Working quickly, she filled two glasses with the beverages table eight had requested. She looked at the Diet Coke to make certain it had just the right amount of ice. She'd had customers like the woman at table eight too many times to count, and she knew any little thing might be an excuse for a complaint.

As she walked toward table eight, she wondered what such a handsome and obviously polite man like the one seated there was doing with such a stuck-up woman. Maybe Whitney had been right. Maybe it was just business.

"Here you go," Poppy said, setting the Diet Coke on a coaster in front of the woman before placing the glass of water on a coaster before the man. "Do you need more time with the menu?"

"My, my," the woman said. "You are in a hurry, aren't you?"

"No, ma'am," Poppy said. "Just thought I'd ask while I was here."

"Do I look like a 'ma'am' to you, sweetie?" the woman asked. Her voice was thick with arrogance, irritation, and self-superiority.

"I-I…" Poppy stammered. She was completely caught off guard. She'd never had anyone criticize her for trying to be polite and respectful.

"*Miss*," the woman instructed. "Miss Reginald," she said. "Susan Reginald, but you'll address me as Miss Reginald."

"Um…of course, Miss Reginald," Poppy said as a large lump began to form in the back of her throat. She felt extra moisture begin to gather in her eyes but willed it to stay at bay.

"This is our first meeting together," the handsome man said to Poppy.

She looked to him and felt somewhat comforted when he winked at her, smiling with understanding. He knew he was with a wench and had made it clear he was with her for a meeting, not a date.

"I'm Mark," he said. "Mark Lawson—and I'm actually ready to order."

"Yes, sir," Poppy said. She tried to still her trembling hand as she held her pen ready to jot down the man's order on her tablet.

"I'd like the filet mignon," he said.

"H-how would you like that cooked?" Poppy stammered. She was still far too unsettled and nervous to have completely regained her composure.

"Medium-well," he said.

"And for your sides?" Poppy asked.

"What are my choices?" he asked, smiling and winking at her again.

"Loaded baked potato, garlic mashed potatoes, mixed vegetables, or you can specify a particular vegetable. Oh, and sautéed mushrooms. You may choose two, of course," Poppy said.

"Mmm! Sautéed mushrooms and garlic mashed potatoes," Mark said.

"What if he wants three vegetables?" Susan Reginald interrupted.

"That's fine. We can do whatever you prefer," Poppy said.

"Well, I want the grilled chicken breast, steamed broccoli, and carrots. Does your cook know how to properly prepare carrots? I don't want them mushy," Susan, the arrogant wench, said.

"The cook in the kitchen right now is the best in the city," Poppy answered. She couldn't help herself. She was starting to really loathe the woman at table eight.

"That's quite a statement," Susan Reginald said. "Are you willing to back that up somehow?"

"He's a professional chef and in high demand," Poppy said.

"Why then, if he's so great, is he working here?" Susan asked.

"He likes it here," Poppy answered. "He's been working here forever. It's a family business and—"

"Just finish up our orders please," Susan interrupted.

"Yes, ma'am…I mean, Miss Reginald," Poppy said. "That's one filet mignon, medium-well with…"

"No need to read it back—unless, of course, you're feeling incompetent somehow," Susan Reginald said.

"Of course not, Miss Reginald," Poppy said. Her entire body was hot with fury! What a nightmare this woman was. She glanced to Mark Lawson to see him scowling with annoyance. "I'll put your order in right now."

"Well, I can't imagine why you'd wait," the woman said.

Poppy had had enough! With a nod to the woman and smile at the handsome Mark Lawson, Poppy turned and made for the kitchen.

"You all right?" Swaggart asked, smiling.

"You would not believe the woman at table eight!" Poppy said through clenched teeth.

"Isn't that the table with the guy who has all you girls breathless with his good looks?" Swaggart chuckled.

"Yes!" Poppy admitted. "But the woman he's with is a total nightmare!"

"Really?" he asked.

Poppy leaned toward the order counter and lowered her voice. "She wanted to know if you knew how to cook carrots properly," she told him. "She, like, wanted your whole background! And she was so rude to me! I'm supposed to call her *miss*, not *ma'am*. Miss Reginald to be specific."

Swaggart shook his head, smiling with understanding. "Well, I hope the guy is worth it."

"You're making fun of me again," she said, smiling at him.

"Me? When have I ever made fun of you, Poppy?" he chuckled. "Give me their order."

"Medium-well filet mignon, garlic mashed, sautéed mushrooms, and she wants a grilled chicken breast, steamed broccoli, and perfectly, properly cooked carrots," Poppy said.

Swaggart frowned. "Do you want me to get back at her for you?"

"Yeah," Bobby said. "Maybe he could undercook her carrots or something."

"Yeah," Swaggart said. "Worse yet—I could overcook them."

Poppy rolled her eyes, and Swaggart smiled. "You can't. I told her you were the best cook in the city."

"Oh, great," Swaggart mumbled.

"Well, you are," Poppy said, smiling at him.

"It's true, man," Bobby said.

Swaggart glanced past her for a moment as he said, "Well, I think waiting on Miss Reginald might prove to be worth it…if the guy headed back here is the famous 'hot guy at table eight.'"

"What?" Poppy gasped.

"Well, he's not quite as hot as me and Bobby," Swaggart said, lowering his voice. "But he's a good third."

"Excuse me."

At the sound of his voice, Poppy's hand flew up to cover her gaping mouth. Swaggart simply raised his eyebrows and returned his attention to whatever he was cooking behind the order counter.

"Poppy? Right?"

Poppy turned to see Mark Lawson himself smiling down at her. He was tall—tall, dark, and incredibly handsome!

"Y-yeah?" Poppy stammered. "Did I forget something?" she asked.

"No," Mark said. "I just wanted to apologize for the behavior of my dinner companion. It's a business meeting and pretty awkward for me too."

"It's all right," Poppy said, smiling.

"No, it's not," Mark said. "I'm sorry. I'll try to do something to tone her down a bit. I just wanted to offer my personal apologies."

"Thank you, sir," Poppy said, smiling. How could anyone not smile at Mark Lawson? He was so gorgeous! Poppy's heart was pounding like a hammer on an anvil!

"Mark," he said, offering a hand to her. "Call me Mark."

"Okay," Poppy said, accepting his hand. He grasped her hand for a moment, sending goose bumps rippling over her arms. "I'll have your order out as soon as it's ready."

"Thank you," Mark said. "And again, I am sorry."

"It's okay," Poppy said.

Mark Lawson nodded, and Poppy released a heavy sigh as she watched him saunter back to table eight.

"Wow," Swaggart said once Mark Lawson was gone. "He *is* hot. I thought you were going to melt into a puddle right there at his feet."

Poppy turned to Swaggart, her eyes narrowing as she sneered at him. "You hush up," she said.

Swaggart chuckled and winked at her as he said, "I'll make sure his filet mignon is perfect so he'll ask for your number."

"Like a guy like that would ever ask for my number," Poppy said.

"Oh, believe me," Swaggart began, still smiling, "he's already thought about asking you for it. Trust me."

"The last time I trusted you, I ended up on Barn Door Road with a flat tire," Poppy said.

"You wanted a short cut to Whitney's house, and I told you about one. It wasn't my fault you picked up a nail," he said. "Anyway, I told you that I would've come out there and changed it for you."

"Make that a perfect filet mignon, and we'll see then, won't we?" Poppy said, smiling. She loved when Swaggart teased her. It wasn't the sort of attention she once dreamed of receiving from him, but it was attention all the same.

"You got it, Poppy-seed," Swaggart said. "And I'll bet you ten bucks he asks for your number."

"You've got a deal," Poppy giggled. "I could use ten bucks."

"Me too," Swaggart said. "I'll call you when that order is ready."

"You do that," Poppy said. "And keep your wallet handy, buddy." Swaggart chuckled, and Poppy turned, intent on checking on her tables.

Something inside her chest fluttered. Perhaps Swaggart was right—maybe the total hottie, Mark Lawson, would ask for her number! Yet she knew he wouldn't, and that made her wonder why the something inside her chest was fluttering. She wondered for a moment if it was her friendly banter with Swaggart causing the sensation or the hope that Mark Lawson really would ask for her number.

Shaking her head, she headed to table five to check on the family of four seated there. She couldn't help glancing at table eight as she went, smiling when she saw Mark Lawson glance at her and smile.

"Perfect filet mignon *is* one of your best, Swaggart Moretti. For my sake, let's hope you pull it off this time," she whispered to herself.

CHAPTER TWO

"That meal was absolutely fabulous," Mark Lawson said. Poppy smiled and filled his empty water glass with more ice water from a pitcher. "You weren't kidding about the cook here."

"No, sir. I was not," Poppy said.

"Even I'll admit the carrots were done to perfection," Miss Reginald said. "I was very pleasantly surprised. What's the cook's name?"

"Swaggart Moretti," Poppy answered, smiling at Mark as he smiled at her.

"Swaggart Moretti?" Miss Reginald said. "That's an odd name combination."

"Would you like to see a dessert menu?" Poppy asked, skirting the comment. This woman didn't deserve to even speak Swaggart's name, let alone discuss it.

"I'm fine," Mark said. "Susan?"

"I couldn't eat another bite," Miss Reginald said.

Poppy eyed her suspiciously. Experience told her that had Miss Reginald been in the company of other women, instead of a man she was trying to impress, she would've been more than willing to indulge in dessert.

"We'll just have the check then," Mark said, smiling at Poppy. Something in his smile caused her to blush all over. Oh my heck! He was *so* handsome!

"Of course," Poppy said. "I'll be right back."

"This Diet Coke needs freshening, Poppy," Miss Reginald said, stalling Poppy. "It was a bit watered down when you brought it. I need a new one."

"Yes, Miss Reginald," Poppy said, picking up the glass and heading toward the beverage fountain.

"Well?" Swaggart asked as she approached. "Did he ask for your number yet?"

"No," Poppy said, feeling entirely disappointed. "You owe me ten bucks."

"He ain't gone yet," Swaggart said.

"The filet mignon was perfect—in case you want to know," she said. "And the carrots too."

"You sound surprised," Swaggart said, flashing a dazzling smile in her direction.

Poppy mused that standing there with Swaggart Moretti on one side and Mark Lawson on the other was a lot like having peach pie in one hand and apple pie in the other—too delicious!

"Just get your wallet out, buddy," Poppy said as she turned and headed for the order computer.

Poppy printed out a receipt and returned to table eight.

"Here you go, Miss Reginald," she said, setting the fresh drink on the coaster before the woman. "And here you are, sir," she said, handing the check to Mark Lawson. "I'll be your cashier when you're ready."

"You just assume he's paying?" Miss Reginald asked. "That's a pretty sexist assumption."

"I'm sorry," Poppy said, retrieving the receipt from Mr. Lawson's hand and offering it to Miss Reginald.

"He *is* paying," the arrogant woman said. "I just thought you needed to know your assumption was inappropriate and therefore offensive to me."

Releasing a heavy sigh of irritation, Mark Lawson rather snatched the receipt from Poppy's hand. His eyes narrowed as he reached for his wallet while looking at Miss Reginald.

"Thank you, Poppy," he said, opening his wallet and removing a gold credit card. He started to hand Poppy the card but paused.

"Susan," he began, "After having spent the evening with you, I've come to a decision."

"Yes?" Miss Reginald said. A triumphant and rather seductive smile spread across her perfect-makeup face.

"Our firm won't be representing you," Mark said.

"What?" Susan exclaimed, her smile vanishing.

"We're not interested in taking on your account," he said.

"*I* came to you! This dinner is your interview, not mine!" Miss Reginald nearly growled. "I have a ten million dollar advertising account, and you're telling me you don't want it?"

"Yes," Mark said, handing Poppy his credit card. He looked to Poppy then and added, "Would you have your hostess call a taxi for Miss Reginald as well?"

"A taxi?" Miss Reginald screeched in a barely controlled whisper. For a moment, Poppy thought the woman's head might explode. She was furious!

"Y-yes, sir," Poppy said. She could feel the tension hanging in the air and did not want to be present when Miss Susan Reginald lost her snooty cool.

"You won't even have the decency to drive me home?" the woman screeched in a louder whisper as Poppy turned to leave.

"You've been a nightmare for this girl from the moment we walked in," she heard Mark say. "I won't work with someone like that."

Poppy couldn't help but smile as she ran Mark Lawson's card for $35.85. He was dishing off a ten million dollar advertising account because Miss Reginald had been rude to *her*! It was too wonderful! Of course, for a moment Poppy felt bad about his losing such a sum of money. However, in the next moment, she giggled with delight.

Once the receipt for Mark Lawson was printed, Poppy swung by the hostess podium and asked Whitney to call a taxi.

She was bit nervous about facing Miss Reginald again. Still, it was obvious Mark Lawson would champion her if the woman attacked her in any manner. So, she returned to table eight to deliver the check.

Miss Susan Reginald sat silent, but obviously infuriated. Her anger was evident by the way her plentiful bosom rose and fell with quickened breathing, the way her mouth pinched into a firm frown.

"Here you are, sir," Poppy said, handing the credit card and receipt to Mark Lawson. "Is there anything else I can do for you?"

"Oh, believe me," Miss Reginald began, "you've done enough."

"Thank you for your patience," Mark Lawson said to Poppy as he signed the receipt. He reached into his wallet and withdrew a fifty dollar bill. "And this is for your trouble tonight," he said handing the fifty to Poppy.

"Oh, no sir! I couldn't possibly…" Poppy began to argue.

"Oh, go on, honey," Miss Reginald said. "You've earned it—somehow!"

Taking hold of Poppy's hand, Mark Lawson placed the fifty dollar bill in her palm, closing her fingers over it. His touch made her entire arm tingle.

"I'm sorry for any inconvenience or distress we caused you," he said, rising from his seat and putting his wallet in his back pocket. "Did you call for a taxi?"

"Yes, sir," Poppy said. "It will be here in five minutes."

"Thanks," Mark said. He turned to Miss Reginald then. "I wish you luck in finding an advertising firm, Miss Reginald. Your taxi will be here in a few minutes."

"You're leaving me here?" Susan Reginald screeched in a whisper.

He paused and turned back to Poppy. Retrieving a business card from his shirt pocket, he handed it to Poppy. "If you ever have need of great advertising, give me a call."

"Thank you," Poppy said accepting the card.

"This is a great place," he said. "I hope I'll see you next time I'm in."

"Thanks," Poppy said. She felt her heart sink to her stomach as Mark Lawson smiled at her and headed for the front door. In another moment, he was gone.

"This is the worst restaurant I've ever been to," Miss Reginald said as she stood and gathered her purse. "With absolutely the worst service I've ever experienced!"

"You have a nice evening...*ma'am*," Poppy said.

Susan Reginald's eyes narrowed as she glared at Poppy. "He'd never think twice about someone like you," she said.

"Your taxi should be here any moment," Poppy said, tucking the fifty and Mark Lawson's business card in her apron pocket. She left Susan Reginald standing with her mouth gaping open.

"I'm taking my break," Poppy told Josh as she untied her apron.

"What a wench, huh?" Josh said, running a hand through his brown hair.

"You have no idea," Poppy said, somehow glad Josh had witnessed the incident.

With a heavy sigh, Poppy headed toward the back of the restaurant to take a much-needed break.

She loved the gardens behind the restaurant. At the height of summer, Mr. Dexter had tables and chairs set up among the trees and flowers and next to the fountain and pond. For now, however, the gardens served as a great place for the employees of Good Ol' Days to spend lunch and break times.

Poppy stepped out onto the back patio and inhaled a refreshing breath of late spring air. The sweet, romantic scent of hyacinth filled her with delight and seemed to relax her a bit.

"What a night, huh?"

Swaggart's voice startled Poppy a little, but she smiled as she looked over to see him sitting at the wrought-iron table nearby. He sat sideways in the chair leaning back against the outer wall of the restaurant.

"What a night, indeed," Poppy sighed, collapsing into the chair across from him.

"Oh, that wench at table eight did her job on me too," he said, taking a sip of ice water out of the glass in his hand. He let his head fall back against the wall and closed his eyes. "She handed a written complaint about the food to Whitney on her way to the women's room a few minutes ago."

"Are you serious?" Poppy asked. Suddenly, the drama and frustration of her own experience seemed to pale a little. "What did she complain about?"

Swaggart lifted his head and looked at her. Instantly, Poppy's stomach did a little loop-the-loop. The dark chocolate of his eyes was intent on her, his great fatigue mirrored in their warmth.

"Chicken was overdone, carrots weren't tender enough," he said. "If it was on the plate—she complained about it," he said.

"You never overcook anything," Poppy said. She was momentarily mesmerized by his pure attractiveness—the perfect angle of his squared jawline, the very masculine five o'clock shadow there, his dark eyelashes and eyebrows, straight nose, and that wonderfully mussed hair! "Never," she added as he grinned at her.

"And you never waitress a table badly," he chuckled, stretching and displaying perfectly sculpted biceps and forearms. He wore his usual work attire, worn-out jeans, basketball shoes, and a white t-shirt, which did little to hide the perfectly chiseled torso beneath.

Poppy sighed at the pure magnetism of him and looked away, out into the garden. He was too wonderful! Swaggart Moretti was not a man a girl could let her mind linger on—too unobtainable. The man at table eight was wonderful too—the way he'd stood up for her, sent that wench packing—it was pure chivalry.

"Brush it off, Poppy," Swaggart said, yawning. She smiled, realizing he was assuming she was lingering on the stuck-up woman and not the chivalry of her dinner companion. "Women like that are all about money and themselves—always looking to step on somebody because their lives are so empty." He looked at her and grinned with mischief. "Besides, she knows you caught the guy's eye."

Poppy felt herself blush, but she couldn't decide whether the blush was caused from the fact that the man at table eight had been her champion—or the fact Swaggart was giving her the time of day.

"He was really nice about it," she admitted. "He didn't even drive her home—just called her a cab."

Swaggart raised his eyebrows, impressed. "Wow! Cool."

"But you owe me ten bucks," she said.

"He didn't ask for your number?" Swaggart asked. His eyebrows arched in surprise.

"Nope. Just gave me his business card," Poppy sighed.

"That counts as the same thing," Swaggart said.

"It does not! You owe me ten bucks!" Poppy laughed.

"You mean he didn't look into your warm brown eyes and say, 'Hey, baby…can I have your number?'" he asked, gazing into her eyes with his own gorgeous ones.

"N-no," Poppy said, momentarily unsettled by his gaze. "And you owe me ten bucks."

"Hey, babe—how's your night going?"

Poppy felt the hair on the back of her neck prickle at the sound of Jennifer's voice. As Jennifer approached, Poppy looked away for an instant, somehow feeling guilty for talking to Swaggart.

Jennifer was tall, runway-model-built, with the bluest eyes and long, perfectly styled cocoa hair. Poppy glanced up to see Jennifer lean forward and firmly kiss Swaggart on the lips.

The familiar heat of jealousy washed over Poppy as she looked at them. She couldn't stand Jennifer! Swaggart deserved so much better, and she could never understand how he could settle for such a shallow, personality-challenged woman. Still, she was beautiful—the kind of woman that turned every male head in every room she walked through.

"Hey, Jen," Swaggart said, remaining seated. "What're you doing here?"

"Oh, I knew it was time for your break and thought I'd just drop in and see you," Jennifer said. She looked to Poppy. Though she couldn't understand why, Poppy always had the feeling Jennifer didn't like her. Jennifer smiled at her, but it was forced.

"Hi, Poppy," she said. "Keeping my man company awhile?"

"Just…taking my break," Poppy stammered, again feeling guilty—but for what, she didn't know. "It's been a pretty busy night."

"Has it?" Jennifer said, running her fingers through Swaggart's mussed hair. Poppy wondered then if Swaggart's hair felt as soft and wonderful as it looked. "I don't know why you choose to work this hard, babe," she said. "An office job would—"

"So how was your day?" Swaggart interrupted. Poppy knew Swaggart liked working at the restaurant and that Jennifer thought it was a waste of his business degree. Obviously, Swaggart didn't want to talk about it.

Jennifer switched subjects easily enough—as long as she was the subject.

"Oh, great! I've got this new client, and he really likes my work," she said, sitting down in the empty wrought-iron chair across from Swaggart.

Poppy knew this was her cue to leave.

"Have a good night, Jennifer," Poppy said as she stood to leave.

"You, too, Poppy," Jennifer said. Then she smiled at Swaggart and ran one hand through his hair again, adding, "Though I don't know how any girl can have a good night if she's doesn't have Swaggart to look at."

Swaggart frowned. He seemed a little irritated with Jennifer's compliments.

"Good luck, Poppy," he said. "Let's hope we've seen the last of the difficult customers tonight."

"Yeah," Poppy said as she opened the back door and went into the restaurant, leaving Swaggart with Jennifer.

The thought of them together in the garden made her feel sick to her stomach. She'd have to think of something else—get her mind off the gorgeous Good Ol' Days cook and his perfect girlfriend.

Nat King Cole's "Unforgettable" wafted through the restaurant as Poppy headed for the hostess podium.

"What a wench!" Whitney whispered to Poppy as she gathered four menus from the podium.

"No kidding," Poppy said. She knew Whitney was referring to the now-infamous Miss Reginald.

"She was so mad by the time the taxi got here, I thought her ears were going to catch fire," Whitney said. "I hope the guy was worth it."

"He was," Poppy said, thinking of the fifty dollar bill and business card in her apron pocket. Mark Lawson was gorgeous, charming, and chivalrous. Dealing with Miss Reginald had been well worth it.

"Troy, party of four?" Whitney called. Two young couples stepped forward from the waiting crowd.

"I'm Troy," one of the men said.

"Poppy will be seating you tonight," Whitney said. "At table seven," she added to Poppy.

"Will you follow me please?" Poppy said. She smiled. She'd seen these two couples before—pleasant people.

Poppy sighed and thought of Swaggart out in the gardens with Jennifer. Better to think on Mark Lawson. He said he hoped to see her again. Poppy hoped he would.

She thought of his dazzling smile as she handed the menus to the four people she'd just seated at table seven.

"He tipped you fifty bucks?" Whitney exclaimed as she and Poppy sat on the sofa in their apartment.

Poppy nodded and smiled. She was so tired! It was two a.m., and she had the midshift the next day, but she couldn't go to sleep without telling Whitney about Mark Lawson.

"And he said he hoped he'd see me next time," Poppy giggled.

"Oh my heck, Poppy! He's in love with you!" Whitney said.

Poppy laughed and said, "Whitney! He won't even remember me tomorrow."

"He'll remember," Whitney said. "Did he ask for your number?"

"No," Poppy said, sighing with disappointment. "And that reminds me, Swaggart owes me ten bucks."

"Oh! The ol' 'I'll bet you ten bucks he asks for your number' line, huh?" Whitney said, shaking her head with amusement. "Swag is so predictable. Still...I've lost a lot of tens that way. He's probably collected hundreds of dollars over the years with that gimmick."

"Well, he lost this time," Poppy said.

"What would you have done if Mr. Mark Lawson *had* asked for your number?" Whitney asked.

"Dropped dead of shock," Poppy said.

"He was so gorgeous!" Whitney sighed.

"He was," Poppy agreed.

Whitney paused and looked at her friend. There was something Poppy wasn't telling her—she knew it. She'd been Poppy Amore's best friend since kindergarten, and she could read her like a book.

"He was gorgeous...but not as gorgeous as Swaggart?" Whitney ventured.

"What's he doing with a skank like Jennifer anyway?" Poppy grumbled. Her smile traded places with a frown.

"Ah ha!" Whitney exclaimed. "Swag's as much under your skin as ever!"

"He's not," Poppy said. "I got over him years ago. But he is my friend...and I can't figure out why he wastes his time with Jennifer Trujillo. There's nothing to her."

"Nothing but long legs, a big chest, and a perfect face," Whitney said.

"You know him better than anybody, Whitney," Poppy said. "What's his deal?"

Poppy never could figure out why Swaggart Moretti gave Jennifer the time of day. She didn't have an ounce of brains in her head—she was all glamour and flattery.

Whitney shrugged her shoulders. "I don't know. Grandpa says Swaggart settles too easy for some reason. He wasn't that way when we were younger. You remember? Every year when our family would have the big reunion dinner at Good Ol' Days, Swaggart was always front and center…confident, the life of the party, and even then he was the best cook in the city. But…I don't know. It seems like—you know, after he finished culinary arts school and went to college for his business degree—somewhere in there, he changed a bit."

Poppy shook her tired head. "All I know is he owes me ten bucks," she said before yawning.

"Well, collect it from him," Whitney said, echoing Poppy's yawn. "And if he doesn't pay up, I'll have our grandpa lean on him. You're Grandpa's favorite waitress, you know. Me, Bobby, and Swaggart may be Grandpa's favorite grandchildren, but you're his favorite waitress."

Poppy smiled. She loved Mr. Dexter. He'd owned Good Ol' Days for nearly forty years. What a name he'd built for himself and his restaurant! Poppy had been overjoyed two years before when Whitney had managed to get her an interview with her grandfather. She had been stunned when he'd hired her too! Whitney had had another cousin who wanted the job, but Mr. Dexter had chosen Poppy over family. Working at Good Ol' Days had been a blast ever since.

"I'm done in," Poppy said. "I've got to get some sleep."

"Me too," Whitney said. "I'm on early tomorrow. See you at two?"

"Yeah," Poppy said, yawning again.

"Okay. Sweet dreams, Poppy Amore," Whitney said. "I hope Mr. Lawson shows up in them."

"I hope so too," Poppy said smiling.

CHAPTER THREE

Mr. Lawson had shown up in Poppy's dreams, charming, handsome, and wonderful. However, it was a nightmare that greeted her the next day. As Poppy walked into Good Ol' Days at five minutes to two, it was to see Miss Susan Reginald herself shaking an index finger at Whitney and demanding to see the manager.

"I want to see the manager this minute!" Miss Reginald said. She glanced over to see Poppy enter the restaurant then and turned to her. "There she is now. That girl—that Poppy—she's the one that waited on us last night...if you can even call it waiting. She was entirely rude, completely unprofessional, and I want to talk to someone about it right now!"

Poppy panicked! She loved her job at Good Ol' Days, and she knew Susan Reginald meant to strip her of it.

"Flirting with my date, rude behavior, you name it...if it was bad, this girl did it," Susan accused.

Poppy wanted to defend herself. In truth, she felt like reaching out and slapping the woman across the face. But she knew the rules at Good Ol' Days—let the management handle any and all complaints.

"If you'll step over here a moment, ma'am," Whitney began.

"*Miss* Reginald," Susan Reginald interrupted.

"Of course," Whitney said. "If you'll just step over here a moment, I'll get the manager on duty. He'll be right with you."

"Doesn't he have an office? Take me to his office," Miss Reginald demanded.

"The manager on duty right now is also the cook at the moment," Whitney explained.

"Oh, no!" Poppy breathed. Swaggart? When Mr. Dexter or Swaggart's Uncle Robert couldn't be at the restaurant or were out, all the managerial responsibilities fell to Swaggart!

"That's right, honey," Miss Reginald said, misinterpreting the reasons for Poppy's horrified expression. "You need to be taught a lesson, and I'm sure once the manager hears what I have to say, you will be."

"I'll be right back, Miss Reginald," Whitney said.

As Whitney started toward the kitchen, she took hold of Poppy's arm and pulled her along.

"Whit! Can't you pretend you're the manager? I don't want Swaggart to have to deal with that woman because of me," Poppy said.

"Because of you?" Whitney said, continuing toward the kitchen. "You didn't do anything! Well, other than catch the attention of the guy she was with. That's why she's ticked, you know. Swaggart will know it too. Wait until he gets of a load of her."

"Whitney!" Poppy pleaded. But it was too late.

As Whitney approached the order counter, Poppy's eyes began to fill with tears. What would the woman say Poppy had done? Would Swaggart fire her?

"Hey, Swag," Whitney began.

"What's up, ladies?" he asked, smiling.

"There's a disgruntled customer up front asking to see the manager," Whitney explained. "It's that super-wench Poppy waited on last night."

Swaggart grinned and wiped his hands on a towel. "She's still ticked off that her date asked for your number, huh?"

"He didn't, and you owe me ten bucks," Poppy said, willing her tears to stay in her eyes and not escape down her cheeks.

Swaggart smiled and said, "I'll be right there." Turning to Bobby he said, "Keep it going in here for a minute, Bobby."

Poppy heard Bobby say, "You got it."

In the next moment, Swaggart left the kitchen and was standing with Whitney and Poppy by the beverage fountain.

"Tell her I'll be right there, Whitney," he said.

"She's a real wench, Swag. I don't envy you," Whitney said as she left.

Swaggart put his fists on his hips and looked at Poppy. "So tell me what went on."

"Nothing!" Poppy exclaimed. "I didn't do anything! I was totally polite…even when she got irritated because I called her 'ma'am' and told me I was supposed to call her 'Miss Reginald.' I was so polite, Swaggart," Poppy babbled. "I didn't even give the guy the time of day until I had spoken to her first. I swear! I didn't do anything!"

"Sure you did, Poppy-seed," Swaggart said.

Poppy frowned. How could he think she had been anything but polite?

"You took the guy's attention away from her."

"But I didn't," Poppy said.

Swaggart chuckled and placed a hand on Poppy's shoulder. "Don't worry about it. I'll go take care of it."

"She'll want you to fire me," Poppy said.

"Then I guess I'll have to fire you," he said.

"Really?" Poppy gasped.

"Of course not," Swaggart chuckled. "And here," he said reaching into his back pocket and retrieving his wallet. He withdrew a ten dollar bill and held it out toward her. "There's your ten bucks. I'm always good for a bet."

"Just don't fire me, and we'll call it even," Poppy said.

Swaggart smiled and tucked the money into the front pocket of her jeans. Poppy smiled, delighted by the gesture.

"Stay here. And don't worry," he said. He winked at her—causing her heart to flutter and her stomach to loop-the-loop—and headed for the front of the restaurant.

31

Carefully, Poppy crept to one side of the restaurant. A large statue of Elvis stood in one corner, close enough that she could hear the conversation at the hostess podium and yet big enough to conceal her.

She watched, heart hammering with anxiety, as Swaggart walked to the podium.

"How may I help you, ma'am?" Swaggart asked Miss Reginald.

Poppy smiled as the expression on Miss Reginald's face turned to utter awe upon seeing Swaggart.

"Oh," Miss Susan Reginald said as she studied Swaggart from head to toe. "Are...are you the manager here?"

"Manager, cook, waiter...whatever I need to be at the moment," Swaggart said.

"Oh...I-I see," Miss Reginald stammered. "Well...well I need to voice a complaint," she said.

"Mmm hmmm," Swaggart mumbled folding his muscular arms across his massive chest. "About my cooking, or about something else?" he asked.

Poppy giggled. Miss Susan Reginald was completely undone! Swaggart Moretti stood six foot three inches, was built like a Greek god, and was more handsome than any dark-haired, square-jawed movie star.

"W-well, about the service here, actually," Miss Reginald stammered.

"Mmm hmmm," Swaggart mumbled, nodding.

"I was here last...last evening...with a male companion...and one of your waitresses was so silly and ridiculous over him. Well, I can't tell you how embarrassing it was. She was completely incompetent in her duties and practically threw herself into my date's lap!"

"What?" Poppy gasped from her hiding place behind Elvis. She felt her face burning crimson with angered indignation. The woman was a liar, as well as a wench!

"Who was it that waited on you, ma'am?" Swaggart asked.

"Poppy," the woman nearly spat.

"Are you sure?" Swaggart asked.

"How could I forget? Some ridiculous song came on, and the entire restaurant was singing to her," the woman said. "Besides, believe me, I would not forget such a goofy name."

"Hmmm," Swaggart said. His brow wrinkled in a frown, and he put a fist to his mouth as if he were thinking very hard. "I find that very surprising because Poppy is our best waitress. In the two years she's worked here, more customers have offered her their high regard than any other waiter or waitress here."

"I find *that* very surprising, considering my experience last night," Miss Reginald said.

"Well, how was your meal?" Swaggart asked then. "Was that to your satisfaction?"

"Oh, the meal was excellent!" Miss Reginald said. "That's what made the experience with your waitress so unfortunate—because the food was fabulous."

Swaggart drew a deep inhale as he withdrew a piece of paper from his apron pocket. Holding it between his index and middle fingers he held the paper out to Miss Reginald.

"Hmmm. Interesting," he said. "Because I believe I received this from you last night."

Miss Reginald cleared her throat and took the paper from Swaggart.

"Well, I was...I was very upset about the service," she stammered. "I suppose I was just upset about that and felt it tainted the meal as well."

Swaggart nodded and folded his arms across his chest once more. "I see," he said. "Well, what is it you would like to see done about this?"

Miss Reginald smiled, eyebrows arched in arrogance. "I'd like to see the waitress in question fired. She cost me a great deal beyond a bad dining experience. The man I was with was an agent from a well-known advertising firm, and your waitress was so unreasonably inept and distracting that he has refused to take on my account."

"I see," Swaggart said.

Poppy was sure her heart would pound its way right out of her chest! Swaggart had said he wouldn't fire her, but Poppy's worry and anxiety told her differently. It was obvious this woman was a liar, but business was business, and Good Ol' Days didn't need any bad publicity.

"Well, I'll tell you what," Swaggart began.

"Yes?" Miss Reginald asked, smiling at him.

"There's the door," he said then, pointing to the restaurant's front door. "I'd like to see you leave through it."

"What?" Miss Susan Reginald exclaimed. "Do you mean to tell me you're not going to take any action in this matter?"

"I am taking action, lady!" Swaggart growled. "You waltz in here wanting me to fire my best waitress because you're ticked off that the guy you were with would rather have taken her home than you? I'm wise to you, lady, and you can just hurry your arrogant a—a—*attitude* out of my restaurant!"

Miss Susan Reginald's mouth dropped in astonishment.

"You're just ticked off because I criticized your cooking," she said, tucking a strand of hair behind one ear as she struggled to regain her composure.

"Sister, if anyone gave an ounce of credibility to every idiot who criticized my cooking, I wouldn't be pulling in a hundred dollars a plate for doing the LaForge Industries VP luncheon this Tuesday," Swaggart said through clinched teeth. "Do you need me to call you a taxi…again?" he asked.

He was angry. Poppy had seen him angry before and wished never to be on the receiving end of his anger. If Miss Susan Reginald knew what was good for her, she'd leave as fast as the pencil-thin heels on her black pumps could carry her.

"What? Have you got a thing for her too?" Miss Reginald asked, defiantly putting one hand on one hip.

"Everybody's got a thing for her, including your little advertising executive. Isn't that right?" Swaggart said. "Now get out of my restaurant," he added opening the door for her. At Swaggart's command, several customers sitting close enough to have heard the exchange began to applaud.

"Well. I can assure you that I will never step foot in this roach-infested shack again," Miss Susan Reginald said as she turned and quickly left Good Ol' Days.

Again the customers applauded and Swaggart shook his head. "Can you believe that woman's sh—shmeeha?"

Again there was applause, and as Ella Fitzgerald began singing "Dream A Little Dream," Swaggart shook his head once more and started back toward the kitchen.

"Poppy! Come here," he growled as he went.

Poppy bit her lip and tried to keep the tears from escaping her eyes. Dealing with rotten customers was just about the worst thing that could happen to anybody, and she felt terrible for being the cause of Swaggart's having to go to bat for her.

Leaving the protection of the Elvis statue, Poppy paused in front of Whitney on her way to the kitchen.

"No wonder Miss Reginald is still a 'Miss,'" Whitney said.

"Yeah," Poppy said, still horrified at what had happened.

Lowering her voice, Whitney asked, "And do you really think Swag pulls in that much for just one moonlighting chef gig?"

"I-I don't know, Whit," Poppy said, shaking her head. She had to face Swaggart—she didn't care how much he made when he was moonlighting.

"What's wrong, Poppy?" Whitney asked. "Swag took care of it. You still look upset."

"She was a total nightmare to him, Whit," Poppy reminded her.

Whitney smiled. "He handled it fine. Now go on back there. I'm sure he's got one of his empathetic pep-talks ready."

Poppy nodded and headed for the kitchen area. When she arrived, it was to find Swaggart leaning one shoulder against the wall in the alcove near the back door.

"She was a real piece of work, wasn't she?" he asked.

Poppy felt the tears brimming in her eyes and knew she would lose the battle with them. As the first tear trickled over her cheek, she brushed at it, frustrated she had failed in holding it back.

"I'm sorry, Swaggart," she mumbled. "You shouldn't have had to—"

"What are you sorry for?" he interrupted, "That some witch intruded on our happy little restaurant home?" He chuckled and added, "It happens, Poppy, and it's not your fault."

"But she was so rude to you and…and…" Poppy began, wiping an escaped tear from the other cheek.

"I'm sure she was much ruder to you last night," Swaggart said.

She heard him chuckle then and gasped as he reached out and pulled her against him, wrapping her in his arms.

For a brief moment, Poppy couldn't breathe! When she could, the feel of his white t-shirt against her cheek, the solid contours of his muscular chest beneath—it was fabulous! The scent of steak and bacon, of butter and herbs clung to him, and she thought it the most wonderful combination of scents she had ever inhaled! His arms were around her too—tight around her, and she loved the deep sound of his chuckle as it began in his chest.

"Don't let her get to you, baby," he said. "That's what she wanted."

Poppy seriously thought she might faint! She knew his calling her "baby" was just his way of comforting her—knew he was simply trying to calm her down and reassure her. Still, for the sake of the past she'd never experienced with him, she imagined he meant it to be more endearing than it actually was.

"Shake it off," he said, and every inch of her flesh erupted with goose bumps as one of his strong hands stroked her hair. "I gotta get back to the kitchen before Bobby sets the place on—"

"Well, isn't this a tender scene?"

Poppy instantly stiffened at the sound of Jennifer's voice and endeavored to push herself from Swaggart's embrace. He seemed less unsettled, however, pausing before releasing her.

"Hey, Jen," he said.

"What's all this about?" Jennifer asked. Poppy dared to look up at her and immediately wished she hadn't. Jennifer's beautiful blue eyes were blazing with anger. She stood with her arms folded across her bosom, tapping one foot.

"Poppy had a bad customer last night, and the witch showed up here a few minutes ago," Swaggart explained. "You okay?" he asked Poppy.

"Y-yeah," Poppy stammered.

"Are you sure you're okay, Poppy?" Jennifer asked. The sarcasm in her tone of voice was as thick as tar. "Or do you need a little more—what was that—*reassurance* you were giving her, Swaggart?"

Poppy felt ill—literally sick! She felt more foolish than ever as well and stammered, "I'm sorry, Jennifer. He was only—"

"You don't have to apologize to her, Poppy," Swaggart interrupted. "You didn't do anything to apologize for."

"Sure she does!" Jennifer exclaimed, instantly furious. "I walk in here to meet you for lunch and find you groping your little waitress! She better start apologizing, and she better start staying away from you from now on!" Jennifer turned her attention to Poppy then. "You hear me, girl?"

"If I was groping, then why does *she* owe you an apology?" Swaggart growled.

"Swaggart, I-I—" Poppy began.

"Don't you talk to him!" Jennifer exclaimed. "You've got no right to talk to him!"

Poppy held her breath as Jennifer took a step toward her. Stepping between her and Jennifer, Swaggart said, "It's been a rough day, Poppy. Why don't you just be a runner for Bobby for awhile? Brittany can handle the tables for now."

"Okay," she said, wiping more tears from her cheeks. She looked up into his handsome face and tried to smile when he winked at her.

"Okay," he said. He turned back to Jennifer then and asked, "What's up with this, Jen?"

Poppy quickly left them to their argument, feeling all the more guilty for getting Swaggart in trouble with his girlfriend. Yet a moment later, she quietly admitted to herself she hoped the incident caused them to break up. Jennifer was nearly as much a wench as Miss Susan Reginald. Swaggart deserved better.

"It's really going to hit the fan now," Bobby said as Poppy tied her apron at her back.

"Do you think so?" Poppy asked, though she already sensed he was right.

"Are you kidding? Jennifer won't put up with Swaggart even looking at another female, let alone being nice to one," Bobby said.

Poppy frowned as she looked at Bobby. He was a good-looking young man, and for a moment Poppy wondered how Mr. Dexter managed to have such good-looking grandchildren all the way around. Whitney was beautiful, and Bobby was handsome. Swaggart was absolutely gorgeous! The gene pool had been kind to Mr. Dexter's family.

"Boy!" Poppy sighed. "I guess I've given Swaggart enough trouble for one day, huh?"

"None of it's your fault, Poppy," Bobby said, placing two plates heaping with food on the order counter. "Now, run these burgers to table five for me, will you? The one with the fries goes to the guy."

Poppy wiped the last tears from her cheeks with the back of her hand and nodded. "You got it," she said. She picked up the two plates and headed for the tables.

"So you're saying every girl in this restaurant wants me, huh?" Poppy heard Swaggart say as she passed the small alcove where he and Jennifer were continuing their argument. "Does that automatically mean *I* want every girl in this restaurant, Jen? Whitney's my cousin, for crying out loud!"

Swaggart was angry, and it was no wonder. Having just dealt with Miss Susan Reginald, he now found himself under attack by his girlfriend.

Poppy's guilt was thicker than mud, but she knew she didn't dare try to explain it to Jennifer herself.

"Here you are," Poppy said as she set the burger and fries on the table in front of the man and the burger with onion rings in front of his female companion. "Is there anything else I can get for you?"

"No, thank you," the man said. He smiled at Poppy, but she felt no better. She had suddenly become very paranoid and looked to the woman to see if she was irritated. She was relieved when the woman kindly smiled and nodded at her.

Heading back toward the kitchen, she passed the alcove once more and heard Jennifer say, "Every time I come here, Poppy's stalking you like some stupid lovesick puppy."

"You're way out of line, Jen," Swaggart said.

"I know I just got here, Bobby," Poppy said. "But do you mind if I take a really quick break?"

Bobby smiled with understanding and said, "Sure, Poppy. Get some air. It's a little too close in here today. You know what I mean?"

"Thanks," Poppy said. There would be no going out the back door of the restaurant. Swaggart was still receiving a tongue-lashing from Jennifer in the alcove. So Poppy quickly exited Good Ol' Days by way of one of the side exit doors.

The moment she was outside, she leaned back against the outer wall of the restaurant and inhaled a deep breath. She closed her eyes as more tears escaped them. What a terrible way to start a work shift! Miss Susan Reginald's lies and Swaggart having to volley them—Jennifer's jealousy and Swaggart having to volley it. What else could she do to make his day miserable?

"Bad day?" Mr. Dexter asked.

Poppy gasped and opened her eyes to see Mr. Dexter sitting at one end of the patio tables watching her.

"Kind of," she said.

Mr. Dexter smiled and winked at her, and Poppy instantly felt somewhat comforted.

"Come and tell me about it," Mr. Dexter said, gesturing with one hand that she should join him at his table.

Tentatively, Poppy joined him, studying him for a moment as she sat down. The sight of his half-moon-shaped smiling eyes, silvery-white hair, and understanding grin soothed her.

"What's all this about?" he asked.

Poppy shrugged and said, "I had a rotten customer last night. She showed up to complain today, and Swaggart had to deal with her." She sighed, exhaling the breath she hadn't realized she'd been sort of holding.

"And then?" Mr. Dexter prodded.

"And then…and then I was talking to Swaggart about it in the alcove, and Jennifer showed up, and now she's all mad at him, and…and it's just been a terrible day," Poppy said.

"Well, rotten customers are a part of life, I'm afraid," Mr. Dexter said. "Don't you let it upset you one more minute. And as far as Jennifer…well, personally I hope Swaggart finally gets irritated enough with her to dump her flat on her fanny."

Poppy giggled as she looked at the elderly man. "What?"

"I can't stand that girl myself," Mr. Dexter said. "I think Swaggart only started dating her because she was so obsessively insistent." He smiled at Poppy and said, "You and I both know she's not the girl for him."

"Agreed," Poppy said. "But anyway…that's how my day has started."

"Are you getting tired of working here, Poppy?" he asked.

A sort of panic gurgled in Poppy's stomach. Was Mr. Dexter thinking of letting her go?

"No! Not at all, Mr. Dexter," she assured him. "You know how much I appreciate you giving me this opportunity. I love working here—I love being here!"

"What do you love about it?" he asked.

"Well…well…everything, I guess," Poppy said.

"Give me some examples," Mr. Dexter said.

Poppy shrugged and said, "I love the smell of the food, the sounds of people eating and being happy together. I love the music and the other employees. And I love the atmosphere—it's like all the good things about the past still live here, and when you're sick of the world and all its baggage…Good Ol' Days gives you a reprieve. Do you know what I mean?"

"I do," Mr. Dexter said, still smiling.

"I guess that's why the rotten customers upset me so much," Poppy added, "They try to taint a good thing, and it sort of hurts me somehow."

Mr. Dexter chuckled, his mouth and eyes still smiling.

"But what about your future, Poppy?" he asked. "Or are you planning on being a waitress forever—even after you finish college next fall?"

Anxiety—thick and unpleasant anxiety washed over Poppy again. She didn't want to think about leaving Good Ol' Days. Two more semesters and she would be finished—have her degree. But part of her didn't even want it. Most of her wanted only to waitress at Good Ol' Days for as long as she could.

"Are you…are you needing to cut back on employees, Mr. Dexter?" she asked. Her heart was hammering with anxiety and anticipation of what his answer might be. Maybe her time at Good Ol' Days was at an end after all—even without Miss Susan Reginald's help.

"Oh, no, no, no!" Mr. Dexter chuckled. "I just wanted to know what your thoughts were. You know you have a job here for as long as we can keep you, Poppy."

Poppy exhaled the breath she'd been holding and smiled. "I-I thought you were prepping me to be let go."

Mr. Dexter chuckled again. "Oh goodness, no!" he said. "I just want to be sure you're living your life, Poppy—not just lingering. Do you know what I mean?"

"I think so," Poppy said.

"The rotten customer is gone, the sun is shining, and Swaggart and Bobby are cooking up some fine food inside," Mr. Dexter said. He patted the back of Poppy's hand where it lay on the table. "It's a new minute. Anything can happen."

Poppy smiled. Mr. Dexter always had a way of making people feel better. Poppy knew his love and joy for life spilled over into his restaurant. That's why people loved Good Ol' Days. That's why reservations were hard to get on Saturday nights.

"You're right," Poppy told him. "And I better get back before Bobby has my head on a platter."

Mr. Dexter chuckled and said, "I'd hate to see that. And besides, I'm not sure how good that would be for business."

Poppy laughed as she stood. "Thanks, Mr. Dexter. I feel much better."

"Good," he said.

"Bye-bye," Poppy said as she headed back to the restaurant.

The sun was shining! The rotten customer was gone, and Swaggart and Bobby were cooking up some good food inside! Poppy was sure she'd seen the last of Miss Susan Reginald—possibly Jennifer Trujillo too, and as she entered the restaurant to hear Nat King Cole's version of "Stardust" echoing through the building, she smiled.

"Runner!" she heard Bobby call from the kitchen.

She hurried to the kitchen to find four orders on the counter, ready and waiting.

"Sorry," she said, just as Swaggart entered the kitchen and stepped up next to Bobby to inspect the order tickets.

"Run over, and come right back," Swaggart said. "Things are heating up!"

"That's because..." Bobby began.

"It's Saturday night!" he and Swaggart shouted simultaneously.

"You got it," Poppy said, smiling.

Swaggart seemed no worse for the wear—as if he'd just had a conversation with his grandpa as well. Yet Poppy knew it was impossible. Something else must've lightened his load.

"You've got roses at the hostess podium!" Brittany exclaimed as she skipped up to the order counter.

"What?" Poppy asked.

"Three dozen red roses!" Brittany said. "Huge arrangement! Baby's breath, greens, a big red ribbon, and a card!"

"You're kidding," Poppy said. "Who would be sending me roses?"

Brittany shrugged. "How am I supposed to know? All I know is the delivery guys said they were ordered by somebody from Heaston Advertising."

Poppy gasped as her hand flew to cover her mouth. It couldn't be! Could it? Quickly she pulled Mark Lawson's business card from the pocket of her apron.

"Mark Lawson—Heaston Advertising," she read in a whisper.

"The gorgeous guy from last night?" Brittany asked.

"I'll be taking that ten bucks back now," Swaggart said.

Poppy looked to him to see a mischievous smile on his face.

"He didn't ask me for my number last night, and that was our bet. I'm keeping the ten bucks," Poppy said.

"Maybe you ought to give the ten bucks to this guy," Bobby said. "Three dozen roses? That's gotta cost a wad."

"Holy cow, Poppy," Whitney said as she arrived then, carrying the enormous arrangement of roses. "Where are we going to put these? I need the room up front."

Poppy stood with her mouth gaping open in delighted astonishment. She had never, never, never received such an elaborate arrangement—nothing even close.

"Well?" Brittany said, as Whitney set the arrangement down in the alcove. "Read the card!"

Poppy's heartbeat increased as she plucked the card from the plastic card holder amid the arrangement. Surely it couldn't be from Mark Lawson. Surely!

"Oh my heck," Poppy breathed as she read the card.

"Can you read it to us? Or is it too personal?" Whitney asked.

Poppy glanced up to see Bobby anxiously waiting for a reading as well. Swaggart simply grinned and mouthed, "I want my ten bucks back."

"I-I guess I can read it," Poppy stammered. She still could not believe Mark Lawson had sent her the roses.

"Poppy," she began.

"Ooooo! That gave me chills!" Bobby said, shivering.

"Shut up, Bobby," Brittany said. "Go on, Poppy. He's just being an idiot."

Poppy cleared her throat and read the card aloud. *"Poppy, please accept these as a small token of my heartfelt apologies for being the cause of such a miserable experience for you last night. I look forward to making amends as soon as possible. Hoping to Be Yours, Mark Lawson."*

"Hoping to be yours?" Whitney sighed. "Oh my heck, Poppy! I can't believe it!"

Poppy stood reading the card again. She couldn't believe it either. Mark Lawson, the handsomest customer she had ever waited on, had sent her roses—implied he was going to see her again. It was too good to be true! Wasn't it?

She glanced up to see Swaggart smiling at her, his eyes bright with amusement. He was so handsome—so charming—so completely unobtainable! For years she'd dreamed of Swaggart Moretti, and for years she'd reminded herself how entirely out of reach he was. And now—now a handsome, charming man seemed to have taken an interest in her. It was as if a door had opened somehow.

She thought of Mr. Dexter, of the conversation she'd had with him only minutes before. *It's a new minute. Anything can happen*, he'd said. Perhaps this was it—perhaps Mark Lawson was the *anything* that could happen.

"Girls!" Bobby said, smacking a palm on the order counter. "This food is going to get cold."

"Oh, yeah!" Brittany said, picking up two plates and scurrying off. "Sorry."

"And look at the line at the front door," Whitney said. She turned to Poppy and hugged her. "I'm so excited! I knew that guy was meant for you" she said before rushing off to the hostess podium.

"Still sorry we had to deal with that wench he brought with him?" Swaggart asked as he set two more plates on the order counter.

"I guess not," Poppy said. She couldn't help but smile. There would always be an order counter between her and Swaggart—an order counter or a Jennifer Trujillo. But it seemed there was nothing but roses between her and Mark Lawson.

Poppy felt her heart flutter a little as she picked up the two plates Swaggart had set on the counter.

"Thanks, Swaggart," she said as she hurried off after Brittany.

Mark Lawson had sent her roses! Not just roses—three dozen roses! Poppy wished Miss Susan Reginald would show up just once more—just long enough to see the roses and read the card accompanying them.

"Poppy Lawson?" Poppy whispered as she headed for table ten. She smiled to herself as she contemplated the way the name fit together so well. Swaggart Moretti was the crush she'd known all through high school, but she was grown up now—time to get on with being grown up. And what better way than with Mark "gorgeous man" Lawson?

Swaggart watched the girls scatter to their different tasks. It felt good to be done with Jennifer, and he wondered why he'd waited so long to break up with her. In fact, in those moments, he wondered why he'd even dated her in the first place. He didn't have one regret about breaking up with her just minutes before—not one. Not one heartache, not one lament. He felt as if some great weight he'd been bearing had just been lifted from his shoulders.

Yet at the same time, he was more than a little irritated by the three dozen roses sitting in the alcove. Poppy deserved better than some showy rich guy. Certainly she deserved better than a cook at the local family restaurant—a part-time chef with no permanent direction. It had been one reason he'd steered clear of his grandfather's beautiful little favorite waitress. What did he have to offer her? Nothing. Yet he didn't like the idea of this advertising guy going for her either.

"What's the matter, Swaggart?" Bobby asked. "Jealous?"

"Of what, Bobby?" Swaggart said, frowning and smiling at the same time.

"I know you better than you know yourself, cousin," Bobby chuckled.

"Maybe you do, and maybe you don't, cousin," Swaggart said.

"Oh, believe me—I do," Bobby said.

Swaggart shook his head and chuckled. "You keep telling yourself that."

Still, as he looked up to where Poppy and Brittany were serving the foursome at table four, he frowned.

He better be good to her, he thought. *And he better not break her heart.*

He shook his head, trying to concentrate on the crème brûlée he was preparing for table three. He tried to be happy for her—she deserved to be pampered, admired, and adored. Still, the sour sensation in the pit of his stomach lingered long into the evening— long after Poppy and her three dozen roses had gone home.

As Swaggart sat relaxing at table two, listening to Dean Martin croon "Kiss" while Whitney finished up some paperwork, he silently hoped the smooth advertising guy turned out to be an idiot. Still, as his thoughts lingered on the cute little brunette waitress at Good Ol' Days, he wondered—was there such a thing in the world as a bigger idiot than he was?

CHAPTER FOUR

The sun was bright, the sky was clear, and as Poppy pulled into her spot in the Good Ol' Days parking lot, she smiled. Spring was making way for summer! No doubt Mr. Dexter would open the patio and garden tables any day, and Poppy loved serving in the gardens.

She locked her car door, dropped her keys in her bag, and headed for the restaurant. She inhaled a deep breath, smiling again as the scent of lilac and hyacinth kissed her senses. Instantly, she thought of the scent of roses still filling Poppy and Whitney's apartment with their fragrant perfume. She'd spent most of the day before gazing at them in disbelief, reading and rereading the card that had come with them, and smiling with delight. Mark Lawson! It was a dream come true!

"How's it going, Whit?" Poppy asked as she entered the restaurant.

"You're early," Whitney greeted. "And it's a good thing. The lunch rush was crazy today! Uncle Robert even has Josh waiting tables."

"Good afternoon, Poppy," Robert Dexter greeted as he approached. "Glad to see you in a bit early. We had a crazy lunch hour."

"That's what I hear," Poppy said, returning Uncle Robert's smile.

Everyone called Mr. Dexter's son, Robert, Uncle Robert. He was Bobby's dad and Whitney and Swaggart's uncle, so it was just easier for everyone to call him Uncle Robert. It avoided confusion when Mr. Dexter was in as well.

"I'll get my apron and jump in," Poppy said.

"Thanks," Uncle Robert said.

Poppy watched as he went to table two and greeted the couple sitting there.

"Guess what I found out this morning?" Whitney said then.

"What?" Poppy asked. Her curiosity was instantly piqued by the way Whitney had lowered her voice and was glancing about to make certain no one was within hearing range.

"Swaggart finally dumped Jennifer," Whitney said.

Poppy felt her eyes widen—felt her heart beat a little faster.

"Are you serious?" she asked.

"Totally!" Whitney whispered. "Saturday afternoon, right before your roses came. Remember how Jennifer showed up here?"

Poppy nodded. How could she forget? Jennifer had been totally ticked off at finding Poppy wrapped in Swaggart's arms. She gasped slightly, her heart beating even more quickly. Could the incident have had something to do with the breakup?

"Do you know why he broke up with her?" Poppy asked.

Whitney shrugged. "No. And who cares? As long as he did it. She was a nightmare!"

"Wow," Poppy breathed.

Whitney raised her eyebrows rather mischievously and said, "So I guess there's nothing stopping you now."

"What do you mean?" Poppy asked, though she had a very good idea what her friend was implying.

"You know what I mean," Whitney said. "Wouldn't now be a good time to—you know—try to wiggle your way into Swaggart's arms?"

"Shhh!" Poppy scolded. "Whitney, are you crazy?" Poppy glanced around to ensure no one had heard Whitney's suggestion.

"Well, you should at least try to finally check item number one off your list," Whitney said.

"Shhh! For Pete's sake, Whitney!" Poppy whispered. "That's the dumbest thing you've said in a long time! You know I'm totally over Swaggart now."

"And on to 'Mr.-Three-dozen-roses,' right?" Whitney giggled.

"I still can't believe he would send me those," Poppy said, smiling. She thought of the massive arrangement sitting in the center of the table back at the apartment—that the likes of Mark Lawson would take notice of her—it caused goose bumps to break over her arms.

"Well, at least he finally dumped her," Whitney said, as a couple walked through the front doors. She picked up her eraser board and turned to greet them.

"At least," Poppy agreed. "See ya later," she said as she headed for the alcove near the kitchen where the aprons hung.

The aroma of lime and garlic shrimp filled her lungs, and she smiled as she stood in the alcove adjusting her apron.

"I've been promoted to waiter!" Josh said as he hurried to the kitchen.

"I know! I heard. Congratulations," Poppy said, returning his smile.

Josh paused and looked around before whispering, "Fair warning—Swaggart's a little uptight today."

"Why?" Poppy assumed Swaggart was irritable because of the breakup with Jennifer. But she played dumb just in case Josh didn't know about it.

"He's got that big thing tomorrow night. You know—one of those deals where he's the hot-shot chef and all," Josh explained. "I think it's got him a bit on edge."

"Thanks for the heads up," Poppy said.

Poppy didn't like the days before Swaggart had special catering jobs lined up. He always seemed a bit touchy and impatient. He wasn't mean or too overly grouchy—just not as relaxed, charming, and fun as usual.

After washing her hands at the sink in the back of the alcove, Poppy headed for the hostess podium.

"Table for four?" Whitney was asking a young family as Poppy arrived.

"Yes, please," the young father said.

Poppy smiled as Whitney turned to her, handing her two adult menus, two children's activity menus, and two boxes of crayons. She loved little families. She didn't care if the kids made a mess or wanted three extra maraschino cherries in their drinks—young families just made her feel happy, and she loved the children.

"This is Poppy, and she'll be your server today," Whitney said. "Table nine, Poppy."

"Thank you," the young mother said.

"If you'll just follow me, please," Poppy said, winking at the little girl dressed all in pink, who stood clinging to her mother's hand.

"We never got sat down by you before," the little boy said.

Poppy thought he must be about six. His sister looked to be about four.

"You haven't?" Poppy said, smiling and winking at him. "Well, I'll just have to make sure you want to come back and see me."

"You guys have good foods," the little girl said.

"We do, don't we?" Poppy said as she grabbed a booster seat from the pile nearby.

"Last time we was here, the man who cooks our food made us Mickey Mouse pancakes," the little boy said as he scrambled into his chair at table nine.

"Mmmm! With a bacon mouth and blueberry eyes?" Poppy giggled.

"And a stwabewwy nose!" the little girl added as her father lifted her onto the booster seat Poppy had put on one chair.

"He's a fun cook, isn't he?" Poppy said. She smiled, thinking of the way Swaggart always asked if the pancake orders were for children or adults.

"He's vewy fun!" the little girl said.

Poppy hoped Swaggart's reportedly less-than-perfect mood wouldn't diminish his thoughtfulness today.

But twenty minutes later, when Poppy picked the children's plates up at the order counter, she smiled when she saw the snowmen pancakes with blueberry eyes, shredded bacon hair and raisin buttons running over their round middle-pancake bellies. She couldn't help smiling at Swaggart as he looked up for a moment and saw her smiling at him.

"Good enough?" he asked.

"Perfect," she said. "They'll love it. I'll be back for the burgers."

He nodded and returned his attention to whatever he was cooking.

The afternoon seemed to fly by, and soon the sun had set and night had descended. Monday nights weren't usually as busy as other nights, and it gave the staff of Good Ol' Days a little reprieve.

All afternoon Poppy's thoughts had lingered on two subjects—Swaggart's breakup with Jennifer and Mark Lawson's three dozen roses.

She was simply elated Swaggart had finally come to his senses and dumped Jennifer. She was so shallow, so empty, so selfish, and entirely self-absorbed. It was obvious she didn't appreciate Swaggart either. Oh, she appreciated his good looks—enjoyed having a trophy-boy boyfriend—but Poppy doubted Jennifer ever knew what she really had her hands on. And thank heaven! What if she had realized what a prize Swaggart was? Swaggart might not have wised-up quite as fast.

Then there were Mark Lawson's roses. The words on the florist's card kept playing in her mind over and over and over. *I look forward to making amends as soon as possible. Hoping to Be Yours, Mark Lawson.*

"Hoping to be yours," Poppy repeated as she washed her hands in the alcove sink. Her heart did a little flutter. It sounded so romantically wonderful!

"Poppy," Josh said as he passed the alcove. "Whitney just had Brittany sit two guys at table two and wants you to get 'em."

"Okay. Thanks, Josh," she said.

She dried her hands and retrieved her order tablet from her apron pocket as she headed for table two.

As she approached, her steps slowed, however, for she was certain she recognized the broad shoulders and dark hair of the person sitting with his back to her. It was him! She was sure of it! Mark Lawson! He'd come back! Her heart fluttered, and she couldn't stop the smile rapidly widening across her face.

"Good evening, gentleman," Poppy greeted Mark Lawson and his male dinner companion. "Welcome to Good Ol' Days. I'm Poppy and—"

"…and you'll be our server?" his friend said, smiling and winking at her.

"Exactly," she said.

"Hi, there," Mark said as she smiled at him. "Remember me?"

"Of course," Poppy said. "And thank you so much for the roses, Mr. Lawson."

"Call me Mark," Mark Lawson said, flashing a stunning smile.

"Okay," Poppy said, blushing to the very tips of her toes.

"And call me anytime," Mark's companion flirted.

"Hey, man—get your own girls," Mark chuckled.

"I'm Braden," Mark's friend said.

"Nice to meet you," Poppy said, shaking the hand he offered in greeting.

"Oh, I know all about you," Braden said.

Again, Poppy felt her cheeks burn crimson.

"Did you like the flowers?" Mark asked.

"They're beautiful! Thank you so much!" Poppy said, placing a hand to her bosom. "I can't believe you would worry about it. We have rotten customers all the time, and that woman…well, she's just part of my job."

"She was an idiot," Mark said. "And I am truly sorry you had to deal with her. I hope the flowers softened the blow a bit."

Instantly, Poppy thought of Swaggart's having to deal with it as well. Mark had no idea the ill feelings the woman had caused—how far-reaching her asinine behavior was. It made the fact he'd sent roses all the more wonderful.

"You have no idea," she told him.

"Good," he said, picking up his menu. "Then when I've finished my meal and ask you out—I hope you'll say yes."

Poppy thought she might burst with delight! He was going to ask her out? It was too dreamy.

"I'm sure I will," she said.

"Finally! Because I'm starving," Braden said, opening his menu. "Now…what's good here?"

"Everything," Poppy said. Her cheeks were on fire with delight and anticipation. She wanted the meal to be over right that very moment—wanted Mark Lawson to ask her out that instant!

"Wow! That's a pretty serious promise," Braden said.

"I'm sure if she says everything's good, then everything is," Mark said. "What do you suggest, Poppy?"

The sound of his deep, smooth voice uttering her name nearly melted her knees.

"Well, it depends on what you're in the mood for," she said. "Or if you're up for a little adventure…" she said, smiling at Braden.

"I'm always up for adventure," Braden said, closing his menu and looking at Poppy expectantly.

"Then you could go for the Chef's Choice," she said.

"What's that? Like the special of the day?" Mark asked.

"No…it's exactly what it says it is," Poppy explained, blushing as he winked at her. "I ask you your meat preference—you know, beef, chicken, pork, or fish—then I find out if there are any vegetables you simply cannot eat…then I give the information to the cook, and he comes up with a meal for you."

"Mmm! I'm intrigued," Mark said, still smiling at her.

"The price varies, however," Poppy said.

"What's the high end?" Braden asked.

"Twenty-five dollars a plate," Poppy said.

"That's what I want," Braden said, handing his menu to Poppy.

"Me too," Mark said. "If that filet mignon was any indication of what the guy can do...I'm up for it."

"Okay, then," Poppy said. "First of all, what can I get you gentlemen to drink?"

"Water with lemon," Braden said.

"Same," Mark said.

"Okay. Any appetizers?"

"I don't think so. We'll just wait for the meal," Mark answered.

"Then we'll begin with you, sir," Poppy said turning to Braden.

"Why? Do you think I'm the girl?" Braden asked her, a teasing smile playing at his lips.

"Well, she sure doesn't think I'm the girl," Mark chuckled. "He's just giving you a hard time, Poppy."

Poppy giggled. Both men were charming and possessed senses of humor.

"Okay, one more time then..." she began again. "Your meat choice?"

"Fish," Braden said. "Let's give this guy a challenge."

"Very well," Poppy said, jotting Braden's choice on her tablet. She smiled. Fish was difficult, but Swaggart had mastered it long ago.

"Any vegetables you may find unpalatable?" she asked.

"Nope. I eat anything," Braden said.

"And for you, sir?" she asked, turning her attention to Mark.

The moment he looked at her, she felt the hot blush warming her cheeks. He was so handsome! Furthermore, she could've sworn his eyes were twinkling as he looked at her.

"Beef...uh...medium-well," Mark said. "And I like any vegetable too."

"Okay," Poppy said. "I'll get your orders started and bring your water."

She started to leave, but Mark Lawson reached out and took hold of her hand. Instantly, her arms broke into goose bumps, and her heart fluttered.

"Can I just ask you out now?" he said. "I don't want to wait until later."

"S-sure," Poppy said. She bit her lip as he smiled at her.

"When's your next night off?" he asked.

"This Thursday," Poppy said.

"If you're not busy…can you pencil me in?" he asked. Again he flashed his stunning smile.

"You bet!" Poppy said.

"Great!" Mark said, still smiling—still holding her hand. "I'll need your number so I can call you to find out where to pick you up."

"Okay," Poppy said. Once he'd released her hand, she tore a corner off the current page of her order tablet and wrote her number on it.

She handed it to him, smiling when he said, "Thanks."

"I'll be right back with your drinks," she said.

Poppy wasn't certain her feet were even touching the ground as she headed to the order counter. "Two Chef's Choices," she said as she tore the page from her order tablet and clipped it on the order line. "One fish, one medium-well beef, and any veggies with both."

Swaggart looked up, and Poppy's heart nearly stopped as his eyes met hers. Sometimes she could swear his eyes were simply little pools of maple syrup. Her stomach did a little loop as he smiled at her.

"I hear your new man is here tonight," he said, winking at her.

"Yeah. He's at table two with a friend. They both ordered the Chef's Choice," she said.

Swaggart's eyebrows arched as he said, "Well, then I better make it good, huh?"

"You better!" Poppy teased.

"Did he ask for your number yet?" Swaggart asked.

"He did," Poppy admitted, ignoring the strange twinge of regret in her bosom. "We're going out Thursday night."

Again Swaggart's eyebrows arched. "Nice. And it only took a truckload of roses to convince you?"

"It only took one look at him the first night he was here," Poppy said.

Swaggart chuckled. "Well, good for you, baby. You go get your boy. I'll make sure he won't forget the meal you serve him tonight."

"Thanks, Swaggart," Poppy said as she stared at him. Just once—she would've liked to have gone out with Swaggart Moretti just once. Just once she would like to have…

"Don't thank me yet," he said. "I'll get nervous and mess up their orders."

"Order up," Bobby said, sliding two plates onto the counter. "It's your table five order, Poppy."

"Thanks, Bobby," Poppy said as she took one plate in each hand and headed for table five.

"Did that salmon get here today, Bobby?" Swaggart asked.

"Oooo! So you're pulling out the big guns for Poppy's new man, huh?" Bobby asked.

"If it helps her get what she wants," Swaggart said.

He shook his head as he thought of the train car of roses the guy had sent to Poppy the day before. He would have to get a look at the guy before he left. He'd make the guy a meal he'd never forget and then visit the table himself—and he better be legit.

Swaggart felt overheated. The muscles in his shoulders and back tightened.

"Here she comes," Braden said.

"She's cute, huh?" Mark asked. Since the night he'd had to endure Miss Susan Reginald's company at dinner, Mark hadn't been able to get the waitress from Good Ol' Days out of his mind! She had entirely bewitched him, and not just because Susan had treated her so badly. She was enchanting, interesting, too adorable, and Mark had decided the minute he'd met her that he had to get to know her.

"Cute?" Braden whispered. "Dude? Are you kidding? She's hot!"

"I know," Mark said as he watched Poppy walking toward them. She had an ice water with lemon in each hand and was smiling at him. She was adorable!

Poppy bit her lip as Mark Lawson winked at her. Setting his glass of water down on the coaster in front of him, she smiled.

"Here you are, gentlemen," she said, setting Braden's water down as well.

"I've given the chef your order. Is there anything else I can get for you?" she asked.

"Well, not in conjunction with the meal," Mark said.

Poppy giggled and blushed.

"Then I'll bring your plates out as soon as they're ready," Poppy said.

Reluctantly, she turned her attention to the table behind Mark's.

He was so handsome! Poppy noticed the way that every woman in the restaurant kept trying to catch a glimpse of him. She had to keep busy! She had five other tables she was waiting on, and she had to be attentive to everyone. Glancing at the clock, she silently told herself Swaggart would have Mark's order up within 20 minutes. If she could just make it 20 more minutes, she could be with him again—even if it was only briefly.

Sure enough, 19 minutes later, Swaggart smiled at her over the order counter as he slid two plates onto it.

Poppy gasped as she saw the two meals Swaggart had prepared. "Oh my heck, Swaggart! Your salmon?" she exclaimed. "And prime rib?" Poppy looked to Swaggart, her stomach doing the usual loop-the-loop as he winked at her.

"Gotta make your boy happy, don't I?"

"Thank you, Swaggart," she said, feeling somehow greatly humbled. He'd done it for her—prepared two fabulous meals because he knew it was important to her.

He looked down, continuing to prepare other food as he said, "The salmon is grilled with unsalted butter, lemon, and topped with sautéed spinach and red onion—served with lemon wedges, steamed asparagus, and mixed vegetable ribbons." It was his habit to explain any Chef's Choice dish to the server so the information could be passed to the customer.

Poppy nodded, astounded by not only the meal but by the presentation. The salmon was grilled to a perfection—color and otherwise—and the yellows, greens, and reds of the lemons and different vegetables were arranged on the plate in Swaggart's signature manner.

"Okay," Poppy said.

"The prime rib is medium-well, with horseradish and au jus, mushrooms sautéed in butter, mixed vegetable ribbons, and minced garlic with cream mashed potatoes. The burgers for table three will be up in a minute," he said.

Poppy was stunned for a moment. How could Swaggart serve up a salmon and a prime rib in one motion and a plain hamburger in the next?

"Th-thanks," she stammered as she lifted the plates and turned to head toward table two and Mark "Gorgeous Man" Lawson.

"The salmon is grilled with unsalted butter and lemon and topped with sautéed spinach and red onion. Served with lemon wedges, steamed asparagus, and vegetable ribbons—I'm sure you'll love it," Poppy told Braden as she set the plate on the table before him. She smiled, feeling triumphant as his mouth dropped open in astonishment.

"All this time I thought this was a burger joint," he said.

Poppy sat Mark's plate on the table before him, twisting it until the prime rib was to his left.

"The prime rib is medium-well—per your request—with horseradish and au jus, butter-sautéed mushrooms, vegetable ribbons, and minced garlic and cream mashed potatoes," she explained.

"Prime rib?" Mark exclaimed. "What? Do you have an in with the cook or something?"

"No, not really," Poppy said. As the two men sat staring at their food in astonishment, Poppy asked, "Is there anything else I can get for you, gentlemen?"

"Order up!" her trained ears heard Bobby call.

"Um…I don't think so," Mark said, still staring wide-eyed at his prime rib.

"Very well," Poppy said. "I'll be back to check on you in a few minutes."

"I hope so," Mark said, smiling at her.

Poppy smiled, biting her lip with barely restrained delight as she walked back to the order counter.

"Well?" Swaggart asked as Poppy smiled at him over the counter.

"You forgot the broccoli on that one, Bobby," Poppy said as she looked at the steak and shrimp ordered up for one of her customers at table four. She smiled at Swaggart then and said, "They were both absolutely blown away of course, chef," she said.

"Well, there you go," Swaggart said with a smile and a nod.

"Thanks again," she said as she watched Bobby add a side of broccoli to one of the plates.

"You owe me," he said. He wiped his hands on the front of his apron and picked up a large knife, twirling it in his palm before using it on whatever was behind the counter that Poppy couldn't see.

"Admittedly," she giggled as she picked up the two plates for table four and left.

"So, I'll call you Wednesday night to get directions to your place," Mark said as he signed his credit card slip.

"Okay," Poppy said.

"I'm trippin' to the men's room, man," Braden said. "You tell your cook that was the best salmon I've ever had in my life! And I'm from Seattle!"

Poppy smiled, delighted with Braden's compliment to Swaggart and by the fact he'd left her alone with Mark.

"I'm already completely smitten with you, you know," Mark said.

"What?" Poppy asked, blushing to the very tips of her toes. She tucked a strand of hair behind her ear as she looked at him. "Smitten? No one says smitten."

As Ella Fitzgerald sang "Misty" over the restaurant sound system, Poppy's arms were suddenly covered in goose bumps as Mark reached out, taking hold of her hand.

Caressing the back of her hand with his thumb, he said, "Smitten. And I mean it. I'm not going to sleep a minute until I can see you on Thursday."

"I think you might be what my grandma calls 'a charmer,' Mr. Lawson," Poppy said.

"I'm only being honest," he said, smiling at her.

"Did you enjoy your meal?" Poppy asked.

"Are you kidding? Prime rib? And by the way, it was the best I've ever had," he answered.

"I'll be sure and tell the chef," Poppy said, biting her lip as the cocoa of his eyes studied hers.

"Good evening, sir," Swaggart said, suddenly appearing beside Poppy. "Was the meal to your satisfaction?"

Poppy was uncomfortable, shy somehow about the way Mark continued to hold her hand. Yet, she was oddly thrilled by his lack of discomfort and timidity about it.

"Are you the cook?" Mark asked.

"Yes, sir," Swaggart said. "Swaggart Moretti."

Mark did drop her hand then, offering his to Swaggart. "Then let me just tell you, that was the best prime rib I've ever had in my life."

"Thank you. I'm glad it was to your liking," Swaggart said, shaking Mark's hand.

Again Poppy was struck by the feeling she was standing with apple pie in one hand and peach pie in the other. Again she wished she could've had just one romantic moment with Swaggart—just one before her "Mr. Right" showed up. She glanced at Mark and wondered if her Mr. Right had shown up.

"Are you the guy who grilled that salmon?" Braden asked as he returned to the table.

"Yes, sir. Swaggart Moretti. I hope you enjoyed it," Swaggart said, accepting Braden's outstretched hand in a firm shake.

"Man, that was incredible!" Braden said.

"Thank you," Swaggart said.

Poppy almost giggled out loud. She knew how difficult it was for Swaggart to accept a compliment—knew his teeth were probably clinched and that all he wanted was to high-tail it back to the kitchen. Still, he always greeted anyone who ordered the Chef's Choice.

"I'm telling everybody about this place," Braden said. "It's fantastic!"

"I'm glad you enjoyed your meal," Swaggart said.

"The meal and the service," Braden said, smiling at Poppy. "You know, my friend has his eye on your little honey here."

"He'd be a fool if he didn't," Swaggart said, winking at Poppy.

Poppy smiled at him, but quickly looked away when she felt Mark take her hand once more. Again her arms broke out in goose bumps at the feel of her hand in his.

The first line of the all-too-familiar song caused Poppy to gasp, "Oh, no!"

"Oh, yes!" Swaggart chuckled as Dean Martin sang "That's Amore."

"All right!" Mark chuckled as everyone working and most of those dining at Good Ol' Days began to sing along.

"You mean…you mean it's happening now?" Braden asked.

Mark nodded as he sang along too. He stood then, joining Swaggart and Braden. Josh appeared and, draping one arm around Poppy's shoulders, the other across Swaggart's, joined in at the chorus.

As the song ended, the usual amused applause erupted, and Poppy thought her cheeks might actually catch flame by the time things settled down.

"That was awesome!" Braden exclaimed as Josh trotted back to work. "This place is wild." Shaking his head he said, "I'll see you outside, man." Nodding at Poppy he said, "I'm sure I'll see you again." He pointed to Swaggart and added, "Excellent meal, my man."

Swaggart smiled and the warm syrup of his eyes lingered on Poppy for a moment. "I've got to get back," he said. Then nodding to Mark he said, "Thank you for coming in."

"Oh, the pleasure was all mine," Mark said.

Poppy watched Swaggart as he walked back toward the kitchen. The feel of her hand suddenly clasped in Mark's again drew her attention to him. He was smiling at her, his eyes warm and twinkling.

"I'll see you Thursday then. Okay?" he asked.

"I can't wait," Poppy said, returning his smile. She bit her lip as he raised her hand to his lips, kissing the back of it lingeringly.

"I'll call you," he said as he left.

As soon as he was out of sight, Poppy collapsed into his recently emptied chair.

"I saw that!" Whitney whispered as she seated a couple at the next table.

"Unbelievable!" Poppy whispered in return.

She sighed, suddenly overwhelmed with sheer delight. Mark Lawson! She had a date with Mark Lawson! And he was smitten with her! It was the stuff of dreams.

Sighing once more, a pleased smile on her face, she glanced down at the plate still sitting on the table—Mark's plate. She gasped a moment later as she saw the fifty dollar bill peeking out from under it. She wondered if it was too late to catch him before he drove off— too late to return the ridiculous tip to him. Yet as she pulled the currency out from under the plate, she smiled. Attached to the fifty was a small yellow Post-it note, which read, *And in case you ever need my number...891-1288.*

Poppy giggled, tucked the fifty and its accompanying note in her apron pocket, lifted the two plates off the table, and headed for the kitchen.

She had a date with Mark Lawson, and he was smitten with her! Nothing could ruin this night—nothing!

Mark smiled as he thought of Poppy and turned out of Braden's apartment complex parking lot. Poppy Amore was completely under his skin. She seemed to radiate beauty and goodness in every respect, and he'd managed to secure an evening with her. He chuckled, pleased with himself and eager for Thursday to arrive.

He thought of the look on Poppy's face when Dean Martin had begun to sing "That's Amore." It was obvious it had rattled her, just as it had the first night he'd seen the spectacle, and he loved it. And what a fabulous meal! He did wonder for a moment if that movie-star-looking cook had a thing for Poppy himself—it was quite a meal he had pulled off. Yet Poppy wouldn't have so eagerly accepted a date with another man if there was anything between her and the cook. Mark smiled again. She did seem pretty delighted when Mark had asked her out—very enthusiastic in agreeing to go.

He thought about the softness of her small hand—how great it felt to hold it in his. He thought about the way her eyes seemed to sparkle when she smiled, how perfect her figure was.

Yep—Thursday couldn't come fast enough.

CHAPTER FIVE

"I dug out our notebook and lists last night," Whitney said as she sat at the table eating noodles swimming in melted butter.

"Why?" Poppy asked, studying her reflection in the microwave door. "Feeling sentimental?"

Whitney shrugged and answered, "I don't know—I guess so." She giggled and slurped a noodle. "We were so funny—and so full of energy and adventure!"

Poppy smiled and giggled too. "Were? What do you mean? Twenty-one isn't exactly elderly, Whit. Besides, you can speak for yourself, but I'm still full of energy and adventure." Poppy fastened a gold hoop earring in one ear and then the other. "Though I will admit to you that you tainted my brain a bit by bringing up that unfinished item on my list yesterday."

"What do you mean?" Whitney asked.

Poppy pulled her lip gloss from her purse. She used her right ring finger to apply a glistening shine to her lips as she continued to look into the microwave.

"You know—when you told me about Swaggart dumping Jennifer and you said I should at least try to check item number one off my list. It tainted my brain a bit," Poppy explained.

"Good," Whitney said.

"What?" Poppy asked. "That's a mean thing to say!"

"I just meant…doesn't it drive you crazy that you have that one thing left?" Whitney asked. "I mean, it's not like you're me with four things left to check off. I'll never finish."

"You'll finish," Poppy said. Then, rolling her eyes, she added, "And it doesn't matter if you finish or not. We made those lists when we were fourteen. It's a miracle we checked off as many items as we did."

"Look," Whitney said, reaching into a canvas bag sitting on the floor near her chair. "Here they are. Let me read the lists off to you."

"I know the lists, Whit," Poppy said, smiling at her friend.

Whitney Dexter and Poppy Amore had been fourteen, freshmen in high school, when they'd started the notebook. It was basically a notebook of handwritten memories, pasted-in mementoes, and other schoolgirl interests. It also included each girl's "Dreams to Do" list— a list of twenty things each girl wanted to accomplish or experience in her lifetime. It was just a fun little list, a list of dreams—most of which the girls had been fortunate enough to see come to fruition.

"You don't know the lists," Whitney said. "Here's mine…I'll read them from last to first." She cleared her throat. "Dreams to Do," she began. "Number twenty: Donate my hair to Locks of Love. Number nineteen: Hike down into the Grand Canyon—"

"You've done both of those," Poppy said, pulling out a chair and sitting down at the table with Whitney. As much as she pretended otherwise, Poppy loved the occasional, "reading of the list," as Whitney called it. Reading the lists not only brought back a flood of wonderful memories but caused Poppy to feel as if she'd already accomplished so much in her young life. It made her feel as if anything were possible. Well—anything but checking off the number one thing on her list.

"Yes, I have," Whitney said, smiling. "Next," she continued, "Number eighteen: Find a starfish while wandering along the beach. Number seventeen: See a tornado in real life—"

"That one freaked us out!" Poppy said.

"I know! It was like…like an angel had read my list and was helping me check stuff off. Imagine—seeing a tornado like that the one time we were in Kansas for drill-team competition."

"Totally weird," Poppy said.

"Number sixteen: Shake hands with Michael Jordan. Fifteen: Visit Mount Rushmore. Fourteen: Learn to surf. Thirteen: Learn to swing dance. Twelve: See the Statue of Liberty. Eleven—now see, this one bugs me big time, but I'm saving up and I'll get it done! Eleven: Visit Prince Edward Island, Canada." Whitney paused and shook her head, discouraged.

"You've got forever to do that one," Poppy said. "Maybe you can honeymoon there when you get married."

"Maybe," Whitney grumbled. "Ten: Visit the U.S.S. Arizona Memorial in Hawaii. Another one that will take forever to check off."

"Oh, just keep going," Poppy said. Whitney had always gotten discouraged when she'd had two consecutive list items that were difficult to fulfill—ever since the day they'd made the list.

"Okay…Nine: Learn to play the piano. I've done that one, at least. Eight: Win a best-of-show ribbon in something—the cherry jelly I entered in the state fair."

"Mmm-hmm," Poppy agreed with nod.

"Seven: Learn to crochet—Grandma taught me. Six: Read all of Dickens's and Austen's works. That one about wore us out, remember?"

"Totally!" Poppy answered. "My brain still hurts."

"Five—visit *The Goonies* house in Oregon." Whitney paused, glaring at Poppy.

"I can't help it if my parents wanted to vacation in Oregon and yours didn't that summer," Poppy said.

"Four: Ride a train coast to coast," Whitney continued. "Three: Memorize 'The Highwayman' by Alfred Noyes. Two: See Bon Jovi in concert."

"That was a hard one to pull off," Poppy commented.

"Expensive too," Whitney added. "And item number one—never to be checked off—Kiss Greg Amore."

"I could've helped you with that one," Poppy said, shaking a scolding index finger at her friend. "But you wouldn't let me."

"I know, I know," Whitney said. "And then you let your stupid cousin move off to Timbuktu, and I'll never get it checked off!"

"I tried," Poppy said.

"You tried to pay him twenty bucks to do it!" Whitney said, smiling. "That wouldn't have even counted!"

"It would too have," Poppy giggled.

"Anyway," Whitney said, turning the page in the notebook. "Let's move on to yours. Number twenty: Photograph the Albuquerque International Balloon Fiesta. Those are still my favorite photos you've ever taken."

"Mine too," Poppy said. She glanced up at the clock. She still had half an hour before Mark was to arrive to pick her up for their date. She was glad Whitney had pulled out the notebook—she was nervous, and the notebook was helping to distract her.

"Nineteen: Serve on a jury—you did that," Whitney continued. "Eighteen: Go fishing in Idaho. I always thought that one was weird."

Poppy giggled. "But I did it," she said.

"Yes, you did," Whitney giggled. "Seventeen: Spend eight hours in a Civil War cemetery. Sixteen: Have a chalk-artist do your portrait. Fifteen: Walk the ridgepole of an old Victorian home." Whitney paused, eyebrows arched. "I'm sure Lucy Maud Montgomery and the orthopedist appreciated that."

"Mom didn't though," Poppy said.

"Fourteen: Plant a rose garden," Whitney said with a nod. "Thirteen: Learn the five Latin ballroom dances. Twelve: Own a pair of Levi's 501 button-fly jeans. Eleven: Visit Arlington National Cemetery. What is it with you and cemeteries?" Poppy only shrugged as Whitney shook her head and continued, "Ten: Sing the National Anthem at a college football game. Nine: Eat crawfish in New Orleans. Your parents always took better vacations than mine. Eight: Receive a stamped postcard from Scotland."

"And I have your grandpa to thank for that," Poppy said.

"Seven: Ride a horse along the beach in Monterrey, California—that was a fun senior trip, huh?" Poppy smiled and nodded. "Six: Read all of Dickens's and Austen's works—and your brain still hurts, I know. Five—visit *The Goonies* house in Oregon." Whitney paused long enough to stick her tongue out at Poppy. "Ride the rollercoaster at the top of the Stratosphere in Las Vegas is number four. Three is memorize 'The Lady of Shalott' by Tennyson. Number two: Shake the hand of the President of the United States. And your number one, and only unfulfilled dream to do—make out with Swaggart Moretti!"

"It says, 'Kiss Swaggart Moretti!'" Poppy argued.

"It says, 'Kiss make out with Swaggart Moretti,'" Whitney corrected.

"The 'make out with' is crossed out," Poppy said, pointing to item number one on her Dreams to Do list.

"Only because you thought you'd overshot your goal," Whitney said. "And I still think you should do it."

"That's because you're dumb," Poppy said.

"It's the only thing left to do, and your list would be totally finished!" Whitney said. "And besides," she continued, "I think it still haunts you. In fact, I know it does."

"So what?" Poppy said, shrugging her shoulders and adjusting the silver and gold bracelet at her wrist. "We all have things that haunt us. And anyway, what if he had kissed me and it had been totally gross? That would haunt me even worse—the fact that the guy I always wanted to kiss was a disgusting kisser."

"There's no way Swaggart's a disgusting kisser...he's my cousin!" Whitney said, pointing to herself. "And anyway, it's not like it's the hardest thing to accomplish on your list. You shook the hand of the President of the United States...but you never found the courage to kiss Swaggart? You braved armed members of the Secret Service, but you won't contrive a way to have one make-out session with Swaggart Moretti? You're a weenie, that's all."

"So I'm a weenie," Poppy said. "I admit it."

A mischievous grin spread across Whitney's face as she asked, "And what if Mr. Gorgeous Mark Lawson tries to kiss you good night this lovely, starry evening?"

Poppy smiled, and her arms broke out in goose bumps at the thought. "Well, Mr. Gorgeous Mark Lawson is smitten with me. Swaggart isn't," Poppy said. "And besides, a kiss good night is a lot different than making out, Whitney—you goofball."

"Okay," Whitney said, still grinning. "But tell me this—and be honest—if Swaggart Moretti and Mark Lawson were both standing here in our living room right this minute, each holding a sign that said, 'I want to kiss you, Poppy Amore'…which one would you most want to kiss?"

Poppy paused too long, and she was afraid Whitney would be wise to her. Still, she said, "Mark Lawson. Hands down."

"You're lying," Whitney said.

"Okay, yes….I admit it, but it's only because I've know Swaggart seven hundred and sixty-three years. I've only been around Mark twice," Poppy said.

"You have known Swaggart longer—but that's not the reason. Admit it," Whitney demanded.

"It's only because you're forever reminding me about stupid item number one on my list!" Poppy exclaimed. "Maybe if you quit mentioning it—or if we'd never made the lists in the first place—then maybe I could get on with life instead of thinking about it every time another guy…" Poppy sighed, stood up, and studied her reflection in the microwave door again.

Whitney's smile faded. She'd hit the nail right on the head, so to speak—Poppy was still haunted by item number one. More exactly, she was still haunted by Swaggart Moretti.

Mark Lawson was gorgeous! He was charming, obviously had money, and was obviously smitten with Poppy. Whitney knew Poppy wouldn't be able to relax and have fun on their date if Swaggart was still lingering around in her mind's eye.

Whitney loved Poppy—they had been best friends forever, and she wanted to see her happy. If Mark Lawson turned out to be Poppy's Mr. Right, then Whitney didn't want to regret not accepting him because she preferred the idea of Poppy with Swaggart.

"You're right," Whitney said. "I was just teasing you. Sorry."

"It's okay," Poppy said, applying more lip gloss. "It does haunt me, and I admit it."

"But, you're right too. Maybe Mark is the guy to put that particular ghost to rest," Whitney said.

"Maybe," Poppy said. Her smile returned. She did feel better. Whitney just enjoyed reminiscing, that was all. She knew her friend didn't mean to upset her. Furthermore, it didn't take Whitney's reminiscing to unsettle her anyway—Mark Lawson would be there any minute!

Quickly, Poppy looked down, smoothing the light pink and lavender fabric of the skirt of her dress.

"Do I look okay?" she asked Whitney. "He said to dress nice."

"You look fabulous!" Whitney said. "He won't be able to keep his hands off you!"

"Right," Poppy said, rolling her eyes.

The doorbell rang, and Poppy felt her body stiffen.

"He's here!" she whispered.

"Do you want me to get the door?" Whitney asked, wide-eyed and seeming suddenly nervous herself.

"No, I'll go," Poppy said. She raked her fingers through her hair, grabbed her purse off the counter, and went to the door.

Poppy opened the door to find super-gorgeous Mark Lawson smiling at her.

"Hi," she greeted.

"Hi," he said, his smile broadening as he studied her from head to toe. "Are you ready?"

"Yeah," Poppy said. "Bye, Whit," she said over her shoulder as she closed the door behind her.

"You look wonderful," Mark said, taking her arm and linking it through his.

"So do you," Poppy said. And it was true! He wore khaki pants, black loafers, and a lavender dress shirt. She smiled, thinking what a wonderful coincidence it was that they both wore lavender.

"I thought we'd have dinner at the Cliff House," he said. He escorted her to the passenger's side of a silver BMW, opening the door for her.

"That sounds great," Poppy said, smiling at him as he closed the door once she'd situated herself in the passenger's seat.

As the smell of a leather-seated automobile filled her senses, Poppy inhaled a deep, calming breath. She still could not believe a guy like Mark Lawson had even found her interesting enough to look at, let alone take out on a date—but she was sitting in his car waiting for him to drive her to one of the nicest restaurants in the city.

Smitten, he had said. As he got into the car and turned the key in the ignition, Poppy returned his smile. It was going to be a night to remember—she could already tell.

"Yeah. I guess I lucked out," Mark said as the waitress refilled his water glass. "I landed a couple of big accounts early on, so the CEO of the firm moved me up."

"That's great," Poppy said, cutting a piece of the citrus-marinated chicken breast on her plate. "Do you like what you do?"

"Yeah. It's great," he answered. "Of course, I work with some great people—you met my friend Braden—and that makes all the difference."

"I know what you mean," Poppy said. "People are what make a work environment good or bad."

"And you like the environment at the restaurant, don't you?" he said.

Poppy looked up. He was smiling at her—a contented, pleased smile.

"I do," she said. "It's…it's what makes it so fun to work there. Just like the good customers offset the bad ones—the other employees at Good Ol' Days make a bad day worth enduring."

"How long have you worked there?" Mark asked.

"Two years. Mr. Dexter, the owner, he hired me himself. He's a really nice man," Poppy said.

"And do you plan on working there for a long time?" Mark asked. "I mean, it seems like it would be a hard job to leave behind. Though I will say you put up with a lot of…junk."

"You mean, like your Miss Susan Reginald?" Poppy asked, smiling.

"Exactly," Mark chuckled.

"Yeah—she was something else," Poppy said. "I felt bad for you—having to sit there with her."

"I felt bad for *you*!" Mark said.

"You know she showed up the next day, don't you?" Poppy asked. She knew there was no way Mark could know Miss Susan Reginald had made another appearance at the restaurant. Still, she wanted him to know for some reason.

"No way! She came back?" he asked. His smile faded, his brow furrowed, and Poppy could tell he was disturbed. "What reason could she have for coming back? Did she leave something?"

"She came back to get me fired," Poppy said.

"You've gotta be kidding me!" he said.

Poppy could tell he was truly upset, and it delighted her a bit.

"Nope," Poppy said. "She walked in and asked—actually, she demanded—to speak to the manager. She told him she wanted me fired."

"On what grounds?" Mark asked. He was angry now.

Poppy felt guilty for even having mentioned it and endeavored to smooth it over.

"That I was rude, ridiculous, and threw myself at you," she told him. "But Swaggart just showed her the door—literally."

"The cook guy?" Mark asked. "He's the manager too?"

"Sometimes," Poppy said.

"Well, good for him!" Mark said. "What a witch! I'm glad we're not taking on her account—she would've made everyone miserable."

"Oh, I'm sure she would've," Poppy agreed.

"And really—I'm so sorry you had to deal with her," he said, reaching across the table and covering one of Poppy's hands with his own.

"That's okay," she said, smiling at him. "I got a good tip out of it."

He laughed then, and Poppy felt warm all over. She liked the deep, rich sound of his laughter. Not to mention the sudden display of his stunning smile.

They lingered at their table for near to an hour after they'd finished their meal. Although Poppy was delighted with Mark's attention and enjoyed the conversation, the waitress in her was unsettled. She knew their waiter was probably anxious to clear the table so he could seat other guests and work on earning more tips for the night. Still, she hoped Mark would leave a nice enough percentage for a tip to compensate.

"Well, I guess we ought to go," he said, at last.

"I guess so," Poppy said.

Mark reached into his back pocket and withdrew his wallet, rummaging through it until he found the amount of currency he wanted.

Dropping a hundred dollar bill on the table he asked, "Did you enjoy the food? I mean…these guys have a lot to measure up to if that prime rib I had the other night is your cook's average meal."

"Oh, it was delicious!" Poppy said. Certainly, it wasn't as good as any chicken Swaggart prepared, but it was enjoyable.

"Are you up for ice cream at Dairy Queen?" Mark said as he stood and assisted Poppy in standing.

Poppy giggled. How adorable! Take a girl to the fanciest restaurant in town and then top it off with a casual trip to Dairy Queen? She loved it!

"Sure," she said.

"Banana split?" he asked.

"Peanut Buster Parfait," she teased.

"You got it," he chuckled.

"You will go out with me again," Mark said. "And that wasn't a question."

Poppy giggled as she noticed the way her apartment porch light illuminated Mark's head as if there were an invisible halo around it.

"I will," she said.

"When?" he asked, stepping closer to her. Poppy's heart began to beat faster. A little flutter in her bosom told her he meant to kiss her good night.

"When do you want me to?" she ask.

"Well, I'm guessing you work the rest of this week," he said.

"Yeah," she said as he took another step closer.

"What's next week like?" he asked, lowering his voice.

"I'm off Wednesday and all day Saturday," she said.

"Okay then," he said, lowering his voice. His eyes were intense as they gazed into hers. "All day Saturday is my preference."

"All day?" she asked.

"Yep. We could do lunch, and then I think it'll be warm enough to take a canoe out on the little lake at Hollander Park," he said.

Poppy's smile broadened. How romantic! She couldn't wait!

"Okay," she said.

"And I'm going to kiss you good night now—so don't run away," he said as his head descended toward hers.

"O-okay," Poppy breathed.

He kissed her softly, slowly—obviously being careful not to overdo it—not to press her too much on their first date. The first moment his lips touched hers, a vision of Swaggart Moretti popped into her mind—but she managed to push his image aside and enjoy, and return, Mark's nonintrusive good night kiss. Her arms erupted with goose bumps as his lips lingered against hers. As he kissed her, he took her face between his strong hands. The kiss was careful—the kiss of a couple realizing they liked each other, but just starting out.

When it ended, Poppy felt pleased and disappointed at the same time.

"Good night, Poppy," Mark said. "I'll call you next Friday about our Saturday together."

"Okay," Poppy said. She smiled after he bent and quickly kissed her once more.

"This is me being on good behavior, you realize," he said winking at her before he turned and left.

"Thank you for a fabulous evening," Poppy called after him.

He turned and smiling said, "No…thank *you*."

Poppy watched him get into his car and drive away. As she unlocked her apartment door and stepped inside, Poppy smiled and bit her lip, still entirely delighted by the evening and Mark's good night kiss.

"You're home earlier than I expected," Whitney said, raising the remote control and pressing the off button. "It's only ten."

"We had dinner at the Cliff House," Poppy said, tossing her purse into the well-worn armchair nearby. "And dessert at Dairy Queen."

"How funny!" Whitney giggled. "Was it all just too dreamy?"

"It was!" Poppy said. "And we're spending next Saturday together."

"No way!" Whitney exclaimed. "Tell me everything! Did he kiss you?"

"Yes!" Poppy giggled. "And it was wonderful! He was careful, you know? Really—sort of polite about it."

"Polite about it?" Whitney asked, wrinkling her nose.

"You know—a gentleman," Poppy explained. "Not one of those guys who attacks you the first night. Mark is…is…"

"Gorgeous!" Whitney finished.

"He's so nice, Whitney," Poppy said, smiling. "And gorgeous too!"

"I'm glad you had fun, girl," Whitney said. "He seems really wonderful."

"He is," Poppy said as she reached back, unzipping her dress. "Let me change and I'll tell you everything."

"Okay," Whitney said, rubbing her hands together in excited anticipation.

Poppy giggled at Whitney's dramatics and headed for her bedroom.

As she passed the kitchen table, however, she saw the infamous notebook still there. Pausing, she saw that it was still open to her old Dreams to Do list.

Letting her fingers travel over item number one, she thought of Swaggart—thought of his brilliant sense of humor, his fabulous physique, his incredible culinary talent, and his unequaled good looks. Frowning, she closed the notebook and headed for her bedroom.

Stepping out of her dress, she forced her thoughts to linger on Mark and the incredible evening she'd spent with him. He was wonderful! Simply wonderful—and he was interested in her! She smiled, thinking of how fantastic a canoe ride with him would be.

She slipped on some pajamas and headed out to talk to Whitney. Mark Lawson was marvelous, and he was attracted to her. She still couldn't believe it—but it was true.

"So, start from the very beginning," Whitney said as Poppy went to the kitchen sink to get a drink of water. As she turned, her eyes fell to the now closed notebook on the table.

"Well," she said, looking from the notebook to her best friend. "First of all, he drives a brand-new BMW."

"No way!" Whitney squealed. Her smile faded suddenly, however, as she asked, "Did it smell like leather seats or some other girl's perfume?"

"Leather seats, idiot," Poppy giggled.

"Good!" Whitney said. "Go on, go on! I've been waiting for hours!"

Poppy laughed and continued to tell Whitney about her evening. Yet several times as she was doing so, her eyes drifted beyond Whitney to the notebook sitting on the kitchen table.

Poppy arrived at work the next day to find the most beautiful arrangement of spring flowers she had ever seen sitting on a stool near the hostess podium.

Uncle Robert was seating customers. He smiled at Poppy as her gaze lingered on the flowers.

"Well?" he said.

"Am I late?" Poppy said. She opened her purse and began to dig for her cell phone. She was sure she'd left the apartment in plenty of time, but she thought she'd better check the time on her phone just the same.

"No, you're fine," Uncle Robert said. "It's the flowers—they're for you."

Poppy felt her eyes widen, a delighted flutter beginning in her chest.

"Really?" she asked.

"Yep," Uncle Robert chuckled. "And there's a card."

Poppy bit her lip as she hurried over to the stool and retrieved the card from the plastic florist's pick.

"They're so beautiful!" she said.

"That they are," Uncle Robert said. "And, I'm guessing, not too cheap."

Opening the tiny envelope Poppy couldn't help but sigh as she read Mark's message to herself. *Thank you for a wonderful evening...and the best "first kiss" I've ever had. I'm looking forward to the second. Yours, Mark*

Poppy bit her lip, delighted by Mark's message. He was too romantic! She'd never received any kind of note, card, or letter that thrilled her the way Mark's flower-arrangement-notes did!

"Take them back to the alcove when you go, okay?" Uncle Robert suggested.

"I will. Thanks, Uncle Robert," Poppy said, lifting the large vase of flowers and heading toward the back of the restaurant.

"Don't thank me," Uncle Robert said. "Thank your Romeo."

Poppy hurried to the back of the restaurant and set the arrangement on an out-of-the-way chair in the alcove.

"I take it last night went well then, huh?" Swaggart said as he entered through the back door and saw Poppy sniffing one of the flowers in the arrangement.

"*Oh*, yeah!" Poppy said. She tried to ignore the loop-the-loop her stomach did when she looked up at him.

"So I guess my prime rib did the trick," he said, flashing a dazzling smile.

Poppy rolled her eyes but couldn't help but delight in his teasing.

"Your prime rib wasn't there last night, buddy," she said.

"Buddy?" he chuckled. "Well, so that's what I get for helping you out with Mr. Joe Perfect-Face." He shrugged his broad shoulders and wrapped the ties of his apron around his waist.

"His name is Mark," Poppy said, lightly punching Swaggart on one muscular arm. "And I already thanked you for the prime rib."

"I'm just kidding with you, Poppy-seed," he said.

"I know," she said as she was momentarily mesmerized by his appearance.

He wore nothing unusual, nothing out-of-the-ordinary—just his uniform jeans with a white t-shirt—but he was astonishing to look at! His dark hair was already a bit mussed, and Poppy guessed he'd driven his old Chevy pickup to work. Swaggart always drove his old blue and white Chevy pickup with the windows down. He owned another car too—a newer but rather beat-up black Jeep. The Jeep ran better and got better gas mileage, but Swaggart seemed to prefer the old Chevy—and when the weather was good, he always drove it with the windows down.

"Driving your pickup today, are we?" Poppy said. Before she realized what she was doing, she reached up and ran her fingers through his hair, endeavoring to neaten it for him. Instantly, she regretted the action, for the fluttering feeling in her stomach increased tenfold, and her entire body erupted in goose bumps!

"As a matter of fact, yes," he said. Obviously, the gesture had little effect on him—for he reached out and playfully ran his hand over the top of Poppy's head, raking his own fingers through her hair. "And now that we're both presentable—I better get busy." He smiled and finished tying his apron strings at his waist.

"Yeah," Poppy said, smoothing her hair and trying to appear unaffected.

He turned and headed into the kitchen. Poppy sighed when he'd gone. She thought of Swaggart—the peach pie—and of Mark—the apple pie. Yet, what fool would linger at the bakery window staring at the peach pie when the apple pie was already in her hands?

Mark was wonderful—a gentleman, polite, romantic, and gorgeous!

Poppy shook her head. "You're a goofball, Poppy Amore," she mumbled to herself as she headed for the hostess podium. She smiled as the memory of Mark Lawson's tender kiss and striking good looks filled her mind. He was fabulous—and smitten!

CHAPTER SIX

The following day found the restaurant so busy that Poppy and everyone else working at Good Ol' Days struggled to keep utter chaos at bay! Summer had arrived, and the regular customers knew the garden and patio tables would be open. A constant stream of customers and a forty-minute wait to be seated gave Poppy little time to reflect on Mark or her upcoming date with him.

The dinner rush was even worse than the lunch rush had been. As Poppy headed to the kitchen with her newest table's order, she glanced out the front window of Good Ol' Days to see at least twenty people waiting to be seated.

"I need two Chef's Choices," Poppy said as she added her order to a long line on the order rack. "One beef, any veggie—one chicken, no asparagus," she said.

"Okay," Swaggart mumbled, handing a knife to Bobby. Poppy felt bad for him as she looked up to see the heavy frown furrowing his brow. Chef's Choices were more time-consuming, more demanding, and she was certain he would rather have been told there were simply two more hamburgers needed.

"Poppy," Swaggart said as she started to leave.

"Yeah?"

He looked up at her. The deep brown of eyes reflected fatigue, and Poppy's heart experienced a sharp pang of compassion.

"Have Uncle Robert come back here to help us," he said. "We're gonna get backed up if he doesn't. Grandpa can help Whitney with seating."

"Sure," Poppy said.

She hurried to the hostess podium to deliver Swaggart's message.

"Uncle Robert," she said.

"Hmmm?" Uncle Robert asked as he handed four menus to Brittany and gestured toward a waiting party of four.

"Swaggart needs you in the kitchen," she said. "Do you think Mr. Dexter can assist here?"

"He's in the office," Uncle Robert said. "I'll let him know. And you need to take your break."

"Ten minutes," Poppy said. "I promise."

"Okay," he said as he left.

"Whew!" Whitney breathed. "It's crazy in here!"

"I know!" Poppy agreed.

"I've got a bottled water in my bag, Poppy," Whitney said. "Next time you're near the alcove, will you grab it for me, please?"

"You bet," Poppy said.

"Rhonda—party of two?" Whitney called as she handed Poppy two menus.

Poppy smiled as a familiar, forty-something, short brunette stepped up to the podium.

"I'm Rhonda," the woman said. Another short brunette stepped up beside her.

"Great! Poppy will be seating you today," Whitney said.

"If you'll just follow me," Poppy said, smiling at the two women.

"It's really jumping in here today," Rhonda said as she sat down at table four.

"It is!" Poppy agreed, handing her a menu. She handed the other menu to her friend.

"Can I start you off with anything to drink?" Poppy asked.

Rhonda smiled and lowered her voice. "How about that tall drink of water you all keep in the back here?"

"What?" Poppy asked. The woman was so approachable and cute, and her smile was utterly contagious. Yet Poppy wasn't sure what she meant.

"Well, let's just say I always order the Chef's Choice here—just so I can get a look at that handsome cook you all have," Rhonda explained. "Wait 'til you see him, Venessa," she said to her friend. "He's reason enough to come here."

"Oooh," Poppy giggled. "So you've seen Swaggart before, have you?"

"Oh, yes!" Rhonda said. "That's why I always order the Chef's Choice!"

Poppy smiled, delighted by the woman's admiration of Swaggart. Though she worried a bit that two more Chef's Choices might put a little too much stress on Swaggart to keep him happy.

"He's a fabulous chef," Poppy said.

"He's a fabulous *man*!" Rhonda exclaimed. "What's his last name again?"

"Moretti," Poppy answered. For a moment she wondered if she should have kept Swaggart's last name to herself. What if the woman was some weird stalker sort?

"Oh, yes, that's right," Rhonda said. "I knew it was something unusual. I wonder how he came to be named 'Swaggart' with such an obviously Italian last name?"

"I guess you'll have to ask him when he comes out to see how you liked your Chef's Choice," Poppy said, winking at the woman.

"I don't know *how* you keep your hands off him," Rhonda said, wagging an index finger at Poppy.

"She doesn't."

The sudden smile of pure delight spreading across Rhonda's face coupled with the sound of his voice from behind her were Poppy's first indications that Swaggart was standing behind her.

"You scared me," Poppy scolded, twisting an elbow into Swaggart's solid stomach.

"And how are you today, Ms. Andrews?" Swaggart asked Rhonda. "Are you in for the Chef's Choice today?"

"We're in for the chef today, Mr. Moretti," the older woman flirted. "This is my friend Venessa Lions."

Swaggart nodded at Venessa and said, "It's nice to meet you." The woman blushed so red Poppy couldn't help but smile. Looking from Swaggart to Rhonda and back, she giggled, delighted with the effect his charm had on them.

"If you ladies will excuse me a moment," Swaggart began, taking hold of Poppy's elbow, "I need to consult Poppy about an order."

As he turned her to face him, she asked, "Is something wrong?" Had she made a mistake? Oh, his eyes were tired—gorgeous, but tired.

"Don't be mad, but I can't remember—on that second Chef's Choice a minute ago…did you say 'with asparagus' or 'no asparagus'? It's not on the ticket."

"Oh, I'm sorry, Swaggart," she said. "It was no asparagus."

"And which table was it?" he asked.

"This one—table three," Poppy said, pointing to the couple sitting at the table behind Rhonda and Venessa's. He looked so tired! It worried her.

Reaching out, she placed a hand on his chest and whispered, "You need a break, Swaggart. We have hours and hours left tonight."

"I know," he said. "I'll get all these special orders finished and take a break." He grinned at her and reached out, tweaking her nose as he said, "You're sweet to worry about me."

Poppy felt a pleasant shiver quickly travel through her body as he brushed something from her forehead and winked at her.

Looking past her, he said, "I'll see you ladies in about twenty minutes, all right?"

"We'll be waiting," Rhonda flirted.

Poppy watched Swaggart pause at table three and greet the couple there before heading back to the kitchen. She sighed as she watched him go. Even his walk was attractive, entirely cool.

Turning back to the two women at table four, she said, "Now, where were we?"

"We were all drooling over that cook of yours," Venessa said.

"It's hard not to, isn't it?" Poppy said. "What did you want to drink?"

"Just water for me," Rhonda said.

"Me too," Venessa said.

"And are we having two Chef's Choices this evening?" Poppy asked.

"We are," Rhonda answered. "I'll have chicken and any vegetables."

"I'll try pork and any vegetables," Venessa said.

"Any appetizers?" Poppy asked, scribbling two Chef's Choices on her tablet.

"Oh, no," Rhonda said. "He was just here."

Poppy nodded and giggled. What a couple of fun women!

"I'll get that order in then, ladies, and be right back with your water," Poppy said.

"Thank you," Rhonda said. "And thank you for being a good sport as well."

❦

Twenty minutes later, Poppy sat on a bench outside the restaurant. Her feet were sore, and she felt worn to the bone. She wondered how a fifteen-minute break was ever going to revitalize her—help her make it through the rest of the evening until closing.

The bench sat against a wall at one side of the restaurant, and the warm summer breeze felt soothing on her tired body.

"What a night," Swaggart said as he turned the corner.

He rather collapsed onto the bench beside Poppy, leaning back and stretching for a moment. Poppy looked away, somewhat disturbed by the display of rippling muscles beneath his t-shirt.

"Where do all these people come from? You'd think there weren't any other good restaurants in town."

"There aren't," Poppy said, smiling at him. He looked so tired. Again, it worried her. "You should take more time off," she told him.

"Naw," he said. "I just haven't been sleeping too well these last few nights."

"How come?" she asked.

85

He shrugged his broad shoulders, and his arm brushed hers, causing goose bumps to ripple over her body.

"Just have a lot on my mind, I guess," he answered.

"How were your lady admirers at table four?" Poppy asked, smiling at him. "I handed the table over to Brittany just now. Your Grandpa said he would paddle me if I didn't take a break."

Swaggart chuckled. "They're just fine. I like Ms. Andrews," he said. "There's nothing pretentious about her. She just says what she thinks."

"She sure likes you," Poppy said. "She was asking me about your name—how you came to be named 'Swaggart' when your last name is so purely Italian."

Again he shrugged, and again his arm brushed Poppy's. Poppy gently rubbed her forearms to dispel the increasing goose bumps.

"My mom was born in Texas—grew up there before Grandpa moved the family out here," he said. "She says she always liked the name Swaggart. And my dad—well, my last name is Moretti, but the Italian is pretty watered down otherwise."

"Same here," Poppy said. "About the watered-down Italian, that is."

"That's one of the great things about America," Swaggart said. "You really can't tell how many nationalities a person is made up of."

"That's true," Poppy said, smiling at him as he tried to stifle a yawn.

She watched him for a moment as he closed his eyes and let his head rest on the outer wall of the restaurant. Every part of her wanted to reach out and run her fingers through his hair, press an index finger against one of his pectoral muscles to see if they were really as rock-solid as they looked.

"So, Whitney says you're going out with Mr. Joe Perfect-Face again," he said. His eyes were still closed.

"Um…yeah," Poppy said. She realized then she hadn't thought about Mark for hours. Work had been too demanding.

"Oh, no!" she exclaimed then. "I was supposed to take Whitney's water bottle to her." She stood up from the bench, intending to fetch the bottle and take it to her friend, but Swaggart reached out, taking hold of her hand and pulling her to sit back down.

"It's all good," he said. "She told me where it was, and I got it for her." He opened his tired eyes and looked at her, scowling. "Which reminds me—how do you women get anything done with all that junk you drag around?"

"What?" Poppy asked.

"Whitney sends me to the back to get her water—'It's in a canvas bag,' she tells me. That thing was like a suitcase!" he said. "It looked like she had packed for a two-week trip—makeup, an extra shirt, wallet, breath mints, and some big blue binder with pictures of Jon Bon Jovi all over it. And that was just the first level, mind you," he said. "The water bottle was all the way at the bottom of the—"

"A blue binder with Jon Bon Jovi all over it?" Poppy gasped.

"Yeah," Swaggart said.

"Oh no!" Poppy breathed. "What on earth would she have that here for?

"I have no idea," Swaggart said. "Why? Is it yours?"

"Yeah! I mean, no—sort of," Poppy stammered. "Y-you didn't see anything that was inside the notebook, did you?"

Swaggart's eyebrows arched as he said, "No. Why would I care what's in Whitney's notebook?"

"Oh, you wouldn't. Of course—you wouldn't," Poppy stammered. Poppy watched as her hands began to nervously twist her apron in her lap.

"Have you got any plans for your day off?" she asked, desperate to change the subject—divert his attention.

"No," he said, frowning. "Right now all I can think of is a good long nap."

"Me, too," Poppy said, a nervous giggle escaping her lungs. "Well, I suppose I better get back," she said. All she could think about was getting to Whitney's bag and hiding the notebook—the notebook that contained her and Whitney's Dreams to Do lists.

"You just started your break," Swaggart said, taking hold of her arm again as she stood. He pulled her to sit back down on the bench and added, "And you better see it through. I'm sure Grandpa's watching the clock. If you show up early, he'll have your head on a platter."

"That's true," she said, more to herself than to Swaggart.

"Tell me about Mr. Flowers," Swaggart said, again closing his eyes—this time resting one elbow on the arm of the bench and propping his head on his fist.

"Mark?" she asked. Somehow she didn't want to talk to Swaggart about Mark.

"Yeah," Swaggart said. "Does he treat you right? I mean—other than strewing flowers in your path?"

"Yes," she said. "He's very nice."

"Nice?" Swaggart asked, looking at her through narrowed, tired eyes. "That's it?"

"He's very polite and charming and witty," she said.

"That sounds better," Swaggart said. "You had me worried."

"He took me to the Cliff House the other night," she told him. She wanted him to know another man had taken her to a fancy restaurant—seen her as worthy enough to do so.

"That's a good place. I know one of their cooks," Swaggart said. "What did you have?"

Poppy smiled, relaxing a bit. Leave it to Swaggart to be more interested in the food of a restaurant than what happened between her and Mark afterward.

"I had the citrus chicken—and, no, it wasn't nearly as good as yours," she told him.

He chuckled, flashing one of his dazzling smiles. At the sound of his laughter and the sight of him smiling, Poppy felt warm and tingly all over.

"You're on to me," he said. Poppy smiled at him as he said, "Well, I'm glad you had fun and that Romeo is so 'nice.'"

"What is your favorite meal to cook anyway?" she asked. She'd seen Swaggart Moretti cook everything from the most delicate, difficult dish imaginable to simple meatloaf and potatoes. It was a constant amazement to her—the versatile nature of his culinary skills.

"Do you want the honest truth?" he asked, tired eyes glowing warm and sultry.

"Yeah," she said.

He laughed. "I don't know if I should tell you," he said.

"Why not?"

"Because I've never told anybody. Besides…you'll probably think I'm a fool for it."

Poppy smiled. How could he be a fool for liking to prepare a certain meal?

"Tell me," she said. "Come on. Just tell me."

He raised his head, and she smiled when he actually glanced around to ensure their privacy.

"It can't be that bad, Swaggart," she giggled. "It's no secret you moonlight doing big, fancy catering jobs. Why would I think you're weird for wanting to cook fancy stuff? You went to school to learn how to do it, so I don't see why it would seem strange to—"

"Hamburgers," he stated.

"What?" she asked. He couldn't be serious.

"Hamburgers," he repeated. "There—I've admitted it."

"Hamburgers?" she giggled. "You're teasing me."

But he shook his head and said, "Nope. Hamburgers."

"But…but they're so easy," she said.

He held up an index finger and said, "Not true. Name the best hamburger you've ever had."

Still smiling Poppy said, "Yours, of course."

"That's right. I know you're telling the truth," he said. "Now, tell me…in your entire life—even considering specialty burger places—in your entire life, can you ever remember eating another hamburger as good as mine?"

Poppy thought for a moment and then said, "No."

"Exactly," he said. "A good hamburger is a very rare thing. Hamburgers are a challenge—if you care, that is."

"Hamburgers," Poppy said, shaking her head in delighted disbelief.

"Yep," he said.

Somehow—and she couldn't at first fathom it was even possible—but somehow, Swaggart suddenly seemed even more attractive than before. Here was a highly educated man—a man who had completed culinary arts school, earned a business degree, and managed to become the best cook in the city—and his favorite thing to cook was a hamburger? It was entirely too admirable and endearing.

Poppy felt her mouth begin to water. She couldn't quite tell if it was the memory of one of Swaggart's delicious hamburgers causing it to do so, or the fact she had just remembered the notebook inside in Whitney's bag and item number one on her Dreams to Do list.

"Okay, now you tell me a secret," Swaggart said, closing his eyes once more. "It's only fair."

"I don't have any secrets," Poppy lied, again thinking of infamous item one.

"Everybody has secrets, Poppy. Come on… ante up."

"You'll have to let me think of something," she told him. "But meanwhile…my break really is over."

"Chicken," he said, smiling at her.

Poppy smiled and stood up from the bench. She didn't want to leave him. He was so refreshing, so enjoyable to converse with. He looked so weary, and she couldn't resist running her finger through his soft, dark hair.

"I'll give you a quarter if you do that for two minutes," he said. "That feels really good."

Poppy ran her fingers through his hair three more times before forcing herself to stop.

"I don't have two minutes left, and you never have any change," she said, smiling down at him.

"That's because Whitney's always stealing it to buy cookies from the Girl Scouts who come in," he said.

"Well, you be sure and get some sleep tonight. *And* a long nap tomorrow," Poppy said.

"Tell Uncle Robert I'll be right there, will you?" he asked.

"You bet," she said.

She didn't want to leave him—felt depressed somehow about doing so. Therefore, as she walked away, leaving him on the bench—wondering if he might accidentally fall asleep and forget to come back in—she consciously conjured up a vision of Mark. Next Saturday would be fun! Romantic too, no doubt. She couldn't wait!

Suddenly remembering the notebook in Whitney's bag, Poppy hurried back into the restaurant. She wanted to make sure the stupid Jon Bon Jovi notebook didn't find its way into Swaggart's hands. What a nightmare it would be if he managed to get hold of it and see item number one on her list.

Swaggart rested his head against the outer wall of the restaurant once more. He was wiped out! He hadn't had a good night sleep since Joe Perfect-Man sent Poppy that stupid truckload of roses. It was always like this—anytime she went out with someone, Swaggart got all uptight and nervous. This time, it was even worse because this guy seemed perfect—perfect clothes, perfect hair, perfect face—perfect. Secretly, it ate Swaggart up inside. He hated the smelly flower arrangement sitting in the alcove at that very moment. He wondered what the card that had come with it said. His Uncle Robert said Poppy's face lit up like the Fourth of July when she read it, and it ticked Swaggart off!

Still, who was he to say anything? He'd never made a move on Poppy—how could he have? Here he was, a cook at Good Ol' Days—no fancy career, no massive amounts of money in the bank or invested—just a cook at his grandfather's restaurant, and Poppy deserved far better. This new Romeo sure seemed far better—and Poppy seemed pretty pleased with him.

Swaggart wondered if the guy had kissed her good night after their date the other night. Most guys who dropped the dough for dinner at the Cliff House would've expected at least a good night kiss. Did she kiss him? The thought caused his ears to burn with jealousy and near rage. Yet what right did he have to be jealous?

All at once, part of the conversation he'd just had with Poppy pushed its way to the forefront of his mind.

"Hmmm," he mumbled to himself. Poppy was a little too uptight about the notebook he'd mentioned seeing in Whitney's bag. Now that he thought about it, she seemed pretty desperate to change the subject. What? She didn't want him to know she and Whitney had been in love with Jon Bon Jovi when they were in high school? What high school girl wasn't in love with the famous rocker at one time or another? Still, she'd seemed pretty rattled about it being at the restaurant.

Swaggart opened his eyes and sat up straight on the bench. In fact, hadn't she asked him if he'd seen inside it? She was sure she had.

You didn't see anything that was inside the notebook, did you? she had asked—and then she'd abruptly changed the subject.

What could be in Whitney's notebook that Poppy didn't want Swaggart to see? At first he thought perhaps she'd slipped the note that had come with Romeo's flowers into it. No—why would she put a no doubt personal note in Whitney's stuff? All at once, Swaggart's mind burned with curiosity. What didn't she want him to see? Whatever it was—he had to see it!

Standing up, he headed back to the restaurant. Poppy had probably moved the notebook or Whitney's entire bag the second she'd gotten back inside. But it had to be there somewhere. Whitney and Poppy were both working the same shift he was—two to closing. Both of them had already had their lunch break too. The bag wasn't going anywhere yet.

"Oh, no! I already took my break!" Poppy said. Mark looked wonderful! He wore jeans, a blue t-shirt, and basketball shoes. "In fact, I just got back." She had been so delighted to see him waiting for her at the hostess podium when she'd returned from her break.

"That's okay," he said. "I was just driving by and thought I'd see if you had a free minute." He smiled at her, and she felt warm all over. "Did you get the flowers?"

"Yes," she said, biting her lip. "They're beautiful! Thank you."

"Good," he said. "I'll let you get back to work, but I'm stoked about Saturday."

"Me too," Poppy told him. She was so disappointed! If Mr. Dexter had let her work just a little longer before forcing her to take her break…

"I'll call you tomorrow—okay?" he asked.

"Of course," Poppy said, blushing as an elderly woman waiting to be seated winked at her with understanding.

"Okay, then—bye," Mark said.

"Bye," Poppy sighed.

He left, and Poppy wondered how she would ever concentrate on work with so many thoughts and feelings clattering around in her mind. Swaggart liked to cook hamburgers? She thought of the fact he could use some bigger t-shirts—the ones he had were pretty form-fitting and left little to the imagination concerning the definition of his muscular torso. Mark was going to call her tomorrow? What would he say? What would they talk about?

Her brain threatened to establish a headache it was so full of questions, anticipation, and fatigue. But as Nat King Cole sang "Pretend," she turned and accepted the three menus Whitney handed to her.

"By the way," she whispered to her best friend, "what are you doing with the Bon Jovi notebook here?"

"I shoved it back in my bag the other night and forgot to take it out this morning," Whitney said. "Why?"

"*Someone* saw it when he got your bottled water for you," Poppy said. "You're lucky he didn't look in it, or I would've had you maimed."

"It's in the alcove. You can move it next time you're back there," Whitney said. She mouthed, "I'm sorry, "and turned to greet a couple entering the restaurant.

Poppy smiled lovingly at her and shook her head. "You're lucky," she mouthed to her friend. "Will you follow me please?" she said to the young family waiting to be seated.

Before putting in her next order, Poppy detoured to the alcove. Whitney's bag, complete with Jon Bon Jovi notebook, was still sitting on the floor near the apron rack. Picking it up, she set it around the corner on the far side of the water cooler. No one ever used the water cooler—no one, that is, except Mr. Dexter, and Jon Bon Jovi surely wouldn't interest him.

"Poppy! Order up!" Bobby called from the order counter.

"I'm here!" she called in return. Breathing a sigh of relief, Poppy headed to the order counter.

"Where's Swaggart?" Bobby asked. It was obvious Bobby and Uncle Robert were beginning to sink.

"He's not back yet?" Poppy asked. "I just saw him a few minutes ago. Did you want me to dig him up for you?"

"No. That's okay. I guess he's really only been gone about fifteen minutes," Bobby said. "But we had two Chef's Choices order up at one of Brittany's tables, and I'm starting to get nervous."

"I'm right here," Swaggart said.

"Man, I'm sorry," Bobby said. "But we're swamped."

"That's all right," Swaggart said, entering the kitchen through the side door.

Poppy breathed a sigh of relief. She'd hidden Whitney's bag with the notebook in it just in time.

"Your order for table five is up, Poppy," Bobby reminded.

"Oh, yeah!" Poppy said, remembering her table two order. "And I need one Jiggy with rings, a pepper with rings, and one kids' grilled cheese with fries."

"Was that Romeo I saw leaving just now?" Swaggart asked. His grin was purely mischievous—Poppy loved it! Still, she couldn't let him get away with such teasing. Therefore, she glared at him for a moment before sticking out her tongue, then quickly retracting it.

"Is that an invitation?" he asked, grinning at her.

Poppy's mouth dropped open in delighted, yet astonished, awe. "I cannot believe you said that!" she scolded. However, the loop-the-loop that rocketed in her stomach at his remark was the most intense he'd ever caused.

He simply winked at her as Bobby said, "Poppy! Order up! It's going to get cold."

"Oh! Y-yeah," Poppy stammered as she picked up the two plates waiting on the order counter.

"Is that an invitation?" she repeated as she headed for table five. Was he kidding? When she was little, her mother had always told her never to stick her tongue out at boys—that it meant you were asking them to kiss you. Of course, she could never figure out why the gesture would invite a boy to kiss you—not until she was much, much older. But surely that wasn't what Swaggart had just teased her about. Was it? Yet, the loop-the-loop racing around in her stomach and bosom told her it was.

"Here you are, ma'am," she said, setting the plate of chicken scampi on the table in front of the nice lady at table five.

"I ordered the filet mignon," the woman said.

"Oh! I'm so sorry," Poppy apologized as she picked the plate up, replacing it with the correct order.

"And for you, sir—chicken scampi," she said, setting the scampi on the table in front of the woman's male companion. Poppy was jittery, trembling, perspiring for some reason. "Can I get you anything else?" she asked, forcing a smile.

"No. We're fine for now, thanks," the man said.

"Are you all right, Poppy?" Mr. Dexter asked when Poppy accidentally bumped into him on her way to the order counter.

"Oh, I'm fine, Mr. Dexter. Just a little frazzled, I suppose," she stammered. *Is that an invitation?* Swaggart's flirtatious remark kept playing over and over in her head. He shouldn't tease her like that! Didn't he know she'd adored him forever? Didn't he know the man of her dreams was at her doorstep? She thought of Mark, of their wonderful evening together and their good night kiss under her porch light. It calmed her, and she was able to smile at Mr. Dexter.

Mr. Dexter looked around for a moment. "Do you know anyone who might be interested in helping us out here on weekends?"

"Oh! Um…not right offhand, sir," she said. "But if I think of someone, I'll let you know."

"It's just too much for you all to deal with on your own, I'm afraid," he said, smiling with compassionate understanding.

"We'll be fine," she said. "Don't you worry about us." Poppy glanced to table one. "I...uh...I see Mrs. Peterson is in tonight."

Instantly, Mr. Dexter's face lit up. Mr. Dexter's wife had passed away nearly five years before. He missed her more than he liked to speak of, but Poppy had begun to notice how his eyes lit up whenever Mrs. Peterson, a regular to Good Ol' Days, was in dining.

"Oh, yes!" Mr. Dexter said, his eyes twinkling all of a sudden. "Wonderful woman! But do you really think she's up to applying for the waitressing job, Poppy?"

Poppy giggled. He was so adorable!

"No, no, no," she said. "I just thought you might like to say 'hello' to her this evening."

"Oh!" Mr. Dexter said as realization struck him. "Of course. Of course. I really should greet her personally—she's such a loyal customer."

"Yes, she is," Poppy said.

As she watched Mr. Dexter set out for table one, Poppy sighed. Life was pretty wonderful at that moment—the man of her dreams would be spending an entire Saturday with her, her roommate was her best friend, and she loved her job *and* the people she worked with.

"Order up!"

Swaggart's voice pulled her from her reflections, and she hurried toward the order counter.

"We're falling behind," Swaggart told her as she looked over the order counter at him. "And you know what that means..." Poppy smiled as Swaggart turned his back to her, lifted his muscular arms over his head and began swirling his hips in what he liked to call his *Risqué Martin* impersonation. "Everybody better shake their tail feathers!" he hollered.

Poppy laughed as Uncle Robert and Bobby turned around and joined Swaggart in the signature dance, orchestrated to relax the stressed-out kitchen staff. As Dean Martin sang "Sway," she watched as the three cooks left the kitchen and made their way to the dining area. As soon as Swaggart stepped into the dining area, the regular customers already familiar with the tradition began to applaud. As he continued to dance between the tables, Bobby and Uncle Robert followed, and many of the customers stood up from their tables and joined in the Latin-flavored dance.

Poppy stood at the order counter, mesmerized, as always, by the spectacle. Swaggart was such a good dancer! His tight white t-shirt and worn jeans only complemented his fabulous good looks and muscular physique as he danced. She wondered what it would be like to dance with him—really dance with him. She wondered if Mark was a good dancer. She was certain that he was.

Poppy giggled as Mr. Dexter took Mrs. Peterson by the hand, helping her to rise from her seat. Taking her in dance position, he led her in joining the dance.

As the song ended, everyone applauded, and Swaggart, Uncle Robert, and Bobby headed back to the kitchen.

"This place is the best restaurant in the city!" Poppy heard someone exclaim. She smiled—because after all, it was true.

CHAPTER SEVEN

Poppy felt entirely wrung out. What a day it had been! Good Ol' Days had served a record number of customers, and Poppy's feet knew it.

"Uncle Robert looked so worn out," Whitney said, putting the mop in the mop bucket and closing the supply closet door. "You aren't mad at me for saying we'd close up, are you?"

Poppy shook her head as she plopped down into a chair at table three. "No. He did look tired. Anyway, we can sleep in a little bit tomorrow."

Whitney disappeared in the alcove for a moment, and Poppy frowned as she wiggled her sore toes.

"We can go as soon as you tell me where you hid my bag, Pops," Whitney called from the alcove.

"I told you—it's by the water cooler," Poppy called in return. "And you better turn off the music while you're back there. Your Grandpa will be upset if we leave the sound system on again all night."

"Are you sure you put it by the water cooler?" Whitney called. "It's not there, and I need my keys to lock up."

"What do you mean it's not there?" Poppy asked, hopping to her feet. Had someone else moved Whitney's bag? A strong, unsettled sensation began to rinse over her as she headed for the alcove.

Poppy stopped, held her breath—startled as the door to Mr. Dexter's office opened suddenly. Her heart nearly stopped as

Swaggart walked out of the office carrying Whitney's bag in one hand, the Bon Jovi notebook in the other.

"What are you doing with that, Swag?" Whitney scolded, snatching the canvas bag from him. He raised the notebook over his head when she tried to take it from him.

"Grandpa found your bag all spilled out by the water cooler. He was afraid something would happen to your things, so he took them to his office," Swaggart said.

Poppy glared at Whitney as her heart began to hammer in her chest. Why had Whitney forgotten to take the notebook out of her bag? What if Swaggart had seen their Dreams to Do lists—seen Poppy's?

"The thing is," Swaggart began, "And you know how nosey Grandpa can be…"

"Give it to me, Swaggart!" Whitney demanded. "It's mine, and you better not have looked through it."

"Oh, I didn't," he said.

Poppy sighed with relief.

"But Grandpa did."

"What?" Poppy heard her own voice exclaim in unison with Whitney's.

"Furthermore, he felt there was something in here that might interest me," Swaggart said. "And it wasn't the twelve trillion pictures of Jon Bon Jovi."

"Oh, no!" Poppy breathed as Swaggart looked at her then. "Oh, no!" She felt tears beginning to fill her eyes.

"Swaggart Moretti!" Whitney scolded, jumping and trying to snatch the notebook from his hand. "You and Grandpa can't just go around reading everybody's personal stuff! Give it! It's private!"

"I can see why," Swaggart said, continuing to look at Poppy.

"Whitney!" Poppy scolded in a whisper.

"I'm sorry, Poppy," she mouthed as she punched Swaggart in the stomach. Naturally, her assault had no effect on him.

"Give it here, Swag," Whitney demanded, reaching for the book.

At last, Swaggart forfeited the notebook. "Quite the lists of Dreams to Do you had here," he said.

"Shut up, Swaggart!" Whitney said. "It's none of your business."

"Oh, it's not?" he said.

Poppy was frantic! She had to escape, but her mind was so confounded that she couldn't remember where she'd left her purse. In a near state of panic, she began to look around, desperately trying to remember where her purse was—her purse had her car keys in it, and she needed to run!

"I didn't know you could surf, Whit," he said.

Poppy held her breath, praying Mr. Dexter had only shown him Whitney's list. Perhaps all hope wasn't lost after all.

Whitney seemed cautiously calmed too and said, "That's right. It's why I talked my mom into taking me to California my freshman year in college."

"Oh," Swaggart said. "And you really saw Bon Jovi in concert?" he asked.

"We both did," Whitney said, looking at Poppy.

Poppy swallowed hard, knowing she was still in danger of having been discovered.

"And you've only got four things left on the list. Number one was pretty interesting," he said smiling.

"Shut up, Swag," Whitney warned.

Poppy's heart began to hurt with beating so hard. Her anxiety was causing her to tremble—causing her stomach to feel queasy.

"Your number one Dream to Do is to kiss Poppy's cousin Greg. You never got it done?" he asked.

"No. Now shut up, and go home," Whitney said.

Again, Poppy looked around for her purse. Where was it? One more minute, and she promised herself she'd just walk home!

"Why didn't you tell me, Whit?" he asked, smiling. "I knew Greg well. I could've totally hooked you up with that one."

"It's not funny, Swaggart," Whitney scolded. "You've snooped through my personal stuff, and I can't believe you're making fun of me."

101

"I'm not," Swaggart said. "I'm serious. I don't know why Poppy didn't hook you up with her cousin—but I could've, and then you would've had almost everything on your list checked off."

"Yeah, yeah, yeah," Whitney said. "We're going home."

"Oh, don't be mad," Swaggart said, taking Whitney by the shoulders and smiling at her. "You know how Grandpa is—he figures if it's in the restaurant…"

"It's his to know about," Whitney finished—and it was true.

Mr. Dexter had a hard, fast rule about anything brought into Good Ol' Days by his employees—if it was brought into his restaurant, then it better be something an employee wouldn't mind him seeing.

"That's right, and I'm sure he didn't mean to upset you—or Poppy," Swaggart said, looking over to Poppy once more. "That's my fault."

Poppy's heart nearly stopped. He knew! By the warm-syrupy look in his eyes, Poppy knew Swaggart had seen her list—seen item number one at the top of it. Forget her purse—she'd walk home. In fact, she'd run!

Turning around, Poppy fled toward the front door.

"Hey!" she heard Swaggart call.

When she reached the front door, she remembered Uncle Robert had locked it on his way out.

"Where do you think you're going?" Swaggart asked, taking hold of her shoulders and turning her to face him. Poppy couldn't look at him—kept her head down, angrily willing her tears to remain at bay.

"Swaggart," Whitney began.

"See you later, Whitney," Swaggart said. "Poppy will be right behind you."

Poppy didn't look at Swaggart, but she did lean over, looking around him to Whitney.

Whitney shrugged, helplessly shaking her head.

"Whitney?" Poppy pleaded.

"Good night, Whit," Swaggart said. "Let me talk to her for just a minute, okay?"

Again, Whitney shrugged.

Poppy gasped as her friend started to leave. "Whitney Dexter!" Poppy exclaimed. She tried to struggle free, but Swaggart's powerful hands now gripped her arms just above her elbows.

Poppy's eyes widened as Whitney smiled at her then, gestured a check mark in the air, and mouthed, "Check it off!"

"What?" Poppy mouthed.

As Whitney turned and started for the back door to the restaurant, Poppy called, "Whitney! Whitney Dexter, you come back here this minute!" But she didn't, and in the next moment, Poppy was alone with Swaggart Moretti.

Poppy felt the color drain from her face. Humiliation rose in her like a painful sickness. He'd seen it! Swaggart had seen her Dreams to Do list. He knew—Swaggart Moretti now knew Poppy Amore's one unfulfilled dream had been to kiss him!

"Why didn't you tell me, Poppy?" he asked. She could feel his gaze boring into the top of her head like a hot branding iron. "All you had to do was ask."

Entirely stunned by the remark, Poppy finally dared to look up at him.

"What?" she breathed. Swaggart was a flirt and a tease, but he was never cruel. She was surprised he would mock her about it.

"I'm serious," he said. He wasn't smiling. In fact, he appeared to be speaking the truth. "Why didn't you just ask me?" he asked. "I would've been more than willing. I mean, apparently you talked your parents into driving all the way to Astoria, Oregon, just to see *The Goonies* house—but you never found a way to ask me to kiss you?"

Poppy didn't answer, only silently cursed the tears begging to spill from her eyes. She began to tremble, her body now unable to flee because of pure, realized defeat.

"So ask me now," Swaggart said. His voice was deep, lowered, coaxing.

"What?" Poppy asked, still unable to believe what was happening was actually happening.

Swaggart smiled, shrugged his shoulders, and said, "We can check it off that list right now. What do you say?"

Poppy had never in her life known the kind of hurt filling her bosom at that moment. How could he be so cruel? As the first tear escaped one eye, she began to struggle again. She had to escape him—had to run away and drown in humiliation.

"Hey, hey, hey," he said. He lightly squeezed her arms, but she couldn't face him. How could she ever face him again? "Come on, Poppy," he said.

"I don't feel like being made fun of," she said, wiping the tears from her cheeks. "It's been a long day, and I'm tired, and I don't want—"

"But I'm not making fun of you," he said. "I'm offering to help you check that last thing off your list."

Poppy swallowed hard as he continued.

"Come on, Poppy—don't be mad at me," he said. "It's nothing to be upset about. It was like…seven years ago. I know you were a kid. Come on—don't be mad at me. Besides, you owed me a secret—remember?"

"I'm not mad at you," Poppy said, wishing he would release her. His touch was too unsettling to her senses. In truth, she wanted nothing more than to throw herself against him and beg him to go ahead and fulfill her ridiculous, adolescent Dreams to Do list. "It's just embarrassing, that's all," she said, fighting back more tears of humiliation.

"No, it's not," he said. "It's cool. I'm flattered. I think my self-esteem just improved a little."

Poppy rolled her eyes. Yet, if there was one thing the incredibly attractive Swaggart Moretti did need for some reason, it was better self-esteem. She'd never quite been able to figure why his was so low, but it was.

"Come on, Poppy," he said again. "Don't be mad at me—and don't be mad at Grandpa." She still couldn't look him square in the eye, but she did glance up to see him smiling at her—the warm brown of his eyes sparkling with delight and the pure mischief she so adored in him.

"Whitney had the worst crush on my cousin Greg at that same time," Poppy said, suddenly babbling as if a random explanation of Whitney's list items would somehow lessen her own embarrassment.

"Greg was cool," Swaggart said still smiling. "I could've hooked her up."

Poppy grinned. He hadn't meant to be cruel—she understood that now. "Greg's moving back here to help my dad with his business," she said. Maybe if she made enough trivial small talk, he'd forget the incident ever happened. Maybe if she made enough trivial small talk, *she* would forget it ever had.

But she was not to be so lucky.

"So," Swaggart began, "I'm the only thing left to do on your list, huh?"

Poppy smiled, unnerved by his touch, for he still held her arms. "Well, I was a freshman when I wrote it down. And I was crazy…kiss Swaggart Moretti? It was a tall order," she said, shaking her head and trying to dispel the goose bumps suddenly breaking over her arms at the knowledge he still held her.

"Nah," he said. "I'm not that tall." Poppy felt her smile broaden for a moment at his wit. She was beginning to relax just a little. After all, this was Swaggart! She'd known him for years—worked with him for two. They were friends. Surely he wouldn't tease her for much longer.

Poppy's smile faded at once, however, when he said, "But I think I'm tall enough to still fill that short order."

"What?" Poppy breathed. It almost sounded as if he were implying he would truly be willing to…

"Only…I think the number one thing on that old list of yours was actually *make out* with Swaggart Moretti," he said. "Not just kiss him."

"Well…I-I…I changed it," Poppy stammered. It seemed her humiliation was to be of the mortally wounding nature after all.

"I noticed that," he said. "Why did your cross out 'make out' and leave it just 'kiss'?" he asked.

"I-I knew it was an impossible thing all the way around, and I thought…I thought if I lessened the expectation, a little my chances might be better. You know—statistically," she explained.

Swaggart smiled—his eyes warm and somehow inviting. "Never minimize your dreams, Poppy," he said. "Keep them where you want them."

"Okay," Poppy said, trying once again to move out of his grasp. But again, Swaggart held fast and stayed her.

"Seriously, though…wouldn't you like to finally finish that list?" he asked. "You know, check off that last little item?"

Poppy shook her head and laughed a breathy laugh as she looked up at him. "It's okay, Swaggart," she said. "I'm embarrassed, and I admit it. Will you just take pity on me and let it go?"

"So…you don't want to kiss me anymore, huh?" he asked.

"Well, of course! I mean, no! I mean, yes! I mean…I mean…" she stammered. The very thought of kissing Swaggart was sending her thoughts into utter chaos. A vision of Mark Lawson flashed through her mind—she had a date with him on Saturday, didn't she? She wasn't sure—all she could comprehend in that moment was the splendor of Swaggart Moretti's handsome face before her, the feel of being held captive by his powerful hands, the excess moisture flooding her mouth.

"Well, I wanna do it," he stated.

"What?" Poppy breathed.

"I wanna do it," he repeated. His smile had faded, and she could tell—he was entirely serious.

"Why?" she couldn't help but ask. Even as her body began to quiver at the thought of finally, at long last, being kissed by Swaggart Moretti, she couldn't fathom why he would be willing to do it. Pity—that could be the only answer. He felt bad for her—for discovering her humiliating secret regarding him. Sure, she owed him a secret, but the fact he preferred to cook hamburgers paled by miles in comparison.

"Because once you thought I was cool enough to want me to," he said.

I still want you to, she thought.

"Swaggart...you don't have to say that. I know you're just trying to—" Poppy began.

She was interrupted, instantly rendered silent and breathless, as he took her face between his strong hands. Her gaze fell to his mouth, to the perfect shape of his lips. The moisture in her mouth increased a hundred times, and as her heart pounded like a hammer on an anvil, she hoped he wasn't simply taunting and mocking her.

"I want to check it off that list for you," he mumbled.

Poppy couldn't say a word. It was a struggle to merely breathe! His face was so close to hers she could feel his breath on her lips.

"It won't change your life, Poppy," he said, his voice low and rich like a warm drink laced with molasses. "And it probably won't be the best kiss you'll ever have," he added.

Her entire body erupted into goose bumps as his thumb traveled slowly over her lower lip.

"But I'll try to make it worth your time—worth having been on that list of yours."

"S-Swaggart," she breathed as his head descended toward hers. Her entire body was tremulous—inside and out! Her mouth was literally watering in anticipation! In her entire life, she'd never wanted anything as desperately as she wanted to feel Swaggart Moretti's lips pressed to hers in that very moment.

She thought of Mark, of the kiss they'd shared only days before. Mark's kiss had not affected her the way the mere anticipation of Swaggart's was affecting her now! Furthermore, one date did not a steady boyfriend make—there was nothing disloyal about letting Swaggart check the number one thing off the ol' Dreams to Do list. Right?

"Only," he began. His lips hovered a breath above her own. "Only I wanna go for the real deal."

"The real deal?" Poppy breathed, certain her knees would give way and find her in a dead faint on the floor at his feet.

"I want the real item number one…I want the make-out version, Poppy," he whispered. "Right here, right now."

"But…but we can't. I mean…I mean…" she stammered, her arms and legs feeling as if they'd just turned to pudding.

"Shhh," he whispered.

In the next moment, Poppy was certain she would faint, or at least burst into flames caused by blissful euphoria—for as Dean Martin began crooning "Innamorata" over the sound system, Swaggart Moretti kissed her! Instantly, she was his—without hesitation, without attempting any sort of resistance. She melted against him as he wrapped his powerful arms around her, pulling her against his rock-solid body.

Administering several slow, sweet, and measured kisses, Swaggart then wasted no time with coyness. Instantaneous passion, immediate fiery fervor erupted between them. Poppy let her arms return his embrace, cared nothing for the fact his five o'clock shadow wore rough against the tender flesh around her mouth. As the warm moisture of Swaggart's mouth worked to lead Poppy's in the exchange, she was conscious that their mouths seemed to work together as if they'd been kissing this way their entire lives!

And he was fabulous! The feel of being in his strong arms, the flavor of his mouth, his pure skill at administering such affection—kissing Swaggart Moretti was even more wonderful than Poppy had ever imagined! And heaven knew she'd spent a very long time imagining it!

As Poppy grasped his shoulders, gathered the fabric of his t-shirt into her fists endeavoring to pull him closer, her mind whirled! It couldn't be! Surely she wasn't really standing in Good Ol' Days, wrapped in Swaggart Moretti's arms, kissing him the way she was—surely he wasn't kissing her the way he was!

Suddenly, he broke the seal of their lips, releasing her for a moment. As he stood, the tempo of his breathing increased, his eyes narrowed as he looked at her. Poppy grew self-conscious and glanced away for a moment.

"Oh, don't you get shy on me now," he mumbled. His hands at her waist, and he pushed her back against the wall, trailing several moist, lingering kisses over her throat. Poppy's breathing literally stopped for a moment—she could not believe the effect he was having on her—and so instantly!

"S-Swaggart," Poppy breathed.

Her heart was hammering so hard it hurt! Her mouth was watering for want of his kiss again—it had to stop—she knew she shouldn't kiss him anymore. What good could possibly come of it? But she was crazy for him! She'd been crazy for him for years and years! She quickly rationalized that if she allowed herself to drown in the pure wonder of finally kissing Swaggart Moretti, then maybe his face wouldn't pop into her mind every time someone else kissed her good night. Maybe—if she continued to kiss him tonight—maybe it would finally purge her heart and soul of the long secreted crush, the tightly guarded infatuation she'd carried for so long. Maybe—if she continued to kiss him tonight—maybe her mind wouldn't always answer *Swaggart Moretti* as the word-association response each time she heard the word *love*.

Therefore, when he paused, looking down at her with his warm-syrup eyes and asking, "Are you done with me already?"

Poppy heard herself answer, "No."

Swaggart smiled his dazzling smile, his eyes twinkling with satisfaction as he said, "Good—'cause I'm not finished with you either—and I just happen to have a few hours of free time on my hands just now."

"Hours?" Poppy asked, biting her lip as she looked at his mouth. "People don't kiss for hours, Swaggart."

Swaggart chuckled—the low, resonate sound of it causing Poppy's body to tremble with delight. "Don't they?" he whispered a moment before the warmth of his mouth took hers once more.

And what magical hours they were! There, in the warm, inviting atmosphere of the Good Ol' Days restaurant, Poppy lived a dream— kissing Swaggart Moretti for hour after hour! He kissed her near the front door, talked with her at table one for awhile, before pulling her into his lap and kissing her again. He led her to the kitchen for a glass of water—pushed her back against the order counter and kissed her more! They stood in the alcove talking for a long time, until Swaggart reached out, pulling her into his arms and further endeavoring to keep the butterflies afloat in her stomach.

After a time, she became conscious of the way he caressed her before he kissed her—if he planned to kiss her cheek, he caressed it with the back of his hand first. If he planned to kiss her neck, he caressed the area with his fingertips before pressing his mouth to her skin. As for Poppy—she couldn't seem to satisfy her need to feel the softness of his hair. Whenever he'd pull her body flush with his, wrap her tightly in his arms, she couldn't resist letting her hands travel over his shoulders, to the back of his neck, and up through the dark softness of his hair.

"You know," he whispered as they stood in the kitchen two hours later, enjoying a bowl of ice cream. Two spoons and one bowl—Poppy thought the gesture sweetly romantic!

"What?" she asked.

"Poppy seeds really can contain or carry opium alkaloids," Swaggart said.

"Really? I thought that was just an urban legend," Poppy said, taking a bite of ice cream.

"Well, eating a poppy seed muffin probably won't find you failing a drug test," he said. "But ingest a ridiculous, unhealthy amount of the seeds, and you might be able to skew one."

"Really?" she asked.

He shrugged his massive shoulders and said, "Or so a botanist once told me."

As Dean Martin began to sing "Innamorata" once more, Poppy frowned.

"Hey, how come this song always plays twice during this loop?" she asked.

"I think it's programmed in there twice," Swaggart answered. "I think Grandpa really likes it."

"So…is it a city in Italy?" Poppy asked.

"What?" Swaggart said as he finished the last bite of ice cream.

"Amorata," Poppy said. "You know, a city. He says something about their lips meeting in Amorata," she explained as Dean sang.

Swaggart chuckled. "It's not 'in Amorata.' It's 'inamorata'—the *word* inamorata," he said.

"Oh," Poppy said, smiling at her own ignorance. "I get it—it's an Italian word."

"Yep," he said, putting the bowl and spoons in the sink.

"Do you know what it means?"

"It means *sweetheart*," he told her. "In other words…if our lips should meet, *sweetheart*," he said.

"Wow," Poppy giggled. "All this time I thought it was a place."

Swaggart leaned against the sink and smiled at her.

"Either way…it's a good song."

"It is," he agreed. "Even at two o'clock in the morning."

"Oh, my heck!" Poppy exclaimed. "Are you kidding me?"

"Nope," he said.

"I'm so sorry, Swaggart," she said, suddenly feeling ridiculous.

"For what?" he asked, walking to her and letting his hands tighten around her waist.

"For…for everything!" Poppy stammered. The humiliation she'd begun to feel when she'd realized Swaggart had seen her Dreams to Do list began to return. "For keeping you up so late, for one thing! I mean…I mean you were tired at six tonight, and here I've…"

"Shhh," he breathed, his head descending toward hers.

"Swaggart," she whispered. "You don't have…you don't have to…"

"Baby, don't go all bashful on me now," he said, smiling at her.

As he placed one hand against her cheek, Poppy reached up covering it with her own. She still couldn't believe he was touching her, that he'd held her, kissed her.

"I really am at heaven's door," he whispered in reference to the song Dean was singing. He kissed her lightly on the lips, and she was instantly at ease. He continued to whisper, sing the romantic song lyrics in unison with Dean a moment before he kissed her more firmly. All at once he gathered her into his arms, kissing her with such a passion's fire she feared it might melt her bones.

Breaking the seal of their lips, he looked down at her—the warm syrup of his eyes drizzling into hers. "Thank you," he said.

"Thank me?" she said. He was the one who'd made her dreams come true. What had she done?

"For putting me at the top of your list a long time ago," he said.

You still are at the top of my list, Poppy thought.

Instead she said, "Thank you for…for…"

"For checking it off your list," he said, smiling at her.

"Yeah," she said.

It was over. Her dream had been fulfilled and it was over. As Swaggart ended their embrace, taking her hand and leading her toward the alcove, sudden heartache mingled with bliss in Poppy. He'd kissed her, yes—and it had far exceeded her expectations! Swaggart Moretti was everything he appeared to be, and more! His kiss was the stuff of romantic fiction—of fairy-tale dreams! And it was over.

Poppy watched as Swaggart flipped the switch, sending Dean Martin's voice to sleep for the night. Reaching behind the large plant in the corner, he handed her purse to her as he opened the back door and stepped aside for her to exit first.

Poppy didn't want to leave! She wanted to turn around, linger in Good Ol' Days and in Swaggart's arms forever! But as she watched him lock the door behind them, she knew it was over.

"I hope you can sleep in a bit," he said as they reached her car.

"You, too," she said.

Poppy could feel the tears beginning to gather in her eyes. She prayed she could get in the car and drive out of the parking lot before they began to fall.

"A-and…" he stammered.

She pushed the unlock button on her key chain, took hold of the car door handle, and pulled. Her body rippled with goose bumps when Swaggart reached out and shut the door as it began to open.

"Promise this won't freak you out tomorrow," he said.

"Okay," she said, unable to look up at him.

He took her chin in his hand, however, forcing her to look up at him. "I mean it," he said.

"Okay," she said, smiling at him.

He continued to hold her face in his hand for a moment. Poppy feared her tears would betray her heartache as he bent toward her, still singing along with Dean. It was such a romantic song!

Once more! Just once more! She had to taste his kiss just once more!

Suddenly, Poppy reached out, pulling Swaggart's head toward her own, kissing him firmly on the mouth. Instantly, he took her neck between his hands, pushing her back against the car as he took control of the kiss.

Poppy's lips burned, her jaws aching as she allowed their last kiss to consume her.

All at once, however, Swaggart broke the seal of their lips and opened her car door. "You need to get home," he said.

"S-so do you," she said, a tear trickling down her face as she moved into the driver's seat of her car.

"Good night," he said as he closed the door for her.

Tears streamed down Poppy's face as she turned the key in the ignition and watched Swaggart jog toward his old blue Chevy pickup. It was very much like waking from a dream—the very moment when the dream finally vanishes, no matter how hard the dreamer tries to linger and tries not to wake up.

Poppy began to sob, unable to believe it when she turned on the car radio only to hear Dean Martin singing "Innamorata" over the oldies station.

She closed her eyes for a moment as she heard Swaggart's pickup engine rumble to life. He was more wonderful than any man she'd ever known, and she'd kissed him! She determined she would fight the heartache and bathe only in the blissful memory of owning his attention to such an intimate extent for a time. She had kissed Swaggart Moretti. Her Dreams to Do list had been fulfilled. She thought of her upcoming date with Mark—of the finality of Swaggart's asking her not to let what had happened between them freak her out. She could still sense the warmth of his kiss, the flavor of it in her mouth. Again she thought of Mark—of Saturday and the canoe ride. Perhaps—perhaps it was time to start fresh. Maybe it was time for a new Dreams to Do list.

Poppy pulled the gear shift into drive. She turned left onto Montgomery Avenue and headed for home—left the past in the past and drove toward the future and a new list of dreams.

CHAPTER EIGHT

In the days following her romantic, fantasy-fulfilling tête-à-tête with Swaggart Moretti, Poppy found herself dithering between elation and misery. She knew the incident had been an isolated one—that Swaggart wasn't going to take her in his arms and slather her with passion every time she entered a room. Still, she wanted him to do so! Each day following the blissful night she'd spent in his arms— each day after, as she'd enter the restaurant to begin her shift and see him working in the kitchen, her mouth would begin to water—her body take to some delighted trembling.

Yet, true to her word, she maintained a perfectly settled outward appearance. And Swaggart treated her exactly the same way he always had—pleasant, playful, and as if they were simply very good friends.

Whitney acted as if nothing whatsoever had transpired between her cousin and her best friend as well. Oh, certainly she had waited up for Poppy's return that night, smiled when Poppy had confessed to her that "item number one" on her infamous Dreams to Do list had been successfully checked off—but beyond that, she did not tease Poppy or linger on the subject for very long. Therefore, as Poppy's emotions rode a rollercoaster of confusion and polar-opposite emotion, she kept the tumultuous feelings to herself.

Poppy tried to focus on her upcoming date with Mark. He'd called nearly every night, claiming he was afraid Poppy would forget about their plans and "stand him up." Mark's attention also stirred her emotions with confusion. She was delighted to see Mark's number on the caller ID each time he called. Yet she felt guilty somehow, as if she were being dishonest with him, keeping secrets she shouldn't keep about her feelings and, now, experience with Swaggart. Still, she was all too conscious of the fact she'd been out with him once! It wasn't like he'd proposed marriage, and she had accepted—it wasn't as if she were even steady-dating him. They'd been on one date! Sure, they had another one planned, but it didn't mean she'd committed some great crime of disloyalty where Mark was concerned. Furthermore, Swaggart had never asked her out in her life. Thus, there was no hope, nothing to keep her from pursuing a relationship with Mark.

In truth, Poppy simply felt trapped, helpless—adrift on an ocean of uncertainty. And her promise to Swaggart—her promise not to let their evening together "freak" her out—right! Yet Saturday was just around the corner, and she hoped her day with Mark would settle her anxieties—her uncertainties. Monday came and went, as did Tuesday, Wednesday, and Thursday, so by Friday afternoon, as Poppy waited on a party of six businessmen at table eight, she hoped the next day, her day with Mark, would quiet the confusion in her soul.

As he sat in a chair in the alcove, attempting to take a quick break from the demanding chaos of a busy Friday afternoon, Swaggart watched Poppy as she hurried from table to table, to order counter, and back. He gritted his teeth as the flesh on his arms involuntarily broke into goose bumps at the thought of her warm, sweet kiss. He'd been mentally flogging himself from the moment he'd slid his key into the ignition of his pickup and watched Poppy pull out of the Good Ol' Days parking lot at 2 a.m. five nights before.

The thing was, Swaggart couldn't quite settle on the reason for his self-inflicted, ongoing abuse of mind. He couldn't settle on whether he was distraught because he'd given in to a weak moment and kissed her or because he'd given in to self-doubt and let her go. What he did know was he'd wanted her for himself for years, and now he was going to have to stand by and watch some other guy win her. He knew this Mark guy would win her too. Swaggart was no fool. He'd seen the guy: business suit, executive type with loafers, and probably some expensive sports car. Oh, there was nothing wrong with the business suit, executive type. Nothing wrong with the sports car.

A few different career decisions probably would've found Swaggart in the same race—but it wasn't what he wanted. Swaggart loved the restaurant—loved making Mickey Mouse pancakes for kids, loved to see people talking and laughing together, affected by the fantastic endorphins released in their brains by the taste of great food and the feel of a pleasant atmosphere. He knew he could simply put his business finance degree to better use and waltz into Good Ol' Days in a suit and loafers. On second thought, no loafers. Loafers were a little too on the "soft" side—but he could give that Mark guy a run for his money in the career area if he wanted to. Yet the thing of it was, he knew it would be to his misery. He was using his degree—it wasn't like he had wasted his time getting it. His grandfather's financial success had quadrupled since Swaggart had secretly taken over the business end of things. No one but his grandpa knew Swaggart was the brains and financial manager behind the restaurant's incredible financial success. No one even knew how crazy its financial success was! That's the way Wally Dexter, owner of Good Ol' Days Family Restaurant, wanted it. The day he'd handed off the business finances to Swaggart, he made him promise to keep the information strictly confidential—and Swaggart had.

Therefore, as Swaggart sat watching Poppy, contemplating the successful business executive who was hot on her tail, he allowed a tiny shred of pride to lift his spirits for a brief moment. He'd done wonders with his grandfather's business. This Mr. Joe Perfect-Face after Poppy wasn't any better than Swaggart Moretti.

The confident moment was short-lived, however.

"Poppy just ordered up two Chef's Choices, Swag," Bobby called from the kitchen.

"All right," Swaggart said. "I'll be right there."

What was she doing? It seemed to Swaggart that Poppy's tables ordered Chef's Choices three or four times more often than anybody else's. Was she campaigning for them or something?

He stared at her, heat flooding his limbs as she caught his gaze and smiled at him as she walked toward the alcove. Every kind of emotion poured through him as he watched her advancing—fury funneled toward this Mark guy—jealousy, resentment. Other emotions were alive in him too—possessiveness, passion, desire. If he knew one thing about himself, it was that, in that moment, he was in trouble. He'd spent too long contemplating Poppy Amore there in the alcove. He'd allowed his mind to nest on inconceivable thoughts of out-jousting this Mark guy and winning her over.

"Taking a break?" Poppy said as she stepped into the alcove.

"Yeah," he managed. The back corner of the alcove was out of the line of vision of the entire restaurant, he realized in that moment. "You?" he asked, rising from his chair as she went to the apron rack.

"No," she said, rummaging around in a canvas bag hanging on one of the rack hooks. "Just parched. I brought a water bottle…or at least, I thought I did."

"You're thirsty?" he asked, striding to where she stood. What was he doing? He'd lost his mind! Furthermore, his own grandfather would have grounds to fire him for sexual harassment!

"Yeah," Poppy said, still rummaging.

"Well, let me take care of that for you then," he said.

Before Poppy could even blink, Swaggart had taken hold of her arm and maneuvered her to the back corner of the alcove. Taking her face between his strong hands, he rendered her breathless, executing such a passionate, driven kiss that Poppy's arms and legs literally went numb!

It wasn't an unusually long kiss, but it was long enough to allow Poppy to melt against him and return it with the same vigor with which it was administered.

"Sorry," he said as he released her. He stepped back, thick guilt apparent in the expression of his eyes.

"Th-that's okay," Poppy breathed, smoothing her apron and wondering if her cheeks were as red as they felt.

"You still thirsty?" he asked as he turned and headed for the kitchen.

"Not for water," Poppy muttered under her breath.

"Grandpa put a fresh bottle on the cooler this morning," he called to her as he turned the corner and entered the kitchen.

Poppy covered her mouth with one hand, trying to calm her breathing, still her trembling. What use were the five days she'd just spent trying to put her feelings into some sort of manageable order, if she was going to be so easily overcome by Swaggart's attention again?

Inhaling a deep breath, and trying to calm herself, Poppy went to the water cooler around the corner and filled a paper cup with water. After drinking three cups' full, her mouth still bathed in the blissful sensation of Swaggart's kiss, but she had to get back to her tables.

"Everything all right?" Mr. Dexter asked, appearing at his office door suddenly.

Poppy gasped, putting a hand to her bosom.

"You scared me, Mr. Dexter!" she told him, forcing a smile.

"Sorry about that, Poppy. You okay?" he asked.

"Oh, yeah! I just had to pop in for a drink of water. It's crazy out there today," she said.

Had he seen? The far corner of the alcove was invisible to every part of the restaurant except the door to Mr. Dexter's office. Poppy tried to remember if the door had been open when she passed it on her way to the apron rack. She couldn't remember! Still, he didn't seem mad, amused, or unsettled in any regard. She was sure he hadn't seen Swaggart kiss her. Swaggart kissed her! Her cheeks grew warm at the realization and memory.

"Just checking," Mr. Dexter said. "You do seem a little flushed— but I suppose a busy Friday will do that, won't it?"

"Yes, sir!" Poppy nervously exclaimed. "Well, back to work." She was anxious, still uncertain as to whether or not Mr. Dexter had seen her kissing Swaggart in the alcove. Surely he hadn't! She knew Mr. Dexter well enough to know he would've had to tease—he wouldn't have been able to keep himself from it.

Wally Dexter watched Poppy as she hurried off to tend her tables. In truth, he wanted to shout, "Whoopee!" but he managed to keep from doing so. He'd started to come out of his office just in time to see his grandson fairly assault his favorite little waitress, and all he could think was *Whoopee!*

It's time, he thought. *At last, at last, at last!* The time had come, and Wally was glad. He'd been in the restaurant business for over forty years, and he was tired. He'd been waiting for just the right moment to go ahead with his plans—and it looked like just the right moment had arrived—or was about to.

He chuckled at the twinkle apparent in Poppy's eyes, her rosied cheeks, her breathless appearance a moment before when he'd startled her. He knew she had some new Mr. Wonderful in her life, but he was glad to see his grandson hadn't let her go without stamping himself in her mind, if not her heart. Swaggart was coming up out of the mire—Wally was certain of it, and it made him happy for more reasons than anyone could understand.

Whistling a happy tune, Wally Dexter headed for the hostess podium. He felt revitalized and hopeful. He even felt up to greeting a few customers. Maybe Yolanda Peterson would even make an appearance at the restaurant.

"You okay?" Whitney asked, handing Poppy three menus. "Brian—party of three," she called.

"Fine! Just fine," Poppy said. Her hands trembled as she held the menus. "I-I just need tomorrow to get here."

"Oh, so that's it!" Whitney said in a whisper. "A little nervous about our day with Mr. Gorgeous, are we?"

"Yeah," Poppy lied. Poppy frowned for a moment. It was strange—not being able to tell Whitney about the agony and delight where Swaggart was concerned. But she just couldn't—it would be too weird—explaining to Whitney that her cousin was the most magnificent kisser she'd ever imagined. And besides, Poppy was certain her date with Mark would be incredible! She'd just wait and tell Whitney all about that and keep her confusion concerning Swaggart a secret.

"I'm Brian," a tall middle-aged man said as he approached the podium.

"Table five, Poppy," Whitney said.

"If you'll just follow me, sir," Poppy said. She smiled as Brian and two men apparently his same age fell into step behind her.

"Order up!" she heard Bobby call from the kitchen. She'd seat these customers at table five, pick up her order for table two, and try not to faint at the sight of Swaggart when she did so.

For a moment, she worried that kissing Swaggart would be some sort of catalyst to making her work environment uncomfortable somehow. But when she went to the order counter to pick up table two's orders, she smiled as he winked at her. All would be well. She would move beyond the knowledge she'd lived her dream of kissing Swaggart Moretti. And so what if he stole one more kiss in the alcove? The fact made item number one—and the checkmark next to it—all the more wonderful to have experienced.

As Poppy headed for table two, a plate in each hand, she glanced out the window. The sun was bright, the grass and trees were green, and everything about the day was beautiful! No doubt the next day would be just as wonderful—maybe more wonderful—though she had a difficult time imagining anything could be more wonderful than a day at Good Ol' Days when Swaggart Moretti was in the kitchen—or in the alcove!

Saturday dawned bright and sunny with blue skies and the promise of being a perfect day. Mark would be picking Poppy up any minute, and she wrinkled her nose at her reflection in the microwave door. Poppy was never satisfied with her appearance—never. She accepted it, but she was never satisfied with it.

"Are you nervous?" Whitney asked. Whitney was sitting at the table, reading the comics section of the newspaper and eating leftover instant cheesecake right out of the pie pan.

"A little," Poppy said. "It feels like forever since I've seen him."

"Are you afraid you've forgotten what he looks like?" Whitney teased. "'Cause I don't think anybody could ever forget what that guy looks like."

"No doubt," Poppy said. Still, as she used her ring finger to apply a light layer of lip gloss to her lips, she wondered if Mark was really as gorgeous as she remembered. Was he really as gorgeous as Swaggart, or had she just imagined he was?

"A lot has happened since you last saw him," Whitney said, still concentrating on the comics page.

"Like what?" Poppy asked, feigning ignorance. Whitney wouldn't buy it, she knew. Still, she had to try.

"Like you've tasted the manly kiss of my cousin Swaggart, that's what," Whitney said. "And from as rattled and uptight as you've been this week—I'd say he did a real bang-up job of checking that little item off your list."

Poppy put her hands to her cheeks as they turned crimson. "Yeah...well..." she said, trying to downplay the subject.

"Oh, come on, Poppy!" Whitney exclaimed then. "You haven't said hardly anything about what happened, and I've tried to leave you alone about it—but you *have* to tell me! Was it worth all those years of dreaming? Was he as good as you thought he'd be? 'Fess up!"

"He's your cousin, Whitney," Poppy said. "It's weird."

"It is not!" Whitney argued. "Did Swaggart ring your bell or not? You have to tell me! I mean, if he's a terrible kisser, then it's a reflection on me."

"What?" Poppy exclaimed with a giggle. "How is it a reflection on you?"

"He's my cousin! He's family! People might think it's a genetic disposition—bad kissing!"

Poppy laughed. "You are so full of beans, Whitney Dexter! You just want to know if he was worth being at the top of my list."

"Yeah, I do," Whitney admitted, smiling. "But by the way you've fumbled and bumbled around this week—I'd say that's a great big yes!"

"Okay, fine," Poppy said. "I admit it—my bell has been ringing ever since. Are you happy?"

Whitney's smile broadened, and she nodded. "Yes—I am. It reflects well on the family."

"You're an idiot," Poppy giggled.

"Do you think Mr. Gorgeous Mark Lawson can do as well?" Whitney asked, casually returning her attention to the comics.

"I'm sure he can, but I don't plan to find out today—if that's what you're implying," Poppy said.

In truth, she wasn't sure Mark Lawson's kiss could have the same effect on her that Swaggart's had—she wasn't sure anyone's ever could! Still, Mark seemed to be a wonderful man—why couldn't it be possible that, eventually, he could drive Swaggart's kiss from her mind?

"We're just getting to know each other," Poppy continued, making sure she had her cell phone in her purse. "You don't just go kissing somebody—like, you know—making out with somebody when you've never really dated or anything."

"Oh, don't you?" Whitney asked eyebrows curved in a daring arch.

"Swaggart's different, and you know it," Poppy said. "I've known him forever and besides…besides…"

"Besides—he was on the list. He's immune to regular rules because he was on the list—I get it," Whitney said. "I'm just glad you got to finish *your* list. I'll never be able to do that."

"Well, I'm thinking of making a new one," Poppy said.

"With Mark Lawson as item number one?" Whitney teased.

"Shut up and read your comics, brat," Poppy said, smiling.

In truth, she'd already begun a new list. However, she'd been wise enough not to include any items that would demand she found a way to kiss somebody. Though—the thought had crossed her mind at putting Swaggart Moretti at the top of the new list again. Kissing him had been such a euphoric wonderment she'd be lying if she didn't admit she wanted to kiss him again. But in truth, she had!

Poppy smiled, remembering the way he'd so forcefully kissed her in the alcove the day before. All day she'd wondered why he had—had he enjoyed kissing her as much as she had enjoyed kissing him and simply wanted a rematch? Had he simply been teasing her? Had he just wanted to make sure she wasn't all freaky about what had happened between them? Secretly, she wished he'd kissed her because he'd discovered he suddenly had feelings for her—but that was too far-fetched and romance novel-ish to be a true contemplation. Wasn't it?

"I think I just heard a Beamer drive up," Whitney said, abandoning the newspaper and racing for the window.

"Whit!" Poppy scolded in a whisper. "He'll see you peeking through the blinds!"

"Naw," Whitney said. "Guys never think to look for stuff like that. Yep! It's him! He's here, and he looks delicious! Ooooo—I bet you're going to have the time of your life!"

Poppy giggled. Yet, a pang of regret echoed in her bosom—she'd already had the time of her life—last Saturday night in Good Ol' Days Family Restaurant, at the hand of Swaggart Moretti. It was hard to believe anything could ever be as wonderful.

Still, as Poppy opened the door to see Mark's gorgeous, smiling face, she thought she might be wrong. Why couldn't this guy be as wonderful as the other? Why couldn't a girl have loved peach pie her whole life but find out that apple pie was even better?

"Hi there," Mark said.

"Hi," Poppy said, smiling.

"You ready for the greatest day of your life?" he asked.

Poppy giggled. It was as if he'd tuned into her soul and was reassuring her apple pie could be better than peach.

"I sure am," she answered.

"Good," Mark said, his dark eyes glowing with a sort of mischievous twinkle. "Then let's go."

As Mark drove his BMW toward Hollander Park, Poppy quickly studied him and smiled.

He wore brand name jeans, a bright yellow polo shirt, and brown deck shoes. In truth, he looked quite nautical, and completely attractive! Poppy endeavored to push the vision of Swaggart in his jeans and tight white t-shirt to the back of her mind—swallowed the excess moisture that flooded her mouth at the thought of him.

"It's a great day for this," Mark said. "I'm going to make sure it's one you'll never forget."

"Wow!" Poppy said. "I feel all special and stuff."

"Good," Mark said, winking at her. "That's what I want."

Poppy smiled and bit her lip, delighted with his flirtatious manner. This *was* going to be a day she would never forget—she could already tell.

CHAPTER NINE

Lunch was fabulous! Mark had stopped at the little bistro near Hollander Park and ordered them each the pita bread chicken salad. Poppy tried not to think of how much better Swaggart's chicken salad was—just concentrated on the fact that the bistro's was delicious—how delicious Mark was!

The day seemed to grow more beautiful with every passing moment. By the time Poppy and Mark had finished lunch at the bistro, the water of Hollander Park's small lake was as smooth and as calm as any lazy summer day ever was.

Mark helped Poppy into the canoe, set a small picnic basket near her feet, and settled himself across from her. He pushed off, and Poppy's heart fluttered when he smiled at her and said, "I love doing this."

"Do you do this often?" she asked. She wondered how many other girls Mark had paddled around the lake.

"I bring my mom sometimes," he said. "Or my little sisters—but you're the first non-relative I've ever brought."

Poppy giggled and said, "That was a good answer!"

"That was a true answer," he said, flashing one of his stunning smiles.

"So, how has your week been?" she asked him.

He shrugged and answered, "Pretty good. I landed a couple of big accounts this week—sorta made up for my blowing Susan Reginald off."

Poppy smiled.

"How about you?"

"It was pretty busy at the restaurant all week long," she told him. "Summers are always the craziest time!"

"You know, my friend Braden…remember him?" he asked.

"Of course," she said. How could she forget the night Mark had come to the restaurant—after having sent the beautiful roses?

"He loved your place," Mark continued. "Told me over and over it was the best salmon he'd ever had, how fun the joint was—you know, everything."

"It is a great place to work," Poppy said. "You know Whitney, my roommate? She's the granddaughter of the owner—it's how I got my foot in the door. I bet we have at least ten to twenty people a week stopping in to ask if we're hiring."

"Seriously?" he asked.

"Yeah! It's a great place to work, and I think people pick up on that and want to be a part of it," she said. "Mr. Dexter's looking to hire another waiter or waitress, and I don't envy him—having to sift through everyone who is going to want the job."

"No kidding," Mark agreed.

He paddled for a moment in silence, and Poppy took the opportunity to let her eyes and mind linger on the beauty of the scenery. The cottonwood trees lining the banks of the lake hummed with the songs of cicadas, and Poppy had the notion she'd never seen so many different colors of wildflowers in the same place.

The water was still and very clear, and fish jumped here and there around her. There was just a hint of a breeze now and then, and the quiet, peaceful atmosphere was soothing to her senses.

"So," Mark said. "Anything exciting happen in your life since I saw you last?"

Poppy nearly choked! Was he kidding? She'd kissed Swaggart Moretti, that's what! But she certainly couldn't explain that to him, so she simply answered, "Nope. How 'bout you?"

"One of my little sisters just got engaged—this past Tuesday, actually," he said.

"Really?" Poppy asked. "Is it a good thing?" He didn't seem all that excited about it.

He shrugged and said, "I guess so. I think I'm just being paranoid—I mean, she is my baby sister, and I do feel protective. The guy seems nice enough—he's got a good job, drives a sweet ride—but I'm still a little nervous about it."

"How old is she?" Poppy asked. She was curious as to just how old Mark was. Perhaps knowing his sister's age would give her a clue.

"Twenty-two," he said. "She's old enough—but I still worry. Do you understand?"

"I do, and you wouldn't be a good brother if you weren't worried," Poppy told him.

"I suppose," he said. "He seems like a nice guy, and I really can't find anything wrong with him—so I guess I should just relax."

"Probably," Poppy said.

Mark smiled at her and quit paddling for a moment.

"You know you're adorable, don't you?" he asked.

"What?" Poppy asked, blushing to the tips of her toes.

"Adorable *and* beautiful—it's rare," he said, smiling at her.

"Ooo! Mark Lawson—handsome and charming! What a rarity that is," she said, trying to push Swaggart from her thoughts.

"If you're the prize at the end of the rainbow, then I'm sure glad I endured that dinner with Miss Susan Reginald," he said, winking at her.

"Keep it up, Prince Charming, and I might swoon or something," Poppy giggled.

"Yeah! Do it! Then I can wake you up by kissing you again," he flirted.

He seemed too good to be true! Such a romantic! Poppy tried to accept him at face value—tried not to be so skeptical about such a wonderful man finding her interesting.

Mark leisurely paddled them around the lake for over an hour. As they talked, enjoying the warmth and beauty of summer, Poppy began to release her inhibitions, let go of her suspicions. Mark Lawson was unusual in the depth of his character—he seemed to be exactly what he appeared to be, and Poppy grew more and more encouraged.

Eventually, Mark pulled the canoe ashore on the opposite side of the lake. Assisting Poppy out of the canoe, he retrieved the picnic basket.

"What have you got in there anyway?" Poppy asked.

"I stopped off at the bakery and picked up dessert," he said.

Poppy smiled. *How sweet!* she thought. In her experience, men like Mark Lawson—courteous, thoughtful, and romantic—were few and very far between. Men who thought of dessert were even fewer and farther between. In fact, Swaggart was the only other man she could think of who…

Again, Poppy pushed Swaggart to the back of her mind. She was with Mark now, and he was wonderful! Taking her hand, Mark led her to a nearby tree. As she watched, he opened the small picnic basket and withdrew a folded plastic tablecloth, spreading it on the ground beneath the tree.

"Don't want to get our clothes dirty, right?" he explained to her as he sat down on the plastic tablecloth. He patted the space next to him, and she sat down. "Now," he began, reaching into the basket again, "I wasn't quite sure where your dessert preferences run—though I know about your addiction to Peanut Buster Parfaits at Dairy Queen," he teased.

"I'm pretty open when it comes to dessert," Poppy told him. "It would be a challenge to find something I didn't like."

"Good—because I love this Italian cream spice cake," he said, pulling out a plastic bakery container.

Poppy could see it contained two slices of a delicious-looking, three-layer cake.

"And," he added reaching into the basket and withdrawing two small bottles of milk. "I even brought something to wash it down with."

"Now *this* is living," Poppy said as Mark handed her a bottle of milk and a plastic fork. "Cake eaten outside always tastes better."

"Exactly," Mark chuckled.

❧

It was a beautiful few hours spent beneath the cottonwood trees on the banks of the little lake. Poppy couldn't remember when she'd enjoyed a day more. She and Mark talked for hours, about everything imaginable—work, hobbies, family. It was a lovely way to twitter away an afternoon.

"There's a concert at the amphitheater at five," he said. "A string quartet performing John Williams selections. What do you think?"

"Sounds fabulous," Poppy said. It just seemed to be getting better!

"Great," Mark said, standing and stretching. Poppy didn't miss the way the muscles in his arms bulged as he stretched—the fact that the ribbing of his shirtsleeves was distressed into nearly bursting at the seams because of the size of his biceps. She wondered for a moment if Mark would fill out a tight white t-shirt as well as Swaggart did.

"We'll paddle back to the dock and get a good seat on the grass before people start showing up," he said, offering her his hand.

Poppy smiled at him and accepted his hand. He pulled her to her feet but kept hold of her hand, staring at her with a rather mesmerized grin on his face.

"Can I kiss you?" he asked.

Poppy's heart panged as Swaggart's face appeared in her mind's eye. The memory of the night she'd spent in Good Ol' Days kissing him washed over her like a warm rain. Yet it had been an isolated incident—one moment in time when two friends had come together in singular purpose. The thought quickly traveled through her mind—*But what was the purpose?* Then she remembered her list—she and Swaggart had shared those wonderful hours simply because of her list. Hadn't they? She thought of the moment he'd pulled her into the alcove and kissed her again—offering no explanation—no reason.

Shaking her head to try and dispel the thoughts of Swaggart, she smiled at Mark.

"I don't know—*can* you?" she teased. He smiled, and she knew he understood her grammatical witticism.

"Oh, definitely," he said.

Poppy's heart rate increased as Mark took her face between his hands and kissed her. His palms were soft against her face, his lips soft against her own. A tiny flutter began in Poppy's bosom—Mark Lawson was kissing her! He kissed her softly, tenderly several times in succession, and she was conscious he was being careful not to press her. Swaggart's image flashed in her mind, and her heart swelled—yet she could not discern whether the sudden swelling sensation in her heart was because Mark Lawson was kissing her or because Swaggart's image had flashed through her mind.

Slowly, Mark pulled her into his arms. The pressure of his kiss increased, and Poppy frowned, abruptly uncertain as to whether or not she wanted him to continue kissing her. Mark must have sensed her hesitation, for he slowly returned to the soft, tender manner of kissing her. He kissed her for several moments before releasing her, smiling down at her, and taking hold of one of her hands.

"Let's pick this stuff up and get over to the amphitheater," he said.

"Okay," Poppy said, smiling at him. Dang, he was attractive! And she was certain she'd be more comfortable kissing him next time—next time—when she'd known him longer—when Swaggart's recent kiss had faded from her thoughts a bit.

The concert was wonderful, the weather fantastic! She smiled at the thoughtful way he'd spread the plastic tablecloth on the ground for them before the concert had begun. Still, Poppy liked to sit in the grass, and she wished he would've had a little less concern for her comfort. Yet who could fault a man for being so considerate? Mark had been quite attentive to Poppy during the performance too—always an arm around her waist, holding her hand, or brushing a piece of grass from her hair.

Once the concert ended, Mark had stopped and ordered them both a fast-food burger and onion rings. As they sat in his car eating their meal, they discussed the concert, their jobs, and families—casual, comfortable conversation—the best kind of conversation.

"I guess I better be getting you home," Mark said, once they'd finished their meal.

"What time is it?" Poppy asked. She did feel tired. She wondered how she had managed to stay up until all hours of the morning kissing Swaggart and not feel the least bit fatigued—yet a day on the lake had worn her out.

"Ten," Mark said. "Do I get to see the inside of your apartment this time?" he asked then. "Maybe even officially meet your roommate?"

Poppy giggled, delighted with his obvious interest in her life. "Of course," she told him.

She did wish, however, that Whitney hadn't looked quite so starstruck in those first moments when she introduced her to Mark.

"Poppy tells me you've been her friend nearly since birth," Mark said as Whitney stood staring at him in astonished disbelief.

"Yep," Whitney managed. "We've been friends forever!"

"It's a nice apartment you girls have," Mark said, looking around the room.

Poppy still couldn't believe a man the like of Mark Lawson was standing in her apartment. "Thanks," Poppy said. "We really like it here."

"Especially when the garbage disposal is working," Whitney interjected. "I've been trying to get that quarter out of the garbage disposal all night."

"Yeah, yeah, yeah," Poppy said, playfully frowning at Whitney. She knew she was going to hear about the garbage disposal again, but she'd thought Whitney would wait until Mark was gone, at least.

"It's stuck good, I'll tell you that," Whitney said to Poppy.

"A quarter?" Mark asked.

"I was washing off some tip change," Poppy began, "My lip gloss leaked out all over my tips yesterday, and I was just washing off some of the change this morning, and I dropped a quarter in the garbage disposal."

"It's stuck in there now," Whitney explained.

"And we all know that Whitney can't live without the garbage disposal," Poppy teased.

"Hey, Mark," Whitney said. "Do you know anything about garbage disposals?"

Mark smiled and chuckled. "Nope. If it were me, I'd just call the plumber," he said.

"Naw," Whitney said. "Too expensive. We can probably just wiggle it out with a screwdriver if we try hard enough."

"Have you tried just reaching in there?" Mark asked. Poppy smiled as he walked over to the sink. How sweet—he was going to take a look at it!

"I'm not reaching in there!" Whitney exclaimed. "I've seen that movie one too many times. You know, the one where the lady sticks her hand in the garbage disposal, and it suddenly turns on and chews off her fingers!"

Mark laughed and peered into the sink. "Yeah, I've seen that one too," he said. "Besides, it's probably pretty nasty in there."

"That's what I was thinking," Whitney said.

"I'm sure we can get someone to fix it, Whit," Poppy said. "You'll just have to live an entire day without it."

"Well, I'm going to go call someone to come fix it now," Whitney said picking her cell phone up off the counter.

"It's almost eleven," Poppy reminded her.

"Well, I'll leave a message, 'cause we need to clean the fridge, and I need my garbage disposal for that gross of a project." Whitney began dialing on her phone as she went into her bedroom, closing the door behind her.

"She's too funny," Mark said, still smiling.

"I know," Poppy agreed. "She keeps life entertaining, that's for sure."

"Thanks for giving your whole day away to me," Mark said, taking Poppy's hands in his own. "I had a great time."

"Me too," Poppy said, smiling at him.

"When do you have time for me again?" he asked.

Poppy bit her lip, delighted that he wanted to see her again. She was really starting to believe he truly liked her more than other girls of his acquaintance.

"I'm off Wednesday and Thursday of this week," she told him.

"Thursday?" he asked, tugging on her hands and pulling her closer to him.

Poppy's heartbeat increased as he smiled at her. He meant to kiss her again, and she was glad she'd taken the time to freshen her lip gloss after they'd eaten—shiny lips were always more appealing!

"Sure," she said.

"I hear there's a guy performing at the Comedy Corner next week who's supposed to be hilarious," Mark said. "What do you think? Sound fun?"

"Sounds really fun," Poppy told him.

"Fabulous! I'll pick you up at five thirty, and we'll do dinner first, okay?" he asked.

"Perfect," Poppy said.

He was smiling at her, his head descending toward hers—he did mean to kiss her again.

Poppy was puzzled when he paused, however. Still smiling at her, he reached up and ran his thumb over her lips twice.

"Perfect," he breathed as he kissed her then.

And it was! It was the perfect good night kiss—warm, lingering, noninvasive, yet thoroughly romantic! He kissed her twice more, pulling her into his arms and against his muscular form the third time.

Slowly releasing her, he said, "You're fabulous, Poppy Amore. I'm afraid you've gotten under my skin."

Poppy smiled, blushed, and bit her lip, delighted by his inference.

"As I said before—you're too charming to be true, Mr. Lawson," Poppy said.

"You're lucky you have a garbage-disposal-obsessed roommate, or I'd be tempted to hang around and kiss you some more," Mark said.

Poppy laughed and said, "She's so random." Whitney was a jewel, and Mark was wonderful! She wasn't sure she wanted him to leave yet—she wished he'd stay, that they could talk some more like they had throughout the day and evening.

"You've got something on your shirt," she said as her gaze fell to his broad shoulders. "Right there…it looks like mud," she said, brushing at a dime-sized smudge of mud near his right shoulder.

He looked down at the spot and frowned.

"Oh, man!" he mumbled. "I hope that doesn't stain—I like this shirt."

"I'm sure it won't," Poppy said. His concern over his bright yellow polo amused her. "And I like this shirt too."

He looked back to her and smiled. "How about the guy wearing it?"

"Oh, I really like the guy wearing it," she said.

He leaned forward, kissing her once more. "I better get going," he said. "See you Thursday, okay?"

"Okay," Poppy said. She followed him to the door, closing and locking it behind him.

Releasing a heavy sigh and leaning back against the door, Poppy smiled. What a wonderful day! Lunch at the bistro, canoeing on the lake, the concert, the kisses. All of it was wonderful! Mark was wonderful! Dreamy, charming, and wonderful! She giggled, certain he'd make an appearance in her dreams that night.

She thought of his kisses, expertly applied and truly romantic—just the right kind for these early stages of a relationship. The kisses she'd shared with Swaggart were passionate, fiery, and knee-weakening, and her arms erupted in goose bumps at the memory of them. She wondered if Mark liked her enough, would continue to like her enough—enough to intensify the kisses between them. She wondered if Mark could one day cause her body to ripple with goose bumps—she was sure he could. It would take time—for Pete's sake, they hardly knew each other! It was different with Swaggart—she'd known him for so long. It only stood to reason Swaggart's kisses would've had a more profound effect on her than Mark's did at this point—after all, she'd been in love with Swaggart for seven hundred sixty-three years! Of course he could thrill her! And Mark would thrill her, too—once she got to know him better.

Poppy pulled on one of her dad's old New Orleans Saints t-shirts to serve as pajamas, brushed her teeth, and fell into bed, exhausted. She dreamed of lakes, of trees, of beautiful music. Yet her happiest dream was the reminiscent dream of the first day she'd worked at Good Ol' Days—the day Swaggart Moretti had made her one of his famous Jiggy burgers for lunch. Even in her dreams, she salivated at the memory of the taste of it. It *was* the perfect hamburger—hot, spiced, and delicious in every way—just like his kiss.

"Sheesh!" Whitney said as Poppy staggered out of her bedroom the next morning. "I thought you were never going to get up."

"Why? What time is it?" Poppy asked, blurry-eyed and yawning.

"Nine," Whitney answered. "You already missed Scooby-Doo, by the way."

"Nine?" Poppy whined. "I had some stuff I wanted to get done early today. You should've woken me, Whit."

"You have your own alarm clock," Whitney said. "Besides, I'm still mad at you for breaking the garbage disposal."

"Sorry," Poppy said. She opened the refrigerator and took out a chocolate pudding cup. She took a plastic spoon out of the basket on the counter, opened the pudding cup, and started her breakfast. "Did you call someone about it?"

"Girl, you are *so* groggy when you first get up in the morning," Whitney said, pointing to the sink. Poppy looked over to see a man lying on the floor in front of the sink, his head and torso inside the cabinet, arms struggling with the garbage disposal.

"You sure didn't waste any time," Poppy said. "And who did you find to come out this early on a weekend? It's probably going to cost us an arm and a…"

Poppy froze—she was sure her heart dropped and landed with a thud in her stomach as the man sat up.

"She found the only idiot stupid enough to do it and not charge you anything," Swaggart said.

Poppy could only remain frozen with humiliation. She knew all too well what she looked like—she'd seen herself briefly in the bathroom mirror before leaving her bedroom. Worn off makeup, pillow hair, and wearing her dad's old New Orleans Saints t-shirt. She had one brief moment of being thankful—for at least the shirt was long and covered most of her thighs.

"S-Swaggart," she stammered at last.

"Good morning, Poppy," he said. He smiled as he studied her from head to toe, and Poppy felt the heat of embarrassment rise to her cheeks. He stood up and looked into the sink for a moment before putting his hand down the hole into the garbage disposal.

"Swaggart, don't!" Poppy heard Whitney's voice exclaim in unison with her own.

"What?" he shouted. It was obvious they had startled him.

"Don't put your hand down there!" Whitney scolded. "Haven't you ever seen that movie where the lady gets her fingers chewed off in the garbage disposal?"

"Yes, Whit," Swaggart said. "That's why I unplugged it first."

Poppy still couldn't move. She didn't know quite what to do. She should race back to her bedroom and put some clothes on. Yet she found she was entirely mesmerized by seeing Swaggart standing in her apartment. He was so handsome! He wore jeans and a red t-shirt, and his hair wasn't tousled as it normally was at work.

"You got it jammed in there pretty good," he said, looking to Poppy. He frowned, and she could see his jaw clenching and unclenching as he struggled with the mechanism inside the sink.

"Sorry," Poppy said.

"Can you fix it, Swaggart?" Whitney said. "A plumber will charge us a mint to come out here."

"I don't know," Swaggart said. "It's really jammed in there." He kept frowning, and Poppy could tell by the expressions crossing his face he was really struggling with the quarter.

"Poppy," he said.

"Yeah?" she answered.

"Come here."

Swallowing the lump of humiliation in her throat, Poppy walked over to the sink. She could feel the crimson on her cheeks. What could be worse than having Swaggart see her at her ultimate worst?

"Give me a bite of that," he said, nodding toward the pudding cup she held in her hand.

"What?" Poppy asked. He couldn't be serious. Everybody knew Swaggart Moretti never ate or drank after anybody—never!

"Give me a bite," he said.

Poppy frowned. Was he serious? He seemed to be. Slowly she dipped her plastic spoon into the pudding and held it out toward him. He put his mouth over the spoon and nodded, indicating Poppy could remove it.

"Thanks," he said. "I love those things."

Poppy smiled, amused by his casual manner—as if seeing her standing there looking like an escapee from some mental ward that didn't provide its patients with pajamas was the most normal thing in the world.

"Hold on...wait a minute...wait a minute...I think..." he said, between grimaces.

"Did you get it?" Whitney asked.

Swaggart pulled his hand out of the garbage disposal. He turned on the water and washed his hands with the dish soap sitting on the counter. He pulled an Allen wrench out of his pocket and stretched out on the floor again. Poppy watched the muscles in his arms tighten as he worked on the disposal from underneath the sink for a minute.

Standing, he turned on the water and flipped the disposal switch on the wall. The disposal roared to life, and Whitney clapped her hands with delight.

Poppy smiled and watched as Swaggart washed off the quarter.

"Give me another bite," he said as he dried his hands on his t-shirt.

Poppy smiled and offered the pudding cup to him.

He accepted the pudding cup and said, "Thanks."

"No—thank *you*!" Whitney exclaimed. "The disposal is one of my favorite appliances! I was freaking out without it."

Poppy stuck the plastic spoon she'd been using into the pudding cup now belonging to Swaggart.

"There's more in the fridge if you want," she said. She smiled at him, adding, "And thank you, Swaggart."

"You're welcome, baby," he said.

Poppy's stomach did a big loop-the-loop as he leaned back against the sink, crossed his feet, and began eating the pudding. Even without touching her, he'd caused her arms and legs to break into goose bumps—it was delicious!

"Here," he said, picking the quarter up off the counter and flipping it to Poppy. She smiled and caught it as he added, "I guess the garbage disposal doesn't take quarters."

"Oh, you're a scream," Whitney said, shaking her head.

Poppy giggled, thinking him quite clever.

"Well, girls," he said, licking the last smidgen of pudding off the plastic spoon. "I gotta run."

"Don't you want to stay for breakfast?" Whitney asked.

"Will Poppy be serving me pudding while wearing her scandalous lingerie?" he asked.

Poppy blushed again when he smiled as he surveyed her from head to toe once more.

"We're having French toast today, dummy," Whitney said.

"I'd rather have Poppy serve me pudding," he said.

Poppy held her breath as he walked over to her, stopping right before her.

"I promise to tip you really, really, really well."

"He's teasing you, Poppy," Whitney giggled. "Call his bluff!"

As Swaggart stood staring down at her, the warm syrup of his eyes drizzling over her like summer rain, Poppy tried to breathe.

"So you're a good tipper?" she managed.

"Try me," he coaxed.

What did she have to lose? Swaggart had already witnessed her morning hideousness. Her stomach sickened at the thought. Again she was mortified at how she must look. Still, he was challenging her.

"Fine," Poppy said, smiling at him. She turned around and retrieved another pudding cup from the refrigerator. Opening the pudding cup, she snatched the plastic spoon from Swaggart's hand and began to slowly feed the pudding to him.

In truth, the act of feeding Swaggart the pudding, watching his mouth—which had been so adept at kissing hers—eat the pudding from the spoon she held caused excess moisture to flood her mouth. Her body somehow ached to feel his arms around her—her fingers longing to weave themselves through his hair. Poppy realized that simply being in the same room with Swaggart Moretti had more effect on her senses than actually kissing Mark Lawson did. It worried her somehow.

As Swaggart ate the last bite of pudding he mumbled, "Mmm! I love this stuff."

Poppy smiled and set the empty pudding cup and spoon on the counter.

"Okay, big spender man—where's my tip?" she asked.

"You mean other than 'garbage disposals don't take quarters'?" he asked.

Poppy rolled her eyes. "Yes—other than 'garbage disposals don't take quarters.'"

"I can't think of one," he said, smiling. Mischief danced in his eyes as he added, "I just wanted you to feed me the pudding while wearing that scandalous lingerie."

"Oh my heck!" Poppy exclaimed, playfully smacking him on one solid shoulder. "You brat!"

Swaggart chuckled. "I fixed your garbage disposal, didn't I? Don't I deserve one little pudding cup?"

"You had one and a half, you idiot," Whitney said.

"And they were the best pudding cups I've ever had," he said, winking at Poppy.

Poppy blushed from the tips of her hair follicles to the red polish on her toenails.

"Thanks, Poppy," he said.

"Thank you for retrieving my quarter," Poppy said. "And for fixing the disposal before Whitney had a nervous breakdown."

"Anytime," Swaggart chuckled. "I'll see you girls at work. Go Saints!" he said, raising a fist in the air.

"Thanks for fixing it, Swaggart. Really," Whitney said.

"You're welcome," he said.

He left, and Poppy wasn't sure her heartbeat would ever slow down. Her stomach was looping double time, and she felt overheated, weak, breathless.

Swaggart's mornings were usually very busy, especially when he wasn't at work. Poppy was sure he'd sacrificed something else to help her and Whitney and their injured garbage disposal. She thought about the way he'd simply stuck his hand in the disposal without hesitation, the way he'd tricked her into feeding him the pudding—the way he'd smiled at her when he'd studied her. She was trembling, quivering with the desire to run after him, beg him to hold her, kiss her, talk with her, smile at her.

Swaggart Moretti was dangerous—her heart was in danger from him. Poppy thought about the day before—the wonderful day she'd spent with Mark. How could it be possible? How could ten minutes of Swaggart Moretti fiddling with her garbage disposal manage to thrill her more than an entire day spent in Mark Lawson's gorgeous company?

CHAPTER TEN

Monday was busy—especially for a Monday. All day Poppy tried to think about Mark, about their wonderful Saturday together. Yet no matter how hard she tried, her thoughts could not manage to linger on Mark and his perfectly applied good night kisses. Instead she could only think of Swaggart—of his willingness to fix the garbage disposal, of his wit and humor during and after doing so, of the delightful goose bumps breaking over her whenever she thought of him. And when she thought of his kiss, her mouth watered for wanting it so desperately again.

It's because Swaggart works here with me, she inwardly told herself. Mark wasn't standing in front of her every second, all gorgeous, charming, and entirely attractive in every way, the way Swaggart was. She was certain if Mark was working in the kitchen, winking and smiling at her over the order counter the way Swaggart was, then her thoughts would be totally dominated by Mark instead.

Still, the loop-the-loop in her stomach tried to convince her differently. *Stop it*, she told her stomach. *You can't have Swaggart—he's out of reach, unobtainable, far beyond anything you could even endeavor to hope for*, she told herself.

"You look tired today, Poppy," Mr. Dexter said as Poppy hung her apron on the apron rack.

"Just have a lot on my mind, I guess," Poppy told him. After all, it was true.

"I guess I won't ask you for the favor I was going to ask you for then," Mr. Dexter said.

Poppy smiled, knowing full well he wanted her to encourage him to go ahead and ask. "Oh, I don't mind, Mr. Dexter," she told him. "Go ahead and ask me."

Mr. Dexter smiled and handed Poppy a manila envelope. "Swaggart left already, and I needed to get this to him before tomorrow morning. He's on your way home, isn't he?"

"Yeah," Poppy said. She took the envelope from Mr. Dexter and smiled at the shiny-eyed elderly man. "I'll drop it off. Are you sure he went home?"

"Oh, I'm sure he did," Mr. Dexter said. "But if he doesn't answer the door, please just take it home with you. I don't want it left sitting on the front porch for any Joe and his dog to get ahold of. Okay?"

"Sure," Poppy said.

"Thank you, Poppy," Mr. Dexter said. "You're saving me a trip out of my way."

"Anytime," Poppy said as she exited the restaurant by way of the back door.

Mr. Dexter smiled. Oh, it was a terribly important envelope and had to be delivered at once. At once—and only by Poppy.

Whistling along with the song playing over the sound system, Mr. Dexter went into his office and shut the door. There was paperwork to finish, signatures to obtain. He'd be working late again—but that would soon change.

Poppy's nerves had begun to twitter, and with every mile closer to Swaggart's house, they twittered more. She'd been to Swaggart's house only once before—when Whitney had dropped off some chicken soup when he was sick last fall. Yet she knew the way to Swaggart's house well enough. For weeks after she'd gone with Whitney and discovered where he lived, Poppy had driven by day after day for months, just hoping to get a glimpse of him. Eventually, she realized she was teetering on being categorized as a stalker and ended her drive-bys of Swaggart's house.

Now, however, as she put her car in park and tried to muster enough courage to deliver Mr. Dexter's envelope, she wondered again what Swaggart's home life was like. She knew he'd moved out of his parents' house and into his own long before he'd finished college. He'd said it was a good investment—better than throwing rent down the drain into somebody else's pocket without anything to show for it.

The house was located in a lovely, perfectly suburban neighborhood and looked like something right out of *Leave It to Beaver*. It was cozy and inviting, yet Poppy gulped as she walked up the walk to the front door.

She watched her own finger trembling as she reached out and rang the doorbell. When no one came to the door, she wondered if Mr. Dexter had been wrong—perhaps Swaggart hadn't gone straight home after work.

As she turned to leave, she heard music. It seemed to be coming from the backyard. Poppy's curiosity was entirely piqued, and she walked around the left side of the house. A smile spread across her face at the sight that met her. Swaggart had parked his pickup in the middle of the backyard and was lying on the hood gazing up into the sky. He was lying on his back, hands tucked back under his head, as the pickup's radio quietly played.

"Hey," Poppy called before her good sense could stop her.

"Hey there, Poppy-seed," he said, glancing over at her and smiling. "What brings you here?"

Poppy smiled and held up the envelope as she walked toward Swaggart. "Your grandpa sent me on a mission," she said, handing the envelope to him. He accepted it, studied it for a moment, and then tossed it into the open window of his pickup. "He said you needed to see it before tomorrow."

"Okay," Swaggart said, sitting up. "Come on up here," he said, gesturing she should join him. "You gotta see this."

Poppy paused. Was he actually asking her to climb up on the hood of his pickup?

"Unless you don't want to get dirty," he added.

"Are you kidding? Like I'm so fresh and clean after working eight hours in a restaurant," she said.

"Then come on," he said, offering a hand to her. "Wait…hold on a second," he mumbled. Unexpectedly stripping off his tight, white t-shirt, he spread it over the hood of the pickup next to him. "There you go," he said, smiling.

Poppy had to consciously, yet silently, will her mouth not to drop open in awed, flabbergasted astonishment—not because of his charming act of chivalry in being concerned for her comfort—but for the sake of being witness to the full glory of the flawlessly chiseled, muscular torso she had always suspected lurked beneath his shirts.

Tanned, ripped, and appearing no less than masterfully sculpted, Swaggart Moretti's biceps, shoulders, chest, stomach, and abdominal muscles were unlike anything Poppy had ever seen—in real life anyway. For the very first time, she understood the term "washboard stomach," and it was staggering. She was suddenly nearly overwhelmed with an intimidated, nervous sensation in her stomach and chest. Yet she could not have resisted joining him—even if she'd wanted to. She would not miss the chance to be alone with him—linger in his company—no matter how unsettling and sexy he looked without his shirt.

"Will it hold me?" she asked as she took the hand he offered again, put a foot on the front bumper, and hopped onto the hood of the pickup.

"Are you kidding? This thing's a tank," he said, helping her settle down on the hood. "Now…lay back and just look at those stars."

Poppy giggled and did as instructed. Studying Swaggart's position for a moment, she crossed her feet at the ankles, let her back lay against the cold windshield, and looked up into the night sky. In that moment, she could've sworn she could feel the warmth radiating from his body—his shirtless body.

"Wow!" she breathed as she managed to concentrate on the brilliance of the stars overhead. The night was unusually clear, and the stars and constellations were more brilliant and vivid than she'd ever seen them.

"I know!" he said. "I came home from work and just happened to glance up. It's too good to ignore."

"It is," Poppy agreed.

"You want some jerky?" he asked, producing a package of jerky from beneath one leg.

Poppy giggled and stuck her hand into the open bag, withdrawing a piece of leathery meat. She smiled as Swaggart pulled a piece out for himself, tearing off a bite with his teeth.

He breathed a heavy sigh and said, "Is this the life or what?" Poppy continued to smile and chew her jerky. "I mean, moments like this—you know—when you're all wrung out from hard work and just needing to get to sleep and then—bam! Something like this makes you stop, take a breath, and be thankful you're alive."

"I call them 'wow moments,'" Poppy said.

"Wow moments?" he asked.

"Yeah," Poppy said, still chewing her jerky. "Wow moments. You know, moments that make you go, 'Wow!' It's the same thing you're talking about. I have them at the restaurant sometimes."

"Me, too," Swaggart said. "Like the other day, I was watching grandpa—thinking about everything he's accomplished in his life—a great family, a successful business, and you're right—I thought, 'Wow!' Once he was just a seventeen-year-old kid riding the rails without a dime in his pocket. It's amazing."

"I like wow moments," Poppy said, gazing at one particular star that seemed to be twinkling more than the others.

"Was your date with Mr. Gorgeous a wow moment?" Swaggart asked.

Poppy's smile faded a little. She didn't want to talk about her date with Mark just then. She wanted to talk about stars, the restaurant— she just wanted to enjoy her private moment with Swaggart. She wanted to reach over and run her hand over his washboard stomach and see what it felt like. Still, his question caused her to think about her date with Mark in a new context.

"It was really fun—different," she said. "But—but it wasn't a wow moment," she answered at last.

The realization discouraged her, but she rationalized it was only because she hadn't spent enough time with Mark yet. Surely wow moments with him were just around the corner. Glancing at Swaggart, Poppy was suddenly very conscious of the many, many, many wow moments he had provided for her throughout the years. Realizing that witnessing him so casually unclothed was just another one gave her goose bumps.

"Yeah, I guess they're kind of rare. You can't go looking for them—they just have to happen," he said.

"Did you ever have any wow moments with Jennifer?" Poppy asked. She couldn't help it. Swaggart dating Jennifer Trujillo had nearly driven her mad! She had to know if Jennifer had provided any wow moments for him—she had to know.

"Not one," Swaggart said, shaking his head. "What was wrong with all of you anyway?" he asked. "Letting me go out with her for so long—I must've been on drugs to do it, and you must've been on drugs to let me."

"You're a big boy—you have to make your own choices," Poppy said. "Even if they are stupid."

"Whoa!" Swaggart chuckled. "That's harsh."

"I'm sorry," Poppy said. She'd let her innermost thoughts pop out in verbal form.

"No. You're right," he said. "But I guess everyone's allowed one foolish relationship choice, right?"

"Maybe," Poppy said. She didn't want to talk about Jennifer Trujillo anymore. She thought of Mark—wondered if she continued to date him, continued to develop a relationship with him—would it be a foolish choice or a good choice?

"You want some more?" Swaggart asked, offering the bag of jerky to her again.

"No, thanks," Poppy said.

Swaggart tossed the bag through the window of his pickup. He turned on his side and retrieved a can of root beer from the dashboard inside. He drank from it for a minute then offered it to Poppy.

Poppy's eyes widened. Everyone knew how Swaggart felt about eating and drinking after people—he didn't do it! Yet he had eaten pudding from her spoon—the day he'd managed to retrieve her quarter from the garbage disposal.

"Here," he said, nodding at her. "That jerky's salty."

Still stunned that he was offering her his drink, Poppy accepted it. It was strange—the way the simplest thing, such as sharing a drink with Swaggart, could cause Poppy's stomach to start the familiar round of twists and turns.

"Thanks," she said, handing the can back to him.

"You bet," he said, taking a swig himself before leaning over to set the beverage back inside the pickup.

"So," he began then. "This date you had last Saturday—Whitney says it was quite the event—canoeing, a picnic, a concert in the park. I guess this guy isn't operating in date rut, huh?"

"Date rut?" Poppy asked. "And what is Whitney doing telling you all about my date with Mark?"

"I asked her," he answered.

Poppy felt breathless—he'd asked about her date with Mark? Why? What did it matter to him? Hope took flight in her chest, and she tried to squelch it.

"I mean, just because you didn't care enough to tell me I was a jerk for dating Jennifer doesn't mean I won't keep my eye on you and Whitney—you know, help you watch out for losers."

Her hope was squelched—he was worried about her the same way he was about Whitney.

"Mark isn't a loser," she grumbled. "And, whatever date rut is…I'm sure he's not operating on it." She felt hurt, defensive.

"I'm sure he's not a loser," Swaggart said. "After all, he's hot after *you*, isn't he? And with a prime cut like you in his sights, I'm sure he's got date rut licked already."

"What do you mean by date rut?" Poppy asked. She was blushing, yes—blushing because Swaggart had called her a *prime cut*—implied she was worth Mark's time.

"You know—date rut," he said, gazing up into the night sky. "Jennifer said I was bogged down in it, completely stuck. Date rut—doing the same things over and over and over—never planning anything exciting and out of the ordinary. Like this, for instance." He nodded toward the sky. "Sitting out here looking at the stars, eating jerky, and drinking root beer—this would've been date rut to Jennifer."

Poppy frowned. "You've got to be kidding me," she said. "What? Did she expect dinner and a movie every time?"

Swaggart laughed. "Dinner and a movie? That was her exact definition of date rut. She called it 'the ultimate insult a woman can receive'—the offer of dinner and a movie. She says it's like offering green Jell-O to someone who's been in the hospital for a year."

"Swaggart Moretti!" Poppy scolded. She was angry, furious with Jennifer for having obviously and so thoroughly attacked Swaggart's self-esteem. "What the heck were you doing going out with that wench? Date rut? Who does she think she is anyway?" she rambled. "Date rut? Why—any woman who knows you would practically do anything to go to dinner and a movie with you! Date rut—that's the most ridiculous thing I've ever heard! *I* love dinner and a movie! It's my favorite thing to do! Now, dinner and a double feature…that's even better!"

"Really?" he said, grinning at her. Poppy didn't care if he was grinning at her—if he was amused by her tantrum.

"Yes, really!" she said, sitting up and playfully pushing at him. The feel of his warm skin against her palm caused her goose bumps to return. "Date rut," she grumbled, shaking her head. "You're right—Whitney and I should've taken you out behind the restaurant and slapped some sense into you when you started taking Jennifer out."

Swaggart chuckled and returned his attention to the sky. "Well, she's history now. I guess that's all that matters—as long as I learned my lesson. Right?"

"In theory," Poppy mumbled. She was still angry, irritated at the very thought of Jennifer Trujillo. Still, she leaned back on the windshield and looked into the black canvas above.

"So you don't believe in date rut?" he asked.

"No," she said. "I think if you feel you're in date rut, you're either a self-centered, arrogant wench—like some Jennifers we could name—or you're simply dating the wrong person. If you're dating the right person, then you'll enjoy doing anything. Different and exciting—that's good just for fun—but you should be able to have as much fun together doing nothing as you do doing something."

"I had no idea you were such a philosopher," Swaggart said, looking from the stars to Poppy and smiling.

"Well—you just hit a nerve, that's all," Poppy said, trying to simmer herself down.

"I think I like hitting your nerves," Swaggart said. "It gets you all wound up."

"Well, *that* nerve did," Poppy admitted. "Don't you have nerves that get hit?" she asked.

"Oh, sure," he said.

"Like what?" she asked.

"I can't tell you that," Swaggart said.

"Why not?"

"Because you'll try to hit them on purpose," he answered, winking at her.

"I won't—I promise," Poppy said. Her curiosity was really piqued. "Come on, Swaggart—just one nerve that you're sensitive about."

Swaggart chuckled. "Okay," he said. "Do you want a good nerve or a bad nerve?"

Poppy didn't want him to get angry while contemplating anything. "A good nerve," she said.

"A good nerve that gets me wound up," he mused, frowning as if he were thinking very hard.

"Come on," Poppy said. "'Fess up."

"Can it be a literal nerve?" he asked.

"You mean like—like part of your nervous system or something? Or something like the way you don't want people eating off your plate and drinking out of your glass?"

"Either," he said. "Hey, wait a minute," he added. "Who told you I don't like people to eat off my plate or drink out of my glass?"

"Everybody knows it, Swaggart," she said, smiling at his perplexed expression.

"I let you drink out of my pop can just a minute ago," he said.

"I know! I felt so special," she teased.

He shrugged and asked, "Why would you think it would bother me to drink after you? Seems to me we swapped more germs the other night in the restaurant checking item one off your list than are in my pop can right now. And believe me—that didn't bother me one bit."

Poppy was stunned into silence. He'd mentioned it! He'd actually referred to their hours together spent kissing!

Unlike Poppy, however, Swaggart seemed unaffected and continued their conversation. "One good nerve that I'm willing to tell you about...hmmm," he mused.

Poppy knew her cheeks were crimson. In fact, she felt hot all over. As she continued to look at him, her mouth began to water at the memory of his magnificent kiss.

"Well, if you'll allow a literal nerve," he continued, "you hit one the other night, and I'm guessing you didn't even know it."

"Wh-what do you mean?" she asked. Was he still referring to their blissful hours in Good Ol' Days? She wasn't sure. Nervously, she reached into her pocket and withdrew her lip gloss. With one trembling ring finger, she smoothed the shiny substance over her lips and waited for his answer.

"You know, the other night when we were—you know— checking that item off your list, so to speak," he said. He rolled onto his side, propped himself on one elbow, and asked, "You remember that, don't you, Poppy?"

"Are you teasing me?" she asked. Her heart had begun to ache a little—fearful he was going to make fun of her for having put him on her list.

"No," he said. "I just want to make sure you remember it happened."

"Yes, Swaggart," she told him, trembling with nerves and embarrassment.

"Well, you did something during our...our time together. You hit a big nerve I didn't even know I had—and I'm guessing you didn't know it. Actually, you did it once before that—that was the first time I noticed it," he said.

Poppy applied more lip gloss. She didn't need more, but she was nervous.

"What kind is this?" Swaggart asked, sitting up and taking the lip gloss from her. He sniffed it and asked, "Strawberry?"

"Raspberry," she told him snatching the small plastic jar from him and screwing the lid back on before shoving it into her pocket. "S-so what's this nerve I apparently hit without knowing?" she stammered. "Are you going to tell me or not?"

"Do you know—speaking of that list of yours—I thought of something just now that I've always wanted to do," he said.

"You're changing the subject," Poppy accused. She couldn't help but smile at him—he was so obviously trying to avoid telling her what nerve she'd hit.

He chuckled and hopped off the pickup. "Here," he said, taking hold of her arm and tugging. "Come here."

Poppy moved to his side of the pickup's hood, delighted when he put his hands at her waist and lifted her down.

"What?" she asked.

"Do you know what I've always wanted to do?" he asked.

"What's that?"

Poppy gasped as Swaggart pushed her back against the cab of his pickup, taking her face between his hands.

"Take that lip gloss right off your pretty little lips," he mumbled an instant before his mouth captured hers in a moist, heated, and very driven kiss.

The lip gloss Poppy had so freshly applied filled her mouth with the flavor of raspberries, and she wished she hadn't used so much—wished she could simply savor the natural taste of Swaggart's kiss. As he pulled her into his arms, however—wrapping her in their strength, the power of his body and the warm, smooth sense of his skin against her, protecting her against the cooling night air—the light flavor of raspberry dissipated, wonderfully replaced by the hot, moist flavor of Swaggart Moretti's mouth.

He kissed her breathless—until the butterflies in her stomach were in a winged uproar—until her knees were weak and her arms ached from wanting to hold him tighter. When he broke the seal of their lips, Poppy inhaled a deep gasp of air—yet preferring to have fainted rather than give up the feel of his mouth commanding her own.

"Delicious," Swaggart mumbled. His eyes narrowed as the warm syrup of them looked at her.

"It's raspberry," Poppy breathlessly corrected. She smiled as she looked up at him to see the remnants of lip gloss shine on his lips and around his mouth. Her stomach looped at the knowledge her lip gloss was on his mouth because he'd just kissed her. She was self-conscious under his gaze and wiped at the remaining lip gloss on her own lips with her fingertips.

"I didn't mean the raspberry," he said, and Poppy smiled as he wiped his mouth with the back of one strong hand. "I meant you."

Poppy was certain her heart swelled to ten times its normal size! Standing before him, being held against him, gazing up into his perfectly handsome face, she struggled to breathe normally. Goose bumps rippled over her body as Swaggart slowly caressed her arms with his strong hands. Poppy could feel the calluses on his hands as they traveled over her arms, and the sensation only served to enliven her more.

"Still want to know what that nerve was you hit the other night?" Swaggart asked, his voice low, alluring, exciting.

"Yeah," Poppy breathed. She only wanted to melt to him—feel her body wrapped in his arms, his kiss raining passion and bliss upon her.

"Well, I'm a little too shy to tell you," he whispered. "The only way you'll ever find out is to spend another hour kissing me."

"Okay," she breathed. She felt entirely intoxicated, absolutely hypnotized by the alluring expression in his eyes.

Swaggart smiled at her as he gathered her into his arms. "Okay, baby," he whispered. "But you better pay attention—or you might miss it when you do hit that nerve."

As Swaggart's mouth took her own, Poppy felt tears spring to her eyes—her emotions in an utter turmoil of bliss, confusion, and something like panic. Swaggart's kiss, his arms around her, the scent of him, the feel of his smooth skin and of his whiskers against her cheek—it was heaven! It was the only thing she ever wanted to do again—kiss him! Yet a tear trickled from one corner of her eye as she wondered how she would ever find the desire to kiss anyone else ever again! How could she go out with Mark on Thursday when all she wanted to do was wrap her arms around Swaggart and kiss him forever? What if kissing him again—spending another hour relishing his affections—what if it really did ruin her, keep her from ever being able to love another man?

Another tear escaped Poppy's eye as she realized then—admitted to herself—she was still in love with Swaggart Moretti! She'd loved him for years—talked herself into believing she did not—but she did! She'd loved him before he'd ever kissed her that night in Good Ol' Days—she loved him now! Her heart soared as she let her arms travel over the solid muscles of his chest. It broke as she caressed the breadth of his shoulders, and it silently cried out to belong to him as her hands were lost in the softness of his hair.

Poppy gasped slightly as Swaggart's embrace suddenly tightened, his mouth crushing her own with a ravenous passion! He broke the seal of their lips, his mouth taking respite in the flesh of her throat as she tried to draw a regulated breath. Poppy let her hands fist where they rested in Swaggart's hair. Instantly, his mouth left her neck and captured her mouth.

Mid the passion raging between them, a somewhat rational thought managed to strike her suddenly: it was his hair. Her fingers in his hair—it was the good nerve he hinted about—the one she'd unknowingly hit before! She was certain of it by the way it seemed to drive him into passionate madness. Poppy wrapped her arms around his neck, enchanted by the sudden realization. Running her hands from the back of his neck, up through his hair, Poppy giggled as Swaggart wrapped his arms around her waist, lifting her off her feet and increasing the intensity of their kiss.

"I know what it is," Poppy breathed as his embrace finally relaxed, allowing her to stand again.

"What?" he mumbled, kissing her softly several times in succession.

Poppy stopped his affectionate aggression by taking his face between her hands and caressing his lips with her thumbs. "It's your hair," she whispered. "You like to have fingers run through your hair."

He grinned and said, "I like to have *your* fingers run through my hair."

He leaned forward, kissing her softly, tenderly toying with her lips. He blew into her mouth, and the gesture sent a rapturous thrill traveling through her. She trembled when he did it again a moment before pressing his lips to hers in a soft, lingering kiss. Poppy quivered as goose bumps erupted over every inch of her flesh, as the butterflies fighting for space in her stomach caused her breath to catch.

"Wow," she heard Swaggart breathe in unison with her own breathy exclamation.

Poppy Amore was in trouble, and she didn't even know it. Swaggart knew it, however, and he struggled to keep his physical desires for Poppy in check. What he wanted to do and what he would allow himself to do were two different things. For the moment he was simply glad she found him attractive enough to let him kiss her—grateful she liked him enough to kiss him back. He grimaced, hoping Whitney was right and that the only kiss the Mark guy had enjoyed where Poppy was concerned was the polite, good-night kiss kind.

As Swaggart felt Poppy pull herself more snugly against him, sigh as he deepened their kiss, he tried to convince himself she liked him more than she did Mr. Romeo Advertising Executive. Surely it was true. If that guy had only managed a good-night peck so far and Swaggart had twice managed to coax her into such passion as they were exchanging at that moment—he had to have the upper hand. Didn't he?

Poppy was so sweet, so beautiful, so clever and kind—far too good for the likes of Swaggart Moretti. Yet he wanted her, and he worried he wouldn't be able to give her up if this Mark guy turned out to be what was best for her.

Again her hands found their way to his hair. Inhaling a deep breath of self-control, he ground his mouth to hers, unable to satisfy his thirst for her. Forget what was best for her! At that moment, she was in *his* arms, kissing *him*, and he would enjoy it!

Poppy's lips hurt, her heart ached inside her chest—worn out from the constant elation she was experiencing in Swaggart's arms—but she didn't care. She loved the feel of the rough calluses on his hands against her cheeks, the euphoric sensation he sent racing through her each time he kissed her neck.

"You all right, baby?" he asked in a whisper.

"I'm fine," she breathed. She loved when he called her "baby"! She liked to imagine that he always would call her baby—that she'd walk into the restaurant to work the next day and he'd say, "Hey, baby," as a greeting.

Poppy knew she was only daydreaming, however—and some dreams were just too impossible to come true. Still, as she stood there, her back pressed against Swaggart Moretti's pickup door, her front pressed up against Swaggart Moretti himself—she dared to dream it could come true. She'd worry about reality in the morning. For the moment, she'd allow herself to bathe in the wonder of belonging to Swaggart—even if it was a fleeting thing.

Poppy pressed one to hear the message again.

"Hey there, beautiful...it's Mark. The VPs are sending me to Chicago this week, so we won't be able to go to the Comedy Corner on Thursday night...*but* I want to make it up to you. I bought us two tickets to this huge charity gala dinner thing on Saturday. It starts at six thirty, and it's all black tie and formal. The food will be really good, and they've got some great live entertainment lined up. So we'll go to that instead, okay? Be sure you can get work off for it...again, it's Saturday. Give me a call in the morning. I'm yours, you know."

Though the hour was late, so many thoughts were rattling around in Poppy's head that it ached! She thought of the way Swaggart had told her he always wanted to take the lip gloss off her lips and then kissed her—Mark, she realized now, had wiped the lip gloss off with his thumb before kissing her. Swaggart had simply used his hand to wipe the residual lip gloss off his lips, while Mark had been upset about a mud stain on his shirt. Swaggart had gotten down and dirty with the garbage disposal, never pausing to question what needed to be done to fix it. Mark had said to call a plumber—had cringed at the idea of sticking his hand down the sink to fix it. Mark's hands were soft when he'd held her face to kiss her good night—but Swaggart's strong, callused ones felt a million times better against her skin.

Brushing a tear from her cheek, Poppy consciously admitted to herself—she'd loved Swaggart forever, and he was, and always would be, her dream man. Mark was kind, polite, gorgeous, and very attentive, but Swaggart was still the perfect man of Poppy's dreams—whether she could ever have a chance of owning him or not.

"You sure got in late, Pops," Whitney said, sitting down next to Poppy on the couch. "And you look a little stressed. What's wrong?"

Poppy let a tear trickle over her cheek—the warmth of Swaggart's arms, the taste of his kiss still fresh to her senses. She turned off her cell phone and sat it on the arm of the couch.

"Nothing," she said. "It's just…I realized tonight that, for the rest of my life, I'd rather stand on the street outside the bakery window and stare at the peach pie on the other side than settle for the slice of apple pie in my hand."

CHAPTER ELEVEN

Through the whole of the next day, Poppy was entirely distracted. She even made two order mistakes! She couldn't seem to keep her mind on work—especially with drop-dead-gorgeous Swaggart Moretti in the kitchen. She had to tell Mark—somehow she had to tell him she couldn't see him anymore. Oh, sure she knew it was impossible to ever own Swaggart. Yet the previous night, spent gazing at the stars from the hood of his pickup and kissing him for over an hour afterward—she knew she couldn't go out with Mark anymore. She didn't want to. Maybe she couldn't ever have Swaggart—the whole peach pie—but she'd still rather dream about the peach pie from outside the bakery window than settle for the apple pie readily available. Besides, it wasn't fair to Mark—dating him when she knew she could never give her heart to him.

But how would she tell him? What would she tell him? She couldn't very well say, "Mark—I can't go out with you because I'm in love with Swaggart." She couldn't tell Mark he was less attractive to her because he didn't have enough calluses on his hands or because he wasn't willing to try to get her quarter out of the garbage disposal. It was a terrible dilemma. Poppy had decided to go ahead and go with Mark to the gala dinner thing on Saturday—he'd already invested in tickets, and besides, maybe an opportunity to be honest with him would arise. She could only hope. Either way, she knew it would be her last date with him. Was she making a mistake? Perhaps, but it didn't matter—she loved Swaggart.

And then there was Swaggart himself! Every time she had to put in an order, or pick one up, she thought she was going faint, tremble to death, or scream! To Poppy, he seemed more gorgeous, more charismatic, and more the object of her obsession than ever before. Yet nothing seemed to have changed in the way he treated her at work—he still smiled and winked at her like he always had—still teased her. Poppy couldn't understand how he could appear so calm, cool, and collected when her insides were freaking out! Then again, maybe he wasn't as calm and cool as he appeared to be. Still, every time she looked at him, her mouth watered or she got goose bumps—or both. How would she manage to keep from being distracted at work? How would she manage to keep from throwing herself into his arms and begging him to love her in return?

With so much turmoil in her mind and body, Poppy was relieved when her lunch hour finally arrived. Finding an empty table near the fountain in the gardens behind the restaurant, she sat down, her plate heaping with Swaggart's seasoned steak fries and a Jiggy burger. Such a big meal would threaten to make her pretty darn tired for the rest of the day, but she didn't care—she wanted a good meal she could sink her teeth and her stress into.

"Mind if I eat lunch with you?" Swaggart asked, just as Poppy dipped her first fry into the small bowl of ranch dressing on her plate.

"Of course not," she said, nervously popping the entire steak fry into her mouth. How could she possibly eat now—with the man of her dreams sitting across from her, looking so wonderful and tempting?

"You like that Jiggy burger?" Swaggart asked. Poppy smiled, realizing his plate was also heaped with a Jiggy burger and seasoned fries.

"Yeah," she said. "It's my favorite."

"Mine too," he said. Picking up a steak fry from his own plate, Poppy's smile broadened as he reached across the table, dipping it in her ranch dressing before popping it into his mouth.

Poppy sighed as she ate another fry. "Why is it called a Jiggy burger?" she asked. She'd often wondered about the strange name of Good Ol' Days' most popular hamburger but had never before thought to ask anybody at the restaurant.

Swaggart chuckled. "You won't believe me if I tell you," he said.

"Yes, I will," Poppy said. "Tell me."

He was gorgeous! Simply delicious! As she gazed at him casually lounging in the wrought-iron chair across the table from her, Poppy's heart fluttered and her stomach began a cycle of its familiar looping.

"There's this song," he began, "by Will Smith…"

Poppy giggled, "You mean, 'Gettin' Jiggy Wit It'? You're kidding me?"

Swaggart smiled and shook his head. "Not kidding," he said. "It was on the radio the first time I ever made this burger. Me and Bobby were messing around in the kitchen—you know, dancing around and being stupid to that song—and then I tasted the burger and…"

"And the Jiggy burger was born," Poppy laughed. "Unbelievable!"

"Believe it, baby," Swaggart said, eating another fry.

Poppy held her breath for a moment—tried to remain calm—he'd called her *baby* again.

"I like the cracked peppercorns in it," Poppy told him.

"Me, too," Swaggart said. He leaned over his plate, picked up his Jiggy burger, and took a big bite. "Mmm! I still love it as much as the first time I ever made it."

Poppy smiled and took a bite of her own burger. It was so good! It never ceased to amaze her—the first bite of one of Swaggart's Jiggy burgers. Cracked peppercorns, garlic, onion, and too many other flavors to identify, just in the meat alone. It was delicious!

"So," he said. "Whitney says you have a date with Mr. Wonderful on Thursday."

Poppy looked at him, studied him as he dipped another fry in her ranch dressing. Did he care? Did he want her to have another date with Mark—or did he *not* want her to have another date with Mark? What was going on between her and Swaggart? Was it just kissing—

just two friends letting physical desire get the better of them? Not for her—she knew that. For her it was much, much more—an affair of the heart—one she'd been dreaming of for years. But what was it for Swaggart? He sat across from her, seeming as natural as ever—as if nothing unusual had ever happened between them. Did he care? Did he care for her—or was she just someone to kiss until his next girlfriend showed up?

"Um…he's out of town for work, so he rescheduled for Saturday," she said.

"Do you like this guy?" Swaggart asked.

Poppy dipped a fry in her ranch dressing, swirling it around for a minute before taking a bite. "He's really nice—I'm sure everyone likes him," she answered. She dared to glance at him. He was staring at her, his eyes narrowed, the smile gone from his face.

"But do you like him?" he asked.

Poppy was feeling uncomfortable, nervous. "I'm not planning on marrying him, if that's what you mean," she said.

"So why are you dating him then?" he asked.

"Probably the same reason you were dating Jennifer—to have a good time and have something to do after work," she said. She didn't look up at him, just took another bite of her hamburger. How could she possibly explain why she had dated Mark? "A handsome, charming man asked me out, and I accepted—does that make me a criminal or something?" she said, her mouth still full of hamburger.

"So you're not exclusive?" he asked.

Poppy looked at him. He was still staring at her, eyes narrowed. It was very disconcerting—as if he were peering into her thoughts, her soul.

"No," Poppy answered, wiping her mouth with her napkin. "If I were exclusive with him, do you think I would have spent last night…talking to you?"

He grinned—most likely amused by her discomfort. "Well, I sure hope not," he chuckled.

The conversation died for a moment. Poppy was uncomfortable—did he think badly of her for being so willing to kiss him while she was dating Mark?

"I do have one question, however," he said at last.

Oh, no! Poppy thought. She had hoped the subject was dead—apparently it wasn't.

"What might that be?" she asked.

"Am I a better kisser than he is?" Swaggart asked.

Poppy looked up at him. His expression was not quite that of mischief, yet not quite that of being serious.

"Oh my heck!" Poppy exclaimed in a whisper. "I cannot believe you're asking me that."

"You're blushing," he said.

"Of course I'm blushing," Poppy whispered. "My heck! I can't believe—"

"You didn't answer my question," he interrupted. Swaggart hadn't lowered his voice to a whisper the way Poppy had, and Poppy glanced to the couple at the nearby table to see if they were eavesdropping. "Am I a better kisser than—"

Before she realized what she was doing, Poppy had reached across the table, pressing her hand to Swaggart's mouth to hush him.

"Shhh," she scolded. "Someone's going to hear you."

Swaggart pulled Poppy's hand away from his mouth and asked, "What? You don't want people knowing we spend hours on end kissing and—"

"Shhh!" she scolded in a whisper, as she pressed her palm to his lips again.

His eyes sparkled with mischief as he chuckled and pulled her hand away once more. "Then answer my question. Am I a better—"

"Yes! Yes, of course you are!" Poppy exclaimed in a whisper. "Though in truth, I never kissed Mark like that. I haven't known him that long at all." She frowned as she looked at him and said, "I can't believe you'd think I would make out with you one night and then someone else another."

"I don't," he said, smiling at her. "I just wanted to hear you say it."

Poppy was puzzled as Swaggart suddenly removed his Jiggy burger from his plate, setting it on a napkin on the wrought-iron table. Next he picked up his plate and dumped the few steak fries he had left onto Poppy's plate.

"You're not gonna eat your food?" Poppy asked.

"Oh, I will," Swaggart said. "But I have to finish this."

Poppy watched as Swaggart turned his plate over and retrieved a folded napkin and a pen from his apron pocket. Unfolding the napkin, he laid it on the bottom of the plate. Poppy could see the napkin already had writing on it, and she smiled as Swaggart leaned over, awkwardly drawing a dotted line border around whatever was written on it.

"Now that we've established I'm the better kisser and that you're not dating Mr. Joe Perfect—here," he said, handing the napkin to her.

"What's this?" she asked.

"A coupon," he said, taking a bite of his hamburger and snatching a fry from Poppy's plate.

"A coupon?" Poppy said, as she looked at the napkin.

"Mmm-hmm," Swaggart said, continuing to eat.

Poppy smiled as she studied the napkin. Written in Swaggart's nearly illegible, very masculine handwriting were the words, *This coupon is redeemable for one night of "date rut"—dinner and a double feature with Swaggart Moretti.* Poppy giggled at the dotted line rectangle Swaggart had drawn around the verbiage.

"It's a 'date rut' coupon," he said, eating another fry. "Read the fine print on the back."

Poppy giggled and turned the napkin over. Written in smaller writing and even more illegibly were the words, *No kissing necessary to redeem this coupon.*

"What do you think of that?" Swaggart said. His eyebrows arched with daring pride, his handsome smile dazzling Poppy to the tips of her toes.

Poppy thought she was going to fly apart! Swaggart Moretti was asking her out? It couldn't be true! It just couldn't be! Yet she held the proof in her hands—it was a dream come true—it was better! She wanted to leap from her seat, throw her arms around his neck, kiss him square on his handsome mouth—but she didn't.

"You are too cute, Swaggart," she said, instead.

"Cute?" he said, frowning and grinning at the same time. "Is that a good thing?"

"Yes," Poppy answered, studying the coupon again. He was adorable! On top of being gorgeous, charming, charismatic, witty, masculine, built like Adonis, and talented—he was adorable!

"So when do you want to redeem that?" he asked. He picked up the white paper his Jiggy burger had been in, crumpling it up and shooting it like a basketball into the nearby trash receptacle.

"I don't know," Poppy said. "When…when can I?"

Swaggart smiled again and said, "Well, a little bird told me you're free Thursday." Poppy giggled and bit her lip. Suddenly she was very, very glad Mark Lawson had been called out of town on business.

"But a double feature…that'll take all day, and don't you work Thursday?" she asked. Her heart was pounding like mad, she felt breathless, and the loop-the-loops going on in her stomach were almost nauseating!

"I'm off Thursday. All day and all night," he said, snatching another fry from her plate.

"If I redeem the coupon," Poppy began, again studying the napkin in her hand, "do I get to keep it?"

Swaggart shrugged his shoulders and said, "If you want."

"Okay then. Let's go Thursday," she said. She was certain her cheeks were going to pop from smiling so hard.

"All righty then," he said, pushing his chair away from the table and standing. "I'll pick you up at ten."

"In the morning?" Poppy asked—hoping he did mean in the morning.

"Well, yeah," he said. "The first matinee movies start at like eleven—that means lunch about one, the next movie at around two thirty or three, and then dinner at six." He put his hands on the table, leaning close to Poppy's face. "And then we could do a late movie if you want or just sit on the grass and check out the stars again."

"But the coupon doesn't include lunch, a triple feature, or stargazing," Poppy said. Oh how she wanted to kiss him! Her mouth was watering, her body trembling as goose bumps poured over her.

"Thursday is double coupon day," Swaggart said. He smiled, reached out, and tweaked her nose. "I've gotta get back to work. I think Bobby's burning something."

"Okay," Poppy said.

"Finish your Jiggy burger—I worked hard on that," he said, as he turned and headed back to the restaurant.

Poppy smiled and breathed a sigh of pure delight as she studied the napkin in her hands.

"This coupon is redeemable for one night of 'date rut'—dinner and a double feature with Swaggart Moretti," she read aloud to herself.

She couldn't stop the tiny squeal of joy that escaped her throat. She had a date with Swaggart Moretti! An honest-to-goodness date! And the way he'd asked her—Poppy looked at the napkin again and giggled—how adorable! She turned it over and read the back again. *No kissing necessary to redeem this coupon*, it said. She knew it was his way of letting her know he wanted to be with her, not just kiss her. It was wonderful! Though she hoped he wouldn't hold too fast to the "no kissing necessary" clause on the back of the adorable coupon.

In those moments, Poppy didn't care how awkward it might be to tell Mark she couldn't see him again. In those moments, she didn't care that this date with Swaggart might be a one-time thing—a singular day of having him all to herself. In those moments, all Poppy could do was try and keep her feet on the ground—she had a date with Swaggart Moretti!

"Swaggart," Wally Dexter called as Swaggart entered the alcove through the back door.

"Yeah, Grandpa?" Swaggart said.

Poppy had liked his coupon! Furthermore, he was beginning to think he had the upper hand over the Mark guy—it was hard to believe, but it looked like it might be true. He smiled at the knowledge.

"Can I see you in the office for a minute?" his Grandpa asked.

"Sure thing," Swaggart said. His light-heartedness was compromised just a bit—his grandpa's serious expression was a little out of character.

Wally Dexter had seen Swaggart having lunch with Poppy from his office window. *Finally,* he'd thought. After all this time, that numbskull grandson of his was finally going to make his move. It had taken him long enough—but it looked like he was finally going to do it. And if Swaggart was ready to make a change, then Wally knew his moment had arrived. Wally had a change he needed to make too—a change that had been in the works for months. He was glad the time had arrived to act on it.

"What's up, Grandpa?" Swaggart said as his grandpa closed the office door behind them. Swaggart felt a bit uneasy. It was unlike his grandfather to appear so serious, so secretive.

He watched as Wally Dexter went to his desk and opened a drawer, withdrawing a set of papers. From the blue cardstock encompassing the papers, they appeared to be legal documents of some sort.

"Did you open that envelope I had Poppy run over last night?" Wally asked.

Swaggart winced and said, "Oh man! I totally forgot about it. It's still in my truck—do you want me to go get it?"

"Not right now," Wally said. "But I do want you to sit down and look at this for a moment. It's your copy."

"My copy of what?" Swaggart said, sitting down and taking the papers when his grandfather offered them to him. He'd seen legal documents folded in blue before—his parents' wills, his grandmother's will. Did his Grandpa want him to look over his will?

Surely not. People didn't give copies of their wills away. Still, Swaggart's heart panged at the thought of one day being without his beloved grandfather.

"Those are your copies of the documentation of the transference of this restaurant from my ownership to yours," Wally said.

"What?" Swaggart breathed.

"I'm giving the business to you, Swaggart."

"Grandpa—you can't just give the restaurant to me. Why would you...you can't just sign your business over to me." Swaggart stammered.

"It's already done," Wally said. "Provided you sign all the necessary documents, of course."

"Grandpa," Swaggart said as he looked at the papers. "Surely you need to consult Uncle Robert, Mom, about this—Aunt Toni…"

"I already have, Swaggart, and they all agree with me—the restaurant should go to you," Wally said.

"Grandpa…I can't just…" Swaggart began. He was dumfounded, flabbergasted, in total shock.

"You love this place, Swaggart," Wally said. "From the time you were a little boy, you've loved this place—everything about it. Tell me I'm wrong."

"You're not wrong," Swaggart admitted. "But—"

"But nothing," Wally interrupted. "It's in your blood; it's in your soul. Not to mention the fact your business sense has quadrupled our profit over the past two years. You'll keep it going. And besides, I happen to know you'd rather flip a Jiggy burger any day for nickels than make ten grand in one night for one of your fancy catered shindigs."

Swaggart smiled. It was true—he would rather flip burgers and create an occasional Chef's Choice at Good Ol' Days than spend his life in some fancy-shmancy restaurant being referred to as "Chef Moretti." It's why he'd gone for his business degree after finishing culinary arts school—he'd realized that, though he liked to cook and had a gift for it, it was the restaurant he loved—not the art of cooking.

"Robert, Toni, and your mother will still continue in profit sharing for the next five years," Wally said. "After that, it's yours—all of it."

"But, Grandpa, I can't possibly accept this. I mean...at least let me buy you out or something," Swaggart said.

"I love this place, Swaggart," Wally said. "I worked over half my life to build it up, make it an icon in this city. The fact of the matter is you're the only one I trust with it—the only one who loves it as much as I do and appreciates where it came from."

"But...but why are you doing this now?" Swaggart asked. "Why not wait until...until you're closer to wanting to retire?"

"You mean, why not wait and simply will it to you when I kick off?" Wally asked.

"Grandpa. Don't say it like that," Swaggart scolded. He didn't like the way his grandfather sometimes referred to death so casually.

"I want this all done now," Wally said. "I'm tired, and I'm old, and I want to sit around and watch the world for a while—instead of feeling like I'm sitting on it while it's going at top speed."

"I just don't think you should...I can't possibly agree to this," Swaggart mumbled, frowning and rubbing his temples where he could feel a headache forming. It was too much.

"What about Whitney, Bobby, all the other grandkids? Don't they deserve to—"

"None of them want it, Swaggart," Wally interrupted. "Nobody loves this place like I do. Nobody but you—and, of course, Poppy."

"Poppy?" Swaggart asked.

"I think her heart is attached to this place as much as yours—only I think you're as much the reason as anything else."

Swaggart shook his head and smiled at his grandfather. "You're imagining things, Grandpa," he said, even though he felt hope ignite in his chest.

Did his grandpa know something he didn't? Swaggart may have managed to secure a day with Poppy, but the Mark guy would still have her on the Saturday after. As long as she still wanted to go out with Mark again, Swaggart was just a guy who'd managed to get her attention back in high school. Maybe he'd held her attention long enough to warrant being able to coax her into some mighty fine kissing—but he'd seen the Mark guy, and that guy was the whole package.

"I never imagine things," Wally said. "I'm just glad you finally found the guts to—"

"She's dating another guy, you know," Swaggart interrupted.

"Well, sure she is! What was she supposed to do all this time you were fiddling around trying to find the courage to reach out and take what you want?" Wally asked.

"I'm just a cook," Swaggart said. "This guy's a big-time business executive. He's got money, position—"

"If Poppy agreed to date him, then I'm sure he's a very nice young man," Wally said. "But he's not for her, and you're not just a cook. Even if there were something wrong with being a cook—which there isn't—you're not just a cook. You're one of the most sought-after chefs in this city, with an incredible talent for business as well. You've seen the numbers for this quarter, Swaggart—you know how much this place is pulling in. It may not last forever, but ride the wave while it does!"

Swaggart looked at the document in his hand. In truth, owning Good Ol' Days would be his dream come true—one of the top two on his list anyway. He chuckled as he realized he'd had his own Dreams to Do list tucked away in his brain for years. Owning Good Ol' Days had been near the top, second only to one thing—owning Poppy Amore.

He thought of Poppy's list—the list he was at the top of. Could he still be at the top of it? Maybe his grandfather was right—maybe Poppy was only going out with the Mark guy because Swaggart had never asked her before.

"Well, maybe we'll talk about this some more, Grandpa," Swaggart said.

"Your owning the restaurant or the fact you're good enough for Poppy?" Wally asked.

"Both," Swaggart said.

"I sent her over there last night because I was tired of waiting," Wally announced.

"What?" Swaggart asked.

"The only thing in that manila envelope is a blank sheet of paper," Wally said.

"You're kidding me?" Swaggart laughed.

"Nope," Wally said, laughing as well. "Did it work?"

"Do you mean did sending Poppy over to my house last night result in any goings-on between us?" Swaggart asked.

"Yep—that's what I mean," Wally said.

"Well, then…yes, Grandpa," Swaggart admitted. "We sat on the hood of my truck, looked at the stars, and ate beef jerky."

Wally Dexter chuckled, his eyes twinkling with amusement. "Good! Now that you've got your hooks in her, get busy and reel her in."

"She's not a fish, Grandpa," Swaggart said. "It's not that easy. And besides, now there's this other guy and—"

"Well, punch his lights out!" Wally exclaimed.

Swaggart laughed. His grandfather was so headstrong. "Oh, believe me," Swaggart said, "It's not like I haven't thought of it."

"Then do it and get it over with," Wally said. "She's only dating him because she thinks you don't have any real interest in her. I thought the minute I showed you that list in Whitney's notebook you'd be after her like a hound after a fox."

"Oh, believe me," Swaggart began, "I have been."

"I knew all you needed was a little encouragement—you know—to be put on the true scent of the prey," Wally said.

Swaggart laughed as he rose from his chair. "She's not a pelt either, Grandpa," he said. "And you know I've had my eye on her since the day she started working here. I just couldn't believe she'd really ever…"

"That's because you're an idiot," Wally said, embracing Swaggart. "And the restaurant is yours, boy. I've called my attorney, and he'll be in Saturday to get your signature on everything. I won't rest a wink until it's a done deal."

Swaggart returned his grandfather's hug, patting him on the back with affection. "I do have one thing to ask," he said when they'd ended their hug.

"What's that?" Wally asked.

"Can we keep it a secret for a while?" Swaggart asked. "I need to adjust. Besides, I think our clientele needs to be eased into something like this. Maybe they don't ever need to know."

Wally smiled. His grandson was a smart businessman as well as a humble one. Both were rare qualities indeed.

"I think I can live with that," Wally said. "We'll keep it quiet until…"

"Until it leaks out, probably," Swaggart said, folding the papers and tucking them into the pocket of his apron.

"Now get back in that kitchen, boy," Wally said. "I think your cousin Bobby is burning something."

"Okay," Swaggart said. He looked at Wally, and Wally could see the emotion, the deep gratitude in his grandson's eyes. "Thanks, Grandpa. You know how much I love this place."

"I do," Wally said.

Swaggart left. As he entered the kitchen Wally heard him holler, "Bobby! What the heck, man? What are you burning in here? It smells like you're smoking a horse."

Wally smiled. The weight of the world was beginning to lift from his shoulders. Furthermore, he could see happiness waiting on the horizon for his grandson. Swaggart would take care of the restaurant. He'd take care of Poppy too—Wally was certain of it.

CHAPTER TWELVE

Poppy slept very little the next two nights—and when she did sleep, it was a fitful sleep. Her anxiety over having to go to the gala with Mark on Saturday, having to explain to him why she couldn't see him anymore, was horrible. Yet the delight, delicious excitement, and anticipation of spending a day with Swaggart were wonderful!

Perhaps Mark would take her to the gala and never ask her out again! Perhaps she could purposely make certain he became disenchanted with her somehow, and even though she knew it would be the coward's way out, she considered it.

Mark Lawson was a handsome, charming, successful man. Yet he just wasn't the man Swaggart Moretti was. Deep in her soul, Poppy knew she'd only been attracted to Mark, only agreed to go out with him, because she had no hope of ever capturing Swaggart's attention. She had been settling for second best, and she scolded herself for it.

As Poppy peeked through the blinds in the front window of the apartment—as she watched Swaggart park his pickup on the street below, her heart soared! Just watching him walk up the sidewalk caused a delicious thrill to travel through her. He wore jeans and a black button-up shirt. Poppy smiled, enchanted by his appearance, elated he was on his way to meet her for an entire day together.

She pulled her lip gloss from her pocket and rushed to the microwave, studying her reflection as she quickly used her ring finger to apply a little extra shine to her lips. She hoped she looked nice enough. She'd chosen to wear jeans and her favorite pink baby-doll top.

Poppy heard the doorbell and felt a little guilty in being glad Whitney had already gone to work and was not home.

Taking a deep breath to try to still the mad pounding of her heart, Poppy opened the door, smiling as Swaggart's handsome everything greeted her.

"You ready?" he asked.

"Yeah," Poppy said. She stepped out of the apartment, locking the door behind her and pushing her house key into her front pocket. She had decided not to bring a purse. She didn't want any distractions—nothing to have to tote around and certainly no cell phone to enable someone to interrupt her day with Swaggart. She patted her back pocket to make certain the debit card, driver's license, and some cash she'd put there were indeed still there.

"Come on then," Swaggart said. Poppy's body quivered with the delightful sensation of erupting goose bumps as he took hold of her hand and began leading her toward the pickup. "I'm stoked," he said. "There's not a cloud in the sky today."

Poppy looked up into the cloudless blue above. The sun was bright and warm, and everything seemed more colorful and inviting.

"Who's in the kitchen today?" Poppy asked. She was so nervous—trembling! She hoped light conversation would serve to settle her a bit.

"Bobby and Uncle Robert," Swaggart said, opening the passenger door of his pickup. "We need a third guy, though."

Poppy climbed into the pickup, and Swaggart closed the door behind her. She watched him, unable to keep from smiling, as he rather sauntered around the front of the pickup to his own side. Sliding into the driver's seat, he turned the ignition, and the old Chevy roared to life.

"You know the great thing about an older vehicle like this?" he asked.

"You mean, besides the obvious fact it's way cooler than a new one?" Poppy asked in return.

"No bucket seats," Swaggart said, smiling. He reached out, taking hold of Poppy's arm and forcing her to slide across the seat until she sat right next to him. "Now buckle up, baby," he said, arm resting on her left thigh as he pushed the gear shift into first. "I printed off the movie schedule," he said, nodding to a white piece of paper on the dashboard. "You need to pick the first one."

As the pickup chugged down the road, Poppy retrieved the paper from the dashboard.

"What if I choose a chick flick?" she asked him. His arm still rested on her thigh as he continued to shift the gears of the pickup. She thought she might simply die of delight! She could sense the softness of his shirt, smell the faint aroma of the aftershave on his face—it was heaven!

"I like pretty much anything," he told her. "My mom used make me watch stuff with her when I was younger—you know, *Pride and Prejudice*, old fifties musicals. I bet I can even answer anything you ask me about Anne," he said.

"Do you mean *Anne of Green Gables*? You're kidding me?" Poppy asked. Already her cheeks hurt from smiling.

"Yep—but I didn't say I enjoyed them all the time," he said. "I mean—if you're worried that I'm girlie or something, I'll lie and take it all back."

Poppy giggled. There was nothing "girlie" about Swaggart Moretti! Furthermore, in Poppy's opinion, his mom had only done right by him by making certain his experience with movies was broad and diverse.

"Test me, if you don't believe me," he said. "Go on."

"Okay," Poppy said, "But you're assuming I've seen *Anne of Green Gables*."

Swaggart rolled his eyes. "Oh, please—every woman I've ever known has either read the book or seen the movie."

"Okay," Poppy giggled. "Um…let me think." Her mind raced for a trivia question concerning the movie, but she was so entirely distracted by Swaggart's proximity, the tickle of his shirtsleeve as it brushed her arm, that she was having difficulty concentrating on anything else. At last, however, she said, "What did Anne do that caused her to hurt her ankle and—"

"Walking the ridgepole of Moody's kitchen roof," Swaggart interrupted.

Poppy's mouth dropped open in astonishment. It was true! At some point in his life, Swaggart had managed to sit through *Anne of Green Gables*! "I'll go one further," he said, smiling. "Someone in this pickup has walked a ridgepole before—I saw it on a certain list of hers one day a while back."

"You're good!" Poppy giggled.

"Oh, you have no idea, Poppy-seed," he chuckled. "So, don't be afraid to pick a girlie movie—I'm man enough to take it."

And he was! The 11:15 showing of the current popular "chick flick" at the theatre proved entertaining to Poppy as well as Swaggart. He seemed to pay legitimate attention, and Poppy was amazed when he chuckled in all the right places. Oh, and what a fabulous experience sitting through a movie with him had been!

Before the movie had started, Swaggart had offered to purchase a beverage and a snack for her. Not wanting to fill up before lunch, Poppy had declined the snack and explained that she couldn't possibly drink an entire large beverage. Therefore, Swaggart had ordered a large beverage and grabbed two straws. "We'll just share then," he'd said. Again Poppy was astounded he would share a drink with her.

As they sat in the darkness of the theatre, arms touching, sharing a beverage, Poppy mused there could be no better moment to the day. Each time Swaggart would lean over and whisper something to her during the movie, Poppy nearly slipped out of her skin with pleasure. She desperately wanted to wrap her arms around his powerful one, lay her head on his shoulder. It had been quite distracting, and she often found herself unaware of exactly what was happening in the movie for brief periods of time.

Everything about sitting in a movie with Swaggart felt wonderful—felt right—as if she was exactly where she wanted to be—exactly where she should be. Poppy wondered if it was simply her deep, long-secreted, true, and obsessive love for him making her feel that way—or if it was something more, perhaps a confirmation of the fact that it was the right place to be—that it was the right person to be with.

For lunch, Swaggart drove them across the street to a little Italian restaurant he told Poppy he liked. He assured her the little restaurant served the best "heart attack on a plate" in the city. Poppy indeed ordered the fettuccine alfredo and agreed—it was the best she'd ever eaten.

During lunch they talked, laughed, teased—it was the most wonderful lunch Poppy had ever known, and she wished the day would never have to end.

True to his word, Swaggart then insisted Poppy choose another movie. She chose the current action adventure romp starring Bruce Willis for Swaggart's sake.

"Hey," Swaggart said as he drove back to the movie complex. "I know you said you didn't feel like dessert at the restaurant—but I have to have my Goobers for this movie. I've got some stashed in the jockey box there," he said pointing to the glove compartment of his pickup. "Get 'em out, and we'll sneak them in."

Poppy bit her lip, entirely amused as she watched Swaggart tuck the box of Goobers into the front of his pants once they'd parked the pickup and were ready to head into the movie.

"They don't sell Goobers here, you know," he told her, taking her hand and starting toward the theatre. "And they're my favorite movie snack, so I always have to sneak them in."

Poppy giggled. He was too adorable. She had a momentary vision of Swaggart strolling into the theatre, a box of Goobers suddenly slipping down his pant leg and onto the floor, giving him away.

"Do you want anything? Popcorn? A drink?" he asked as they approached the concessions stand.

Just you, Poppy thought.

"No, thanks," she said, however. "I'm stuffed."

"I know you picked this movie for my sake," Swaggart said, leading her into the theatre. "But you like Bruce Willis, don't you?"

"Yeah, I do," Poppy said. "Are you sure you're up to another movie, though?" she asked. Most people she knew, especially guys, couldn't sit through two movies and enjoy them both—especially two movies of entirely different genres.

"Of course," he said. "I like movies. You're with the 'date rut' king, remember?"

Poppy smiled. If this was date rut, then she wanted to be stuck in it forever! She giggled when Swaggart pulled the box of Goobers out of his pants before they took their seats, placing it in the cup holder of his armrest.

"I really wish they'd sell these here," he said. "They probably got a little melty in my pickup," he said, frowning as he sat down next to Poppy, taking her hand in his. Poppy's arms prickled with goose bumps because of his touch. She smiled as she glanced away to catch a group of women staring at Swaggart and whispering to one another. It had been that way all day—every female they'd walked past or sat near had done a double-take at the handsome Swaggart Moretti. It didn't bother Poppy in the least—he *was* handsome, and she understood their surprise. Besides, Swaggart seemed completely unaware of his effect on women—a fact which only served to enhance his charm.

Swaggart held Poppy's hand for some time through the movie— sometimes he'd lace fingers with her, sometimes caress the back of her hand or her palm, sending her quivering with delight. In fact, he held her hand through most of the movie. It wasn't until he decided to open his box of candy that he released her.

The movie was phenomenal—or at least, it seemed to Poppy it was. Of course, it may have been that simply sitting next to Swaggart was phenomenal.

Poppy thought of her day at Hollander Park with Mark—how kind he'd been, how polite, how much fun she had. The fun she'd had with Mark was a tiny droplet in a puddle compared to the feelings of delight, euphoria, and pure wonder washing over her while spending the day with Swaggart. She wished she didn't have to go to the gala on Saturday—wished she never had to talk to another man for the rest of her life! She only wanted Swaggart's company, Swaggart's face in her line of vision, Swaggart's attentions and affections.

Once Bruce Willis had blown up several cars and a building, gotten beaten nearly to death, and saved the day, Poppy applied some fresh lip gloss after washing her hands in the women's room. Swaggart was waiting outside for her, and she still couldn't believe it. Swaggart Moretti—waiting outside the women's room—for her! For a moment she wondered if she were just dreaming. Would she wake up any moment to find him gone—to find herself in her bed, never having even received his date rut coupon?

"Your boyfriend's totally hot!" a young woman looking to be about her own age said as she approached, waving her hand under the faucet sensor in order to cue the water.

"Thanks," Poppy said, smiling. Well, sure, she knew Swaggart wasn't her boyfriend—but there seemed no reason to have to explain that to the girl next to her.

"They don't make them like him anymore," the girl said. "You know?"

"I know," Poppy agreed.

"Well, have a good night," the girl said after drying her hands. "I'm sure you will!"

Poppy smiled. She'd had a wonderful day! She couldn't imagine the evening being any more wonderful than the day had already been.

Swaggart smiled and draped one powerful arm across her shoulders as Poppy exited the women's room.

"What do you want to do now?" he asked. "Or are you sick of me and ready to go home?"

"I could never be sick of you," Poppy said before thinking better.

"Really?" Swaggart said, eyebrows arched in surprise. "That's encouraging," he said. "Then, would it be rude or boring to you?—I need to pick up something for Whitney's birthday on Sunday. Would you mind if we stopped by the music box store on 12th Street for just a minute?"

Poppy smiled, delighted by his thoughtfulness. "You know she collects music boxes?" she asked.

"Um…ask her who gave her most of the ridiculous collection she has," he said.

"You're kidding me! I didn't know that," Poppy said. "I mean, she has so many—I sort of just always thought she bought them for herself."

"Oh, she does that too, I think," he said. "Plus her parents and Grandpa buy them for her. But I think mine are the best." He winked at her. "Do you collect anything?" he asked. "Besides admirers, I mean."

Poppy rolled her eyes. "Oh, you're funny," she said. "And yes, I collect a few things."

"Like what?" he asked. They were to the pickup, and he opened the door for her.

"Oh, books, antique postcards, cool photographs," Poppy said. "And probably a bunch of other stuff I don't even consciously realize I collect."

He closed the door and went around to his side of the pickup.

"I think I do that too," he said. "You know…the other day I noticed I have seventeen basketballs."

"Seventeen?" Poppy exclaimed.

Swaggart chuckled. "Yep. I've got every basketball I've ever had starting from the very first one my dad bought for me when I was five."

Poppy smiled. He was too wonderful! Too adorable! Too interesting! He was going to break her heart—she knew he was—but she didn't care. Poppy had decided to live in those moments with him, not worry about tomorrow until tomorrow came.

"Well?" Swaggart asked as he parked his pickup in front of Poppy's apartment. "Did I do okay?"

"What do you mean?" Poppy asked. It was late, but she didn't care. She had the early shift at work the next morning, but she didn't care. She'd just spent fourteen hours in the company of the most wonderful man in the world. She could easily have spent fourteen more and loved every minute of it.

"Did I do okay?" he repeated. "Did you have fun? Or were you wishing you could escape the entire time?"

Poppy shook her head, smiling. How could he even think she didn't have fun? It had been the most wonderful day of her life! A movie, lunch, another movie! It had been fantastic! Not to mention the enjoyment Poppy had experienced in watching Swaggart agonize over a birthday gift for Whitney. In the end, he'd chosen a perfectly Whitney-ish music box—three fairies twirling among autumn trees that played *The Magic Flute*.

After treating Poppy to a late dinner, Swaggart drove to the top of Calvert Hill and parked the pickup in the meadow under the stars. There they'd both lounged on the hood of his pickup and talked—just talked, for hours and hours. The time spent talking with him had been magnificent, and Poppy wanted her day with Swaggart to linger on and on and on. But it couldn't, and now they were parked in front of her apartment building instead—disappointment beginning to overtake her happiness.

"This was the best date I've ever had," she told him at last.

"Don't exaggerate," he told her.

"I'm not," she said.

"Well," he began, "I am pretty proud of myself."

"You should be," she said, glad he hadn't moved to get out of the pickup yet.

"No, I mean for spending fourteen hours in your company and not once putting the move on you," he said, smiling at her. "You do remember the fine print on the back of your coupon, right?"

Poppy smiled. He was gorgeous! The warm brown of his eyes seemed to glow all the more alluring in the moonlight.

"I remember," she said.

"'No kissing required to redeem this coupon,'" Swaggart quoted. "But Poppy," he added. He'd lowered his voice, and it was somehow stirring, entirely alluring. "Who really pays attention to the fine print on anything, right?"

Poppy giggled as the loop-the-loops that had been intermittently performed in her stomach all day long began again.

"I know *I* never do," she answered.

"It's a good thing," he said, smiling as he leaned toward her, caressing one side of her neck with a strong hand. "Because I've been on my best behavior all day, and I'm tired of it."

"Oh, good," Poppy heard herself breathe a moment before the warmth of his mouth met her own.

Once again, Swaggart's kiss was the most powerful experience of Poppy's entire life! Moist, heated, commanding, and she melted to him, letting her hands seek out the pleasant feel of his soft hair.

As her body was alive with a million wonderful sensations, her mind was as alive with a myriad of thoughts. Disbelief at actually being where she was with whom she was, anxiety about having to go with Mark to the gala on Saturday, painfully wishing that she could remain in Swaggart's arms forever! So many thoughts were clanking around in her head when Swaggart initially began kissing her that she was astonished when, in the next moment, everything left her mind! Only one thing was left, the only coherent thought remaining: *I love him! I'll never stop loving him!*

"Poppy," he said, breaking the seal of their lips suddenly.

"What?" she asked, still breathless.

"It's late," he said. "And I need to let you go."

"Okay," she said. Disappointment washed over her like Niagara Falls. She didn't want to stop kissing him, and she certainly didn't want to leave him. She was startled, however, as he suddenly opened his door and stepped out of the pickup, taking hold of her arm and pulling her out behind him. She gasped when he bent over, bracing one broad shoulder firmly against her midsection and hoisting her up like a bag of flour.

"What are you doing?" she asked.

"Getting you home before I lose my good sense," he mumbled.

Poppy couldn't believe it as he carried her all the way to the front door. Setting her on her feet none too gently, he asked, "Do you have your key?"

"Y-yeah," Poppy stammered, reaching into her front pocket and producing the key. She frowned, still confused as Swaggart snatched it from her hand, shoving it into the lock on the apartment's doorknob. He turned the key, unlocking the door and pushing it open for a moment before slamming it shut again and pulling her into his arms, his mouth crushing to hers.

Poppy's arms slid around him instantly as she returned his kiss, wanting never to let go of him. She was surprised and astonishingly delighted as he reached to the back of his neck taking hold of her wrists and pushing them away from his body and back against the apartment door. Swaggart continued to kiss her with a fiery, ravenous fervor, all the while holding her arms pinned against the apartment door.

After several moments during which Poppy wondered if she would faint from lack of oxygen induced by his kiss or the demanding nature of it, Swaggart suddenly released her, opening the apartment door and gently pushing her through the threshold.

"Good night, Poppy," he said. Abruptly, he pulled her house key out of the lock, tossed it into the apartment, and closed the door.

It had been no sweet, timid, tender good-night kiss—it had been produced by restrained passion—tightly guarded self-control.

As the realization rinsed over her, Whitney's voice from behind startled her.

"Oh my heck, Poppy!" Whitney said. "What is going on between you two?"

"We just...we just went out today," Poppy stammered. She was trembling all over—from her hair follicles to her pink polished toenails.

"Like I'm gonna buy that," Whitney said. "But—until you're ready to tell me why my cousin was kissing you like this was the honeymoon suite at the Marriott—I guess I'll just have to wait."

"How will I ever get over him, Whitney?" Poppy asked in a whisper.

"Why do you think you'll ever have to get over him, Poppy?" Whitney asked.

Poppy turned around, tears filling her eyes—tears of love, of joy, of heartache, mingled with desperation.

"Because I'm in love with him, and I can't possibly...he couldn't possibly ever..." Poppy stammered.

"Oh, really?" Whitney asked. "Then you better make an appointment with the optometrist—'cause you're blind as a bat."

Whitney turned and disappeared into her bedroom, leaving Poppy awash with the residual bliss caused by Swaggart Moretti's very existence. Why couldn't he just fall in love with her the way she was in love with him? Why couldn't she just spend the rest of her life kissing Whitney's fabulous cousin?

As Poppy undressed and pulled on an old t-shirt for pajamas, she heard her cell phone beeping from her bedroom. She'd missed a call while she was out and was glad she hadn't taken it with her on her day with Swaggart.

Picking her cell phone up off the bed, she pushed send to retrieve her voicemail.

"Hey, Poppy," Mark's voice said. "This is Mark. Just wanted to remind you that the gala on Saturday is formal, so be sure and dress appropriately. I'm wearing a tux if that helps. Can't wait to see you...I've thought about nothing else all week. I'll call you tomorrow night. Bye, babe."

Poppy's heart sank with a thud into the pit of her stomach. She didn't want to go with him—she should never have accepted his invitation for their very first date. Yet how could she have possibly imagined Swaggart Moretti would even notice her? She knew she was taking a risk by letting herself consciously admit she loved Swaggart. Still, even if Swaggart never asked her out again, never kissed her again—the moments she'd spent with him since his grandpa showed him her Dreams to Do list were worth any heartache. Surely Mark hadn't grown that attached to her yet—had he?

Poppy was suddenly sick to her stomach—sick with longing for Swaggart and sick with worry at having to face Mark. She thought of the roses, the flowers, the day at Hollander Park. She'd tried to lie to herself, tried to see someone beyond Swaggart Moretti, and it had seemed to work for a moment. Yet Poppy knew that even if Swaggart hadn't seen her list, never kissed her—Poppy knew she could never have let Mark kiss her the way Swaggart had. Her heart and mind would've reached that conclusion a little later maybe—but in the end, peach pie would always have been her favorite—always her only choice in the bakery window.

CHAPTER THIRTEEN

Saturday morning dawned bright and cheerful, but Poppy's mood did not mirror it. After spending such a marvelous dream of a day with Swaggart on Thursday, she'd found herself distracted at work on Friday. Each time he looked at her, winked at her, smiled at her, or spoke to her, she wanted to cry, *I love you, Swaggart Moretti! I love you!*

When Jennifer Trujillo showed up with a friend for lunch, asking to speak to Swaggart for a moment, Poppy wanted to wrap her hands in Jennifer's perfect hair and pull as hard as she could—drag her out of the restaurant, slash her tires, and spit in her face. Poppy's emotions were nearly out of control. She felt jumpy, emotional, miserable, and euphoric at the same time. Furthermore, Friday had been a madhouse at the restaurant, as usual, and there had not been one moment to really talk to Swaggart—to draw some kind of reassurance that he really would continue to slather her with attention and affection.

This made Saturday morning almost unendurable for Poppy. She was nervous about Mark, and she didn't want to go to the gala. Still, she'd promised herself she'd act like a responsible adult—tell him face to face she couldn't see him anymore. She'd promised herself she wouldn't take the coward's path by calling him up, cancelling their date, and never again answering his phone calls. Mark Lawson was a nice man, and he'd treated her like a princess—he deserved respect.

Still, when the three dozen red roses arrived at the restaurant Saturday at noon, Poppy began to feel sick to her stomach. She wished Mark hadn't sent them, and she certainly wished he hadn't written on the card accompanying them, *For my lovely lady—I'm living for tonight.* She thought of the handwritten coupon on her dresser at home—Swaggart's coupon—and how much more it meant to her than Mark's expensive flowers did. Furthermore, the roses seemed to do nothing to encourage Swaggart toward her.

"I see the rose truck has been by again," he mumbled over the order counter.

"Y-yeah," Poppy stammered. "I wish he wouldn't do that."

"Really?" Swaggart asked. "Then why are going out with him?"

"I-I have to tell him something," Poppy stammered.

"What? Thank you for the roses?" Swaggart asked.

He was angry, she was certain of it. She so desperately wanted to reassure him—to tell him that she loved him—that she was only going out with Mark in order to tell him she could never do so again. Yet Swaggart had given Poppy no confirmation that he wanted her all to himself. If she simply blurted out she was going tell Mark she couldn't see him anymore, then perhaps Swaggart would ask, *Why?* And if he did ask, it would be an assurance to Poppy that Swaggart did not intend to date her exclusively, and that would break her heart. Therefore, Poppy was torn. Swaggart looked angry about the roses, yet she could not find the courage to tell him she wasn't going to see Mark again.

Poppy jumped when Swaggart slammed two plates on the order counter. "Your order's up," he said.

Bobby frowned and looked to Swaggart, to Poppy, and then back.

"Man, Swag! What bit you on the butt?" he asked.

"Nothing, man," Swaggart mumbled. "I just gotta leave in a few minutes. I've got that gig tonight, and I don't feel like doing it."

"Then that makes two of us," Poppy said, taking the plates from the order counter. Would he recognize her hint? Would he understand that she didn't want to go on the date? She wondered, too, what gig he had lined up. Usually when Swaggart referred to a gig, it was a job—a catered event he'd agreed to. Yet she had seen him talking to Jennifer when she'd been in earlier, and it made Poppy suspicious. Maybe Jennifer was trying to reconcile with Swaggart. She nearly burst into tears then when the thought struck her—maybe Swaggart was considering it! Maybe that's what his gig was—a date with Jennifer.

Poppy served table three with tears in her eyes. She managed to choke them back, inhaling a deep breath and telling herself she had to make it through the day. She had to!

Her orders were ready for two more tables, and she served them before going to the hostess podium to see who else Whitney had waiting to be seated.

"It's crazy today!" Whitney said, checking the eraser board.

"Who's next?" Poppy asked.

"Whitney," Swaggart said.

Poppy jumped, startled by his sudden appearance.

"Yeah?" Whitney asked.

"I have to leave now," he said. "When Josh comes back from his break, tell him he may have to assist in the kitchen here and there if Bobby and Uncle Robert start to fall behind."

"Okay," Whitney said.

"And if—" Swaggart began.

He was interrupted, however, as Mark suddenly stepped up to the hostess podium and said, "Hi."

Poppy held her breath, certain her anxiety and nerves were going to cause her to vomit. What was he doing at the restaurant? Why was he there? Poppy glanced to Swaggart, noting the way his eyes narrowed as he looked at Mark.

"Hello," Poppy managed.

Mark was staring at her, an enormous smile on his handsome face. He wore an expensive-looking business suit, loafers, white shirt, and purple tie—he looked as if he'd just stepped out of a *GQ* magazine ad. Poppy glanced to Swaggart, who stood glaring at Mark and looking as if *he'd* just stepped off the cover of *Men's Health* magazine. There was no contest—none. Swaggart's very presence dominated the room—his appearance infinitely more rugged and masculine—his face far more handsome than Mark's.

Panic began to rise in Poppy. What should she say? How should she act? Perhaps she should just tell Mark then and there that she didn't want to see him anymore—that she was in love with Swaggart, whether or not he was in love with her. She paused too long—missed the opportunity.

"I've got a flat," Mark said, smiling at Poppy. "Right out there in the parking lot. I was dropping in to make sure you remembered you need to be ready to leave by six o'clock and noticed I have a flat."

"Bummer," Swaggart grumbled.

"Oh," Poppy said. "Um…did you need some help?"

"No," Mark said. "I called roadside assistance, but they can't be here for over an hour. So," Mark he added, "I guess I'll just hang out here and wait. I suppose you're busy right now."

Poppy frowned a little. Why call roadside assistance? Couldn't he change his own tire? Poppy started to tell Mark she *was* busy, but Swaggart spoke first.

"We're swamped," Swaggart said. "And since Poppy's going to be busy, we don't want you wasting your time. I'll change it for you."

Mark smiled and said, "Thanks, man. But I can wait."

"I'm on my way out," Swaggart said, untying his apron and stuffing it in Whitney's podium. "I'll take care of it for you."

"Well, if you don't mind," Mark said. "I mean, I'm wearing a suit, and I don't need to add to my already ridiculous dry-cleaning bill."

"It's cool, man," Swaggart said. "I do it all the time."

Poppy was speechless and for several reasons. First of all, she couldn't believe Mark was going to allow Swaggart to change his tire for him. Certainly Swaggart had changed many customers' flats—women, teenagers, and elderly people—but she'd never seen him have to change a flat for a perfectly capable man. This was ridiculous. She'd even seen him change one while wearing a tuxedo once before going to the opera with his grandpa. And that was the second thing—it irked her to think Mark was so worried about his clothes getting dirty that he would allow another guy to change his tire. Third, Poppy was astounded that Swaggart would even offer to do it when she knew Swaggart well enough to know he thought Mark should change it himself too.

"Well, thanks," Mark said. "I'll come help you."

"Just pop your trunk so I can get the spare," Swaggart said.

Mark looked to Poppy, then to Swaggart, then back. "I'll—uh— I'll pick you up at six," he said.

Poppy only nodded. She was afraid if she spoke, she would say something too critical.

"Let's go then," Swaggart said, opening the door for Mark. "See you girls later," he added as he followed.

"Unbelievable!" Whitney exclaimed in a whisper.

"That's ridiculous," Poppy mumbled as Whitney looked over her eraser board.

"So," Whitney said, smiling. "I suppose tonight you're going to tell him you can't see him anymore because you're in love with my cousin. Right?"

"I'm going to tell him I can't see him anymore, yes," Poppy said.

"Well, you better have some good kissing planned for Swaggart—he looks ticked off!" Whitney said.

"At me, huh?" Poppy said, tears welling in her eyes.

"At your pal Mark for being too lazy to change his own tire," Whitney said. She smiled and squeezed Poppy's hand. "Don't freak out, Poppy. Swaggart's hooked—he's just mad because you're going out with Mark tonight."

"But I'm just going with him so I can let him know I don't want to go out with him again after this," Poppy said.

"Yeah, but Swaggart doesn't know that. And anyway, it's good for him to sweat about it a little," Whitney said.

Poppy shook her head. She didn't want to make Swaggart sweat a little—if he really was irritated that she was going out with Mark. She wanted to kiss him, hold him, belong to him, be the cause of the appearance of his dazzling smile—not irritate and anger him.

"Here," Whitney said, handing Poppy three menus. "Seat this party at table five. And don't worry—you've got two hours, and then you're off work and can get this evening over with."

"Yeah," Poppy muttered as Whitney called a name. Three men wearing baseball uniforms stepped up, and Whitney told them to follow Poppy.

As Poppy walked toward table five, she glanced out the big front window of Good Ol' Days. There was Swaggart, hunkered down changing Mark's tire as Mark looked on.

"Unbelievable," Poppy muttered to herself. She knew then—even if Swaggart had never kissed her, even if he'd never unknowingly reminded her how desperately in love she was with him—Poppy knew her enchantment with the charming Mark Lawson would not have lasted. He was gorgeous, sure. But a gorgeous face and body did not a real man make. Swaggart Moretti was a real man—tough, rugged, chivalrous, as well as possessing the natural faults every real man did.

The incident buoyed Poppy somehow—strengthened her resolve and courage to let Mark know that, although he was a nice guy, he wasn't for her. She sighed, feeling less anxious all of a sudden. No matter what—if Swaggart never gave her the time of day again—Mark Lawson was not for her. Still, she prayed Swaggart would give her the time of day—prayed for a miracle and that she could win his heart—some day.

"This is a big deal," Mark said as he drove Poppy toward their destination later that evening. This is the kickoff for Bryant Industries' new line," he explained. "Our firm holds their account, and we've managed to keep them pretty happy so far."

"Oh," Poppy said. She was uncomfortable—having trouble not blurting out that she just wanted to go home. Still, Mark was a nice man who had treated her very well. He deserved the respect of a calm "severing-of-the-ties." She smoothed the black velvet of her dress over her legs and straightened the small ruby hanging from the silver chain at her neck. Even for wearing her fanciest, most expensive formal dress, she felt she suffered in comparison to Mark's perfectly tailored tuxedo. Whitney had sworn to Poppy that she looked fabulous, but Poppy wondered if Whitney was exaggerating as usual.

"Here we are," he said, pulling into the parking lot of the Tinley Convention Center. "This should be interesting."

Poppy smiled at him, taking his offered hand and allowing him to help her out of the car—the car that Swaggart had so recently changed a tire on.

"Dinner is promptly at six thirty, and then there's a concert," Mark explained as they walked toward the entrance to the building.

"Sounds like quite the shindig," Poppy said. She would have to force herself to make polite conversation.

"Oh yeah!" Mark said. "I managed to get tickets last year and it was phenomenal!"

Poppy experienced a massive pang of guilt as Mark smiled at her. He was a nice man—she mentally scolded herself for thinking badly of him. After all, it wasn't his fault she was in love with Swaggart.

"Mark," Poppy began once they were seated at their table. Guilt was washing over her. She kept thinking of the way Mark had stood up for her with Miss Susan Reginald the night she'd first met him, of the fifty-dollar tips and the way he treated her with such respect and admiration. It was going to be hard to tell him she couldn't see him again. She once more considered the possibility he would never ask her out again after the gala. Maybe—maybe she would wait, just a little longer—see how the evening went and if, by some miracle, another venue of letting him know presented itself.

"Yeah?" he asked.

Yes. She'd wait. She'd wait and see if something else happened.

"This is really lovely," she said. "Thank you for inviting me."

"You bet, beautiful," he said, winking at her.

The master of ceremonies welcomed everyone and explained the agenda for the evening. The gala would begin with dinner—guests could choose the citrus chicken or filet mignon—and end with a concert by the famous fiddle-fest group Barrage. Had Poppy not been so miserably preoccupied, the night would've held the promise of being wonderful. She *was* miserable and preoccupied, however. Yet she managed to choose the filet mignon when asked by the attendant and hoped a good meal would add to her courage as well.

"I missed you while I was gone," Mark said.

"Were you able to have any fun on the trip—or was it strictly business meetings and things?" Poppy asked.

She was distracted—Mark had known it from the moment he'd picked her up at her apartment. Something was on Poppy's mind, but he sensed she wasn't ready to share it. He'd decided not to press her, yet he hoped she would be able to relax eventually and enjoy the evening.

Even at the restaurant, when he'd realized he had a flat and pulled over in the Good Ol' Days parking lot to call roadside services—even then she'd seemed a bit distracted. For a moment, he'd imagined it was because of that cook—that Swaggart guy.

Mark remembered the first time he'd ever met the cook. It was the night he'd taken Braden with him to the restaurant to see what his friend thought of the cute little waitress he'd encountered. At first, when the cook had come out to ask him and Braden about their meal, Mark could've sworn he'd seen Poppy's eyes light up like the Fourth of July. Still, he'd convinced himself he'd imagined it. That was until he'd walked into the restaurant earlier in the day to find Poppy and the cook standing with the hostess. The Swaggart guy's eyes shot daggers at him, he was sure. Mark thought it was because he hadn't wanted to change his tire himself. Yet what was wrong with that? *Why do it yourself if you can pay someone to do it for you?* Mark thought. However, now—as he thought back on it—he wondered if the daggers shooting out of the Swaggart guy's eyes were because of Poppy. He wondered if Poppy's obvious distraction right now was because of the Swaggart guy.

Sure the cook was pretty impressive to look at, but Mark was certain the guy didn't hold a candle to him. After all, both times he'd seen the guy, he'd been wearing worn-out jeans and a white t-shirt—

plain as they get. Yet he couldn't ignore the fact that his own sisters probably would've dropped at the cook's feet one by one, begging for his attention. Mark shook his head. What girl in her right mind would choose a fry cook in a t-shirt over an advertising firm executive in a Beamer?

"Just meetings, I'm afraid," Mark answered. "It was tough being in Arizona and not being able to play a round of golf."

"I can imagine," Poppy said, forcing a smile. She couldn't get the vision of Swaggart changing Mark's tire out of her mind. She couldn't get the vision of Swaggart out of her mind—and that vision she didn't want to. It was going to be a long night.

And it did indeed seem to drag. Although it was only twenty minutes between the time the attendant had taken their order and the waiter arrived with it, it seemed like forever to Poppy. She'd managed to hold a fairly interesting conversation with Mark, but all she could think of was Swaggart—long to be with him. She wondered where Swaggart was. Was he with Jennifer? Did he have another date? Had their marvelous date rut day been just another date to him?

"Your filet mignon, madam," the waiter said, setting a dinner plate on the table before Poppy. "And for you, sir, the citrus chicken," the waiter said as he presented Mark's meal.

"Thank you," Poppy told the waiter. She smiled at him, knowing how demanding catered affairs of this magnitude were.

"Wow!" Mark said. Poppy looked to see him studying his plate, a satisfied smile on his handsome face. "Fancy!"

Poppy smiled and looked down at her own plate. She gasped as instant recognition washed over her.

"Oh my heck!" she breathed. Her smile broadened as delight washed over her.

"What? Is something wrong?" Mark asked. "Did they overcook it? I can have it sent back if you want."

Poppy shook her head and tried to keep tears of joy from welling in her eyes. Her heart was pounding like mad.

"No. No, it's perfect," she said.

"How can you tell?" Mark asked. "You haven't even cut into it yet."

"No, it's perfect. I promise," Poppy said.

"How can you be so sure?" Mark chuckled.

"Because Swaggart Moretti cooked it," she said.

"Swaggart?" Mark asked. "The cook at your restaurant?"

"Yeah," Poppy told him. "I'd recognize his presentation anywhere!" Loop-the-loops were going off in her stomach like fireworks on the Fourth of July. "I'll prove it," she told him. "I won't look at your plate, but you ordered the citrus chicken, right?" she said covering her eyes.

"Yeah," Mark said.

"Then on your plate, you'll have two chicken breasts covered in roasted onions with five very thin orange slices fanned out on one side of your plate—three thin lemon slices, alternated with two thin lime slices, fanned out together on the other side. The onions are red onion, and there's a small sprig of thyme resting between the two chicken pieces," Poppy said.

"Exactly," Mark chuckled. "You've got it."

Poppy giggled and let her hand drop from covering her eyes.

"You see?" she said. "The second I saw the presentation of this filet mignon—can you smell the balsamic pan sauce? See the three sprigs of rosemary peeking out from beneath the cut? And the wavy lines drawn through the sauce—he does that with his fingers...but don't tell anyone."

Mark smiled as he watched the light dancing in Poppy's eyes. It was the cook—that he-man, muscle-bound, tousled-haired cook—and she was in love with him! Yet even for the thick jealousy and pang of realization and loss in his chest—how could he be angry with her? What woman wouldn't like a man who could change a fool's tire in one hour and create culinary art in the next?

Poppy Amore was one of the most beautiful people Mark had ever met—one of the cutest, prettiest young women he'd ever known. He was astounded that instead of being enraged—he simply felt bested by a better man.

CHAPTER FOURTEEN

"How long have you been in love with him?" Mark asked.

Poppy's smile disappeared instantly. "What?" she asked.

"With the cook guy?" Mark asked, grinning at her. There was a sort of regret mingled with slight pain and disappointment in his expression, but no true anger or heartbreak. "How long have you been in love with him?"

Poppy swallowed hard. Her initial reaction was to lie, deny being in love with Swaggart, but she didn't. She simply took the time to choose her words with care.

"Seven years," she said.

"Seven years?" Mark exclaimed. "You've got to be kidding me!"

Poppy shook her head. "Since I was a freshman in high school," she answered.

"And he's in love with you?" Mark asked.

Poppy shook her head again, shrugging her shoulders as she answered, "I don't know. He seems to like me, I guess."

Poppy was startled when Mark began to laugh.

"You think it's funny?" she asked him. How cruel! How could he laugh at her being in love with Swaggart? Yet she supposed his reaction meant his own heart wasn't too damaged. She should be glad of it, but it angered her that he would mock her so openly.

"No, no, not at all," Mark said. "I'm just thinking…no wonder he seemed so ticked off about changing my tire! And no wonder he offered to change it—he wanted me out of there!"

"I'm sure he was just being nice," Poppy said. Still, what if Mark was right? What if Swaggart had been irritated by Mark's showing up at the restaurant? What if he had changed the tire just make sure Mark wouldn't be lingering where Poppy was?

"No way!" Mark assured her. "He was furious! I couldn't figure it out at the time—I figured he just thought I was a weenie because I didn't want to change my own tire. But now…" he said, chuckling. "That guy probably wanted to tear me apart."

"You don't seem to be mad at me at all," Poppy said. It was strange—the fact Mark seemed so calm.

"Oh, don't get me wrong," he said, smiling at her. "You're the kind of girl a guy never gets over."

Poppy felt herself blush as she prodded, "But…"

"But I'm humble enough to admit when I'm beaten," he said. "You've left a mark, Poppy—I won't lie to you—but somehow I'm okay. A little wounded, but nothing I can't recover from."

"Wow," Poppy breathed. "Your chivalrous nature sure made that a lot easier than I thought it would be."

"You're just trying to make me feel better," he said. "Though—I do have one question."

"What's that?" Poppy asked.

"Why did you ever go out with me in the first place? If you've been in love with this guy for seven years—why bother dating anybody else?" he asked.

Poppy sighed. It was odd that Mark should ask such a similar question as Swaggart had once before. It was a legitimate question, and he deserved an honest answer.

"I thought I needed to move beyond it," she told him. "I didn't think he'd ever see me as anything more than just another person in his life. I still don't know if he ever will. And you're so wonderful that I…"

"Thought I might be able to purge him from your soul?" Mark finished.

Poppy giggled. "It sounds so dramatic when you say it that way."

Mark chuckled and said, "Well, that's what you meant."

Poppy nodded.

"So now what?" Mark said, leaning back in his chair. "Now that I've been officially dumped…"

"Oh, don't say that," Poppy interrupted.

Mark laughed again. "I'm just teasing you, Poppy," he said. "Tell you what," he began, "let's just enjoy this perfect meal—prepared by Mr. Perfect back there in the kitchen—and be glad we met. What do you say?"

Poppy smiled at him. He was too good! She hoped there was a girl somewhere who would appreciate Mark's unique character—one that wasn't already in love with the most fabulous man on the face of the planet.

"Sounds good," she said.

❦

And it was a pleasant meal. Mark seemed quite painlessly reconciled. Poppy was glad he seemed to be unscathed. They talked about different sorts of things than they had before—more about his work, less about individual goals and experiences.

"Would you care for dessert?" the waiter asked as he cleared their plates.

"What is it tonight?" Mark asked.

"Dark chocolate torte, covered with a layer of ganache, and served with a raspberry puree on the side, sir," the waiter answered.

"Sounds fabulous! We'll have two," Mark said.

"And would you be so kind as to give this to Chef Moretti?" Poppy asked, handing the waiter a folded paper napkin. While Mark had gone to make a phone call, Poppy had taken a moment to write a note to Swaggart. She'd written, *I know you're back there! Perfect…as always!*

"How did you know the chef's name, madam? If I may ask?" the waiter said. "We were told he prefers to work with anonymity."

"I recognized his work," Poppy explained.

"Please give my compliments to the chef, as well," Mark said. "He's an incredible talent—and he changes a mean tire."

"Of course," the waiter said, quirking one puzzled eyebrow. "I'll be back shortly with your desserts."

"Thank you," Mark said. "So he's humble too?"

"Usually," Poppy said.

"I'm lucky I got as far as I did," Mark said.

Poppy smiled as he winked at her.

"A gentleman at one of the tables sends his compliments, chef," the waiter said as he entered the kitchen.

"Thanks," Swaggart mumbled, wishing the infernal event were over. He was tired and grouchy and hadn't been able to think of anything but Poppy and the weasel of a guy who wouldn't even get his hands dirty changing his own tire. It was a miracle he'd been able to instruct the kitchen staff well enough, instruct himself well enough, to pull off a good meal. Why was she out with him? Swaggart couldn't figure it. Hadn't he shown his hand? Hadn't he made it clear he wanted her? Yet he knew he hadn't—not in a way that would let her know for certain.

"And the lady with him asked that I give this to you," the waiter said, interrupting Swaggart's chaotic thoughts.

"What?" Swaggart asked.

"This," the waiter said handing a folded napkin to Swaggart.

Swaggart opened it, his frown curving to a grin as he read the words written in such familiar handwriting. Yes, he'd know Poppy's handwriting anywhere—he'd been reading it off order pages for years.

"'I know you're back there. Perfect...as always,'" Swaggart read. He looked to the waiter and smiled, saying, "Do you think she means the food was perfect or that I'm perfect?"

The waiter, whose name Swaggart couldn't remember all of a sudden, chuckled. "I don't know, but she's hot—so either way, you rock, man."

Swaggart laughed at the waiter's sudden change of demeanor.

"Well, if this lady is hot, with dark brown eyes, brown hair, and lips that make your mouth water," Swaggart began, "then wait just a minute before you take their dessert out. I'm assuming they're both having dessert."

"Yep," the waiter said.

Swaggart tucked the napkin with Poppy's note on it into his pocket. "Hey, Mike!" Swaggart called to one of the cooks he'd hired for the evening. "I'm glad we made that crème brûlée. Grab one out of the fridge for me, would you? And bring me a propane torch too, please."

Swaggart always kept several crème brûlée on hand, in case a guest complained about the planned desert. He knew Poppy loved crème brûlée more than almost any other fancy dessert, and here was his chance to let her know he knew it.

He'd pamper her with a little something special and then pack up his utensils and head for home. Swaggart usually stayed and helped in the cleaning up, even though he was paying other people to do it for him. But tonight, he'd leave early. He had no desire to see Poppy sitting out there with Mr. Perfect. In truth, he was afraid he might lose his cool, knock the guy senseless, throw Poppy over his shoulder, and carry her away. He knew it would be wiser to simply let her finish her date—because if one thing was for sure, it was that this date would be the last she ever had with anybody but him.

"The chef sends this to you, madam, with his personal compliments," the waiter said as he sat a beautiful crème brûlée on the table next to Poppy's chocolate torte.

"Thank you," Poppy said. "I love crème brûlée!"

"I'm thinking he knows that," Mark said, smiling.

Mark was amazed at himself—astonished that he wasn't simply furious or at least humiliated to the core. Yet he wasn't. Oh, certainly he knew what he was missing out on—Poppy Amore was a diamond nestled in a bucket full of coal. Still, he suspected that this Swaggart guy was about as in love with Poppy as any man was with any woman. For some reason, Mark was okay with it. He didn't, however, want to linger too long. If he lingered any longer with the beautiful Poppy Amore before him, he might not be okay with it.

"What do you say we eat dessert and then call it a night?" Mark asked.

Poppy was so relieved. She wanted nothing more than to go home and think about Swaggart. Mark had handled the whole situation so well—it was amazing in fact. And now that the truth was out, what reason did either one of them have to linger?

"That sounds great to me," Poppy said. "Though I do feel bad about your having spent so much on tickets to this."

Mark smiled, a guilty look owning his expression. "I expensed them," he said. "I had to come to this anyway, and I just thought it might be a way to impress you too."

Poppy giggled. "Well, at least you're honest," she said.

"Most of the time," Mark said.

Poppy sighed as she took the first bite of crème brûlée. It was marvelous! Rich and sweet, not very unlike Swaggart's kiss. Oh, how she hoped in those moments she would taste Swaggart's kiss again, feel his arms around her, see his handsome face every day for the rest of forever.

She thought of Swaggart there, in the kitchen, so close to where she sat. She smiled. He was so secretive about his "gigs," as he liked to call them. She wondered for a moment what he did with all the money he made from them. She wondered if he had any others lined up. If she volunteered to work for him during one, would he hire her?

As she walked with Mark toward his car twenty minutes later, Poppy wished she could simply turn and run back to the convention center. She just wanted to see Swaggart, just to see him, that was all. She would be happy with that—just one look at him before leaving.

She glanced over and saw his old pickup parked three spaces away from Mark's Beamer. It was proof she hadn't imagined the meal she'd eaten, hadn't imagined the special serving of crème brûlée he'd sent out to her.

"I saw that truck in the parking lot of your restaurant today," Mark said as he followed her gaze. "And I'm wondering—would you rather just skip the ride home with me and hitch a ride with the local Chef Extraordinaire?"

Of course she would rather ride home with Swaggart than with Mark! But how could she possibly admit it? Furthermore, what if Swaggart had plans or was too tired to give her a lift? She thought about it for a moment. If Swaggart were too busy, or if she chickened out in waiting for him all together, she had her cell—she could just call Whitney to come and get her.

"You really are a wonderful guy, Mark," Poppy said.

"Don't tell me you're going to say, 'You'll make someone a wonderful husband someday,'" he said, smiling at her.

Poppy laughed. "But you will."

"Just not you, I guess, huh?" he asked.

Poppy's smile faded. "No," she whispered.

"Well, can I at least beg one more good-night kiss?" Mark asked.

Instantly Poppy was nervous. She didn't want him to press her. It was over, and she just wanted it to be all the way over.

"A cheek will do," he added, obviously sensing her discomfort.

Poppy grinned and nodded. "Thanks for being so—"

"Oh, sheesh! Don't you dare give me the 'thanks for being so understanding' thing," he said. He smiled at her and added, "In fact, I'll make it easy for you." He took her face in his hands then, kissing her squarely on the right cheek.

"All right, that's enough!" Swaggart growled. He seemed to appear from nowhere, taking hold of the back of Mark's tux jacket and yanking him away from Poppy.

"Swaggart!" Poppy gasped. Her heart leapt in her chest, frenzied butterflies suddenly wildly looping-the-loop in her stomach.

"Hey, man!" Mark said, pulling out of Swaggart's grasp. "Cool off. I was just saying good bye."

"You've said good bye enough," Swaggart growled.

"Swaggart," Poppy said. Although she was delighted by his obvious jealousy, she was disturbed by the barely restrained violence she sensed in him. She stepped between Mark and Swaggart as Swaggart took an aggressive step toward Mark.

"I-I was wondering if you could give me a ride home, Swaggart," she said. She watched as Swaggart's angry glare left Mark and settled on her.

"A ride?" Swaggart asked.

"You win, man," Mark said, smiling at Poppy then. "I never even had a chance. Bye, Poppy," he said. Swaggart watched, obviously confused as Mark got into his car and drove away.

"Well?" Poppy asked when Swaggart looked back to her. "Can you give me a ride home?"

"What's going on?" Swaggart asked. "I thought you were out with this guy because you—"

"I went out with him because I had to tell him I couldn't go out with him anymore," Poppy said. Her heart was hammering so hard in her chest it hurt. She had to know! She had to know if Swaggart cared for her—truly, madly, and deeply cared for her the way she did him.

"Why?" Swaggart asked.

Poppy knew it was taking a minute for his anger to subside.

"Because…because you can't date someone…you *shouldn't* date someone when…when you only want to be with someone else," she managed. She was going to faint—she was sure of it! What would he do? What would he say? Would he tell her he only valued her as a friend? Would he tell her he wasn't ready to get serious with anyone?

"Who's the someone else you'd rather be with, baby?" he asked.

She looked away, to her feet, to the parking lot pavement beneath them—wondering how badly it would hurt when she fainted and fell to it.

When she felt his hand softly caress her cheek, she looked up to find him staring at her. His frown had faded, yet he didn't smile. Still, his eyes were warm and syrupy, alluring, mesmerizing.

"Is it me?" he asked.

Poppy nodded, feeling tears welling in her eyes.

"Why?" he asked. "Why me instead of that rich, handsome guy you just blew off?"

She would tell him! She would! Though it might mean the greatest heartache and pain she'd ever know.

"Because I love you," she whispered.

Poppy looked up to see Swaggart's brow pucker with a frown. He seemed to study her eyes, and when she tried to look away, he took her face between his strong hands, forcing her to look at him.

"You just said the 'L' word," he mumbled.

"I-I'm sorry, Swaggart," she stammered as her tears escaped her eyes and traveled over her cheeks. "I'm sorry...but I can't just..."

"You just said you love me," he mumbled.

"I'm sorry," Poppy whispered. "I didn't mean to..." He didn't love her! He didn't!

But just as Poppy was certain her heart would break in two, she gasped as the heated, moist flavor of Swaggart's mouth met her own. He was ravenous in kissing her—demanding, thirsting, passionate, and Poppy's heartache bowed to elation, euphoric bliss.

Abruptly, he broke the seal of their lips, the warm syrup of his eyes burning into her own. Taking her hand, he pulled her toward his pickup, pushing her back against it as his mouth endeavored to own hers entirely again. Poppy let her hands travel across the broad expanse of his shoulders, caress his neck, to finally be lost in the softness of his dark hair. Instantly, Swaggart's kiss deepened, his hands tightening around her waist until she thought her ribs might give way and break beneath the power of them.

After a time, his mouth left hers, lingering at her neck just below her ear.

"Say you're mine," he whispered. "Tell me you belong to me—because I love you, Poppy. I've loved you for so long."

Poppy felt more tears spill from her eyes as he drew her against him, embracing her and whispering words of confessed love to her.

"Tell me again," he whispered. "Tell me you finally love me too."

"I love you, Swaggart," she whispered. "I've loved you forever—I swear it."

He pulled back a little in order to look into her eyes. He smiled, and she noted the excess moisture in his eyes.

"Then kiss me because—I'm at heaven's door, inamorata," he said.

Poppy smiled, delighted by his quoting the song that had been playing in Good Ol' Days the night he'd first kissed her.

"I love you, Swaggart," she whispered.

"I love you, Poppy—inamorata," he said a moment before his lips met hers once more.

Swaggart Moretti loved her! Poppy could not believe it! She still feared she would wake up to find she'd dreamed it all. But as the warmth of Swaggart's kiss melded with her own, she knew no dream could be so perfect.

CHAPTER FIFTEEN

"All day," Swaggart said. He bent and quickly kissed her neck. "All day tomorrow—you're mine, remember?"

"All day—you're mine, remember?" Poppy said, smiling at him.

"I gotta get back to work," Swaggart said, kissing her quickly on the mouth once more. "Bobby? What are you burning in there?" Swaggart called to his cousin as he pushed the kitchen door open.

Poppy sighed. Her arms were covered in goose bumps, and she still couldn't believe any of it! She couldn't believe she'd confessed her love to Swaggart almost a week before. Tomorrow it would be a week—one week since Swaggart had told her he loved her in the parking lot of the convention center—and they had planned to spend the whole day together. Poppy marveled, still amazed at the fact she'd kissed Swaggart every day since their mutual confession. Kissing him every day only made her want to kiss him every hour, and she wondered how she would endure another eight hours without him when she went home after her shift.

"Wow!" Whitney said as Poppy approached the hostess podium. "Can you believe this crowd?" she asked.

"It is Friday night," Poppy reminded her friend.

"I know, but look how packed we are!" Whitney said.

"There seems to be a ton of regulars too," Poppy said. "I see Ms. Rhonda Andrews is here to check the eye-candy named Swaggart Moretti," she whispered.

"I wonder if she'll be disappointed when she finds out that you and Swaggart finally got your act together and—and got your act together?" Whitney teased.

"I don't know," Poppy said. "But I'll bet it won't stop her from flirting."

"Oh, I'm sure it won't," Whitney agreed. "David—party of five?" Whitney called.

Five young men looking to be about Swaggart's age stepped up to the podium. The tallest one said, "I'm David—and what's your name, cookie?"

Whitney plastered on a pleasant smile and said, "Actually, I'm Whitney. This is Poppy, and she'll be your server this evening."

"Oooo!" one of the other young men said. "Poppy!"

"Have fun," Whitney muttered to Poppy as she handed her five menus.

"If you'll follow me, gentlemen," Poppy said.

"To the ends of the earth, gorgeous," one of the young men said.

After seating the men at table ten, Poppy endured the nightmare of taking their order. They were the worst bunch of insinuating flirts Poppy had ever encountered in her two years at Good Ol' Days!

"I need the ring," Poppy told Whitney after delivering the drink orders to the five flirts at table ten. "I think these guys are drunk or something! They're awful!"

Whitney grimaced and whispered, "Brittany's got a rotten bunch of guys at table twelve, and I already gave her the ring."

"Oh, no," Poppy whined. "These guys are going to drive me crazy—I can already tell."

"Do you want to switch a table with Josh?" Whitney asked.

"Nah," Poppy said. "I can handle it."

Inhaling a deep breath of courage and resolve not to appear affected by the men's flirting, Poppy headed back to table ten.

"Any appetizers for you gentlemen this evening?" she asked.

"Are you on the appetizer menu, honey?" one of the men said.

"Nope," Poppy told them. "But we've got great chips and salsa."

"Hot salsa?" one of the men asked.

"Is the salsa as hot as you?" another asked.

"Did you gentlemen need another minute to look at the appetizer menu? I can come back in a minute?" Poppy said.

"Can't you just stay here with us?" one said.

"Yeah! Can't you just sit down here and—" one man began.

He was interrupted, however, when Swaggart said, "Hey, baby," and kissed her on the cheek.

Poppy smiled. Swaggart must've been greeting a Chef's Choice order and seen her struggling with the group of young men. How chivalrous!

"Baby, you left this on the counter—I wanted to make sure you didn't lose it," he said. Poppy smiled as he took her hand and slipped a ring onto her left ring finger.

"Thanks, baby," she said. She had no idea where Swaggart had gotten his hands on such a beautiful diamond solitaire, but she didn't care. She wondered for a moment if he'd begged it off Ms. Rhonda Andrews. No doubt Rhonda Andrews would do anything for the handsome chef of her choice.

"Man!" one of the men at table ten exclaimed with disappointment. "You mean you're married?"

"Engaged, actually," Swaggart said. "To yours truly."

"You're lucky, dude," one of the other young men said. "She's hot!"

"Thanks," Swaggart said. "I think so too." He smiled at Poppy and kissed her on the mouth, right there in front of everyone in the restaurant. "See you later, baby."

"Okay," Poppy said. She watched him head toward the kitchen, giggling with delight when he paused at Rhonda Andrew's table and did a little of his "Risqué Martin" routine.

"I guess we better lay off," one of the young men said. "I wouldn't want to mess with that guy."

"Probably not," Poppy said.

Swaggart's appearance had settled the young men at table ten way down. Each man gave Poppy their order without the flirtatious remarks she would've endured had Swaggart not shown up with another ring.

As she walked toward the kitchen to give Swaggart and Bobby table ten's orders, she paused and looked at the ring on her finger. It was so beautiful, and she wondered if it was a real diamond or just a cubic zirconia. Yet, in the dimmed light of the restaurant, the large gemstone shined and sparkled like nothing Poppy had ever seen. It sure looked real. She would have to be sure and thank whichever customer had lent it to Swaggart.

"Five Jiggys," she called over the order counter. "Two with fries, three with rings," she added.

"Got it," Bobby said.

"Where's Swaggart?" Poppy asked when she didn't see him behind the counter.

"Oh, he went back out to deliver Rhonda Andrew's Chef's Choice himself," Bobby said.

"Well, when he gets back, tell him thanks—he saved me from who knows what out there," Poppy said.

"I'm sure he did," Bobby said, smiling at Poppy.

As she headed back to the hostess podium to see who else needed seating, she saw Swaggart setting a beautiful plate of citrus chicken on the table in front of Rhonda Andrews. Poppy recognized the woman with Rhonda—she'd been there several times with her friend.

Swaggart said something to Rhonda and then turned to see Poppy approaching.

"You saved my bacon," Poppy whispered to him as he took hold of her arm as he passed. "Thanks."

"Well, you know how I love bacon," Swaggart said. "Especially yours."

Poppy felt herself blush—felt her arms and legs break out in goose bumps because of his simple touch.

"Where did you get it anyway?" she asked in a whisper.

"What? The ring?" Swaggart asked.

"Yeah. It's beautiful!" Poppy said. "Who gave it to you?"

"The jeweler," he said. "But he didn't give it to me—I bought it."

"The jeweler?" Poppy giggled.

"Yeah. The one on Holly Street downtown," Swaggart said. His eyes were warm and bright as he looked at her. She felt as if sweet, warm syrup were being drizzled over her.

"But why would you buy a…" Poppy's words were lost. As Dean Martin began to croon "You Belong to Me" over the restaurant's sound system, Swaggart took Poppy in his arms—in dance position. As he began to sway with her, Poppy's heart began to pound.

"Why would I buy a big diamond ring from a jeweler and then slip it on your finger, you mean?" he asked.

"Y-yeah," Poppy breathed.

"Because I want you to marry me, and I thought maybe an engagement ring would be a nice touch," Swaggart said.

Poppy couldn't breathe! She felt her knees give way beneath her, felt Swaggart's powerful arms go around her to keep her from slipping to the floor.

"Swaggart," Poppy said. "Are you…are you…" she stammered. This couldn't be happening. *Wake up, Poppy! Wake up!* she thought to herself.

"Will you marry me, Poppy?" he asked. Poppy stared at his mouth as he spoke. "I love you, and I want you to marry me. Will you?"

"Of course," Poppy said as tears flooded her cheeks. A sudden and powerful sobbing wracked her body for a moment until Swaggart gathered her into his arms, and she heard the cheers and whistles, the applause of the employees and patrons at Good Ol' Days.

"I love you, inamorata," Swaggart whispered against her neck.

"I love you, Swaggart," she cried in a whisper. "You have no idea how much." She laughed then as he picked her up, spinning her around several times before kissing her with such a passion she thought she might evaporate from the heat of it.

"We've only ever been on one date," she reminded him, as he swayed with her.

"We've been dating for two years," he told her. "Every day we worked here together. And if that's not enough—we can date while we're planning the wedding if you want."

Again the cheers erupted in the restaurant. It wasn't long before a throng of well-wishers had surrounded Poppy and Swaggart.

"Sorry for the hard time we gave you, Poppy," one of the flirtatious young men at table ten said as he hugged her. "He told us we had to make it look good."

Poppy laughed, wiping tears from her cheeks as Rhonda Andrews hugged her next.

"He's something else," Rhonda said. "You're a lucky girl."

"I know," Poppy said as more tears streamed down her face. She could hear people congratulating Swaggart—heard Bobby, Uncle Robert, and Mr. Dexter laughing and patting Swaggart on the back.

"Hey, girl!" Whitney said, wiping tears from her own cheeks. "What did I tell you? Dreams come true every day—sometimes you just have to wait awhile, that's all."

Poppy wiped the tears from her cheeks and hugged her beloved friend.

"Thanks, Whitney," Poppy said. "I know it was no accident that notebook made it to work in your bag that day."

"Consider me your fairy godmother," Whitney said, sniffling.

"Bobby!" Swaggart called above the noise. "You've got the kitchen for the rest of the night. We're out of here!"

Poppy gasped as Swaggart lifted her up in his arms then and headed for the front door. The applause of the crowd in Good Ol' Days echoed out into the parking lot as Swaggart carried her toward his pickup.

"I can't believe it," Poppy cried, burying her face in her hands as Swaggart let her feet drop to the pavement.

"What's not to believe?" he asked, kissing her cheek.

"That you really—that you really love me enough to…to…" she stammered, wiping the tears from her cheeks.

"You love me enough to—that's what's hard to believe," Swaggart said.

Poppy threw herself against his powerful body, broke into thrilling quivers as he embraced her. "Whitney was right," she said. "Dreams come true every day."

"Oh, Whitney's about to find out how true that really is," Swaggart chuckled.

"What do you mean?" Poppy asked, looking up at him. He wore the familiar expression of mischief she loved so much.

"Look," he said, turning her around to face the restaurant.

Poppy smiled at the happy scene before her—there it was, Good Ol' Days restaurant. As its windows glowed with warmth, the scene within brought more tears to her eyes. Families, couples, groups of friends—all smiling, laughing together. Some still seemed to be singing along with Dean Martin. Poppy giggled as she saw Mr. Dexter talking with Mrs. Peterson.

"It's beautiful," Poppy said.

"Watch the hostess podium," Swaggart chuckled.

From where they stood, Poppy had a perfect view of Good Ol' Days front door and the hostess podium. Someone had just stepped through the front door, and Whitney had her back to them as she spoke to Uncle Robert.

"Recognize anybody?" Swaggart said.

Poppy gasped as she recognized her cousin Greg as the man who had just entered the restaurant. She gasped again as she saw Whitney turn around to greet him, her face turning crimson as she realized who was standing in the restaurant.

"I don't know what it is with you two and wanting to kiss each other's cousins…" Swaggart began. "But I figured while we're at it, we might as well all be kissing cousins."

"Oh my heck!" Poppy exclaimed as she watched Greg reach out and gather Whitney into his arms. "He wouldn't!"

"Oh, he will. Believe me," Swaggart said. "I called him up yesterday and found out he's had a crush on Whitney forever."

Poppy's mouth dropped open as she watched Greg kiss Whitney then. It was no sweet little peck on the cheek either. Furthermore, she laughed when she saw Whitney's arms go around Greg's neck as she returned his kiss.

"Did I make any brownie points for that?" Swaggart asked.

Poppy glanced at the diamond engagement ring on her finger. Her tears of infinite joy renewed, and she looked up into the handsome face of Swaggart Moretti.

"Do you really belong to me?" she asked.

Swaggart tweaked her nose and smiled. "Heart, mind, body, and soul, baby," he said.

Smiling, Poppy ran her hands up over the white t-shirt covering his muscular torso to his shoulders and neck until at last her fingers were buried in the dark softness of his hair.

"I love you, Swaggart Moretti," she whispered.

"I love you, Poppy Moretti," he mumbled as his mouth found hers in a long, ravenous kiss.

"Dreams to Do list—part two," she whispered. "Item number one—kiss Swaggart Moretti forever."

"Okay," Swaggart said. And he kissed her.

EPILOGUE

Wally Dexter smiled as he watched little Amore Moretti scramble down from her car seat and out of the car. Every Friday morning, Poppy and Amore arrived at the restaurant to visit Swaggart and have breakfast with "Papa Wally," as Amore called him. As he watched the little dark-haired angel skip across the parking lot, holding tight to her mother's hand, Wally could hardly believe it had been four years since he'd turned Good Ol' Days over to Swaggart. He chuckled, remembering the night Swaggart had proposed to Poppy. What an event that had been! He chuckled again, remembering the way Poppy's mouth had dropped open when Swaggart informed her soon thereafter that the restaurant was theirs.

Wally sighed with satisfaction. He knew he'd done the right thing by giving the business to Swaggart. He shook his head, amazed at how well Good Ol' Days had done since—the incredible improvements and profits Swaggart had made. Yes—he was truly perfectly happy in that moment.

As Poppy pushed the door open, Amore ran headlong at Swaggart's grandfather, arms flung wide, giggles trailing like the sweetest sound on earth.

"Papa Wally!" Amore squealed as Wally gathered her into his arms. "We comed for breakfast!"

Poppy laughed at the pure mirth and delight in Wally's eyes as he hugged his great-granddaughter.

"Did you now?" Wally asked. "And what are we having?"

"Daddy's making pannycakes for us!" the beautiful little girl squealed. Poppy laughed, delighted by her daughter's adorable three-year-old verbiage.

"With syrup?" Wally asked.

"Mmm hmmm!" Amore said, her eyes widening with excitement. "And maybe stwabewwies!"

Wally laughed. "Sounds delicious!"

"I better see Daddy and wemind him about da stwabewwies!" Amore said, quickly kissing Wally on the cheek before skipping off toward the kitchen.

"Good morning, sweetheart," Wally said as Poppy hugged him. "She's up and at 'em bright and early."

"Good morning, Grandpa," Poppy said. "Good morning, Brittany," she said as Brittany stepped up to the hostess podium.

"Hey, Poppy! Amore's in the kitchen with Swaggart—he said to tell you," Brittany said. "She is the most adorable little girl I've ever seen."

"She looks like her daddy," Poppy said. And it was true! Amore was the feminine counterpart to her gorgeous daddy—the same soft, dark hair, the same brown eyes. Everyone noticed it, and she was a beautiful little girl. Poppy secretly hoped the baby boy due in a few months would resemble Swaggart too. She patted her tummy as the baby kicked, seeming to know his mother was thinking about him.

"Which table can we have, Brittany?" Wally asked.

"Table two is free, Mr. Dexter," Brittany said. "And I'm guessing you don't need any menus."

"Amore worked out the menu with Swaggart last night before she went to bed," Poppy explained. "She loves to talk menus with her daddy—I think she likes menus and recipes more than bedtime stories."

"So he's learning not to get her all wound up before bedtime?" Wally asked.

"Oh, no," Poppy explained following Wally to their table. "He still gets her wound up—it's just that now, he winds her back down too."

"Mommy!" Amore squealed, racing toward table two. "Daddy says today stwabewwies *and* bluebewwies!"

Poppy gasped, her eyes widening with dramatic excitement. "Wonderful! Do you think he's teasing us?"

Poppy giggled as Amore put her hands on her hips, tipped her head to one side, and said, "Mommy—you know Daddy nevew teases about stwabewwies."

"You're right. Daddy would never tease about strawberries," Poppy said.

"And he told me Auntie Whitney and Uncle Gweg and baby Jack will be eating wiff us too!" Amore said, clapping her hands with delight.

"Fun!" Poppy said, helping Amore to sit on the booster seat sitting on one chair.

"Oh, Mommy," Amore said, breathing a heavy sigh of pure joy, "I love dis place!"

"Me too, baby," Poppy said, kissing her daughter on the cheek. "Me too."

Poppy let her thoughts travel back for a moment. She'd always loved Good Ol' Days, even before she'd worked there. It seemed she'd always loved Swaggart too. She remembered the night he'd proposed to her—right there, not far from where she sat now. It had been the most beautiful, wonderful, fabulous moment of her life, and she could almost feel the atmosphere of the restaurant that night, almost hear the cheering and Dean Martin singing "You Belong to Me." She'd thought life could never be more wonderful than it had been in that very moment—but it was!

Poppy watched as Wally helped Amore open a small package of sugar, telling her to lick her finger and stick it into the package to make the sugar stick. She shook her head, unable to believe how truly wonderful life was! Certainly there were trials, heartaches, and stress—but the joy Poppy knew through her husband and little girl was infinite and indescribable. Soon there would be another Moretti seated at a table at Good Ol' Days each Friday morning for breakfast, and Poppy couldn't wait!

"Mmmm!" Amore sighed as she stuck her sugar-coated finger in the sugar.

Poppy couldn't believe she was allowing her daughter to eat a packet full of sugar—but how could she deny her little girl such a wonderful memory of her great-grandfather?

Glancing around her, Poppy noticed the regular Friday morning customers scattered throughout the restaurant. Swaggart swore to her that some of the Friday morning regulars showed up simply to see cute little Amore's reaction when her daddy brought out her breakfast.

Poppy guessed he was right when Rhonda Andrews mouthed, "She is sooooooooo beautiful," to Poppy as their eyes met.

"Thank you," Poppy mouthed in return.

"And who are these beautiful ladies sitting with my Grandpa at table two?" Swaggart asked, kissing Amore on the top of the head.

"It's us, silly Daddy," Amore giggled.

"Hey, baby," Swaggart said, kissing Poppy. Poppy couldn't help but sigh as his kiss lingered on her lips, warm, sweet, and so wonderfully familiar. "How are you feeling?"

"Fine," Poppy said, smiling at him. It was incredible—the way her stomach still thrilled with loop-the-loops each time she looked at him. Swaggart seemed to grow more handsome with every passing day, just as Poppy loved him more and more with each sunrise.

"Bobby's gonna bring our breakfast out any minute," Swaggart said to Amore.

"Then you bettew do it now, Daddy," Amore said, giggling and covering her mouth with one hand.

"Now?" Swaggart asked.

"You bettew, Daddy—befowe mowe people come in and see you," Amore giggled.

"Okay, but you have to do it with me," Swaggart said, lifting Amore out of her booster and standing her next to him. "Ask Mommy if she's ready."

"Awe you weady, Mommy?" Amore asked, giggling so hard she could hardly speak.

"You mean for the pancake dance?" Poppy asked. Amore nodded with nearly tangible excitement. "Okay then, I'm ready."

"Okay then—it's time for the pancake dance," Swaggart said, swiveling his hips in his signature "Risqué Martin" way.

Poppy and Wally both laughed so hard tears filled their eyes as Amore and her daddy wiggled their hips, performing their special pancake dance. Amore giggled and giggled, finally wrapping her arms around her daddy's leg in a delighted embrace.

"It worked, Amore! The pancake dance worked again. Look!" Poppy exclaimed, pointing to Bobby as he approached with two plates heaping with pancakes.

"It worked, Mommy! It worked!" Amore squealed, scrambling onto her booster again. "Will you eat wiff us, Daddy?" she asked.

"Of course, muffin," Swaggart said. He sat down in the chair next to Poppy, kissing her on the mouth once more.

"Daddy says Mommy tastes like cake, Papa Wally," Amore said in a loud whisper. "That's why he always kisses her so much."

"Is that so?" Wally chuckled.

"Here you go, Amore," Bobby said, placing a plate of pancakes in front of the little girl.

"Did my daddy make these, Uncle Bobby?" Amore asked.

"Of course," Bobby answered. "Here you go, Poppy. I'll get the others."

"Thanks, Bobby," Swaggart said.

"Look, Amore," Poppy exclaimed. "Mickey Mouse today!"

"I love the Mickey Mouse ones, Daddy," Amore said, dipping a finger in the syrup on her plate and licking it.

"I'm glad, baby," Swaggart said.

He looked at Poppy, and the incredible love evident in his eyes caused goose bumps to ripple over her arms.

"Your old buddy Mark was in here this morning," Swaggart said.

"How's he doing?" Poppy asked. Mark Lawson had been a regular customer at Good Ol' Days since the first night he'd eaten there almost four years before.

"Good," Swaggart said. "His new fiancé was with him." Poppy smiled as Swaggart propped one elbow on the back of her chair, caressing her cheek with the back of one hand.

"He's engaged? That's great!" Poppy said.

"Yep," Swaggart said, twisting a strand of hair around his index finger. "She seems like a really nice girl. They're getting married in June. They came in to ask me if I'd do their wedding dinner."

"You never do weddings," Poppy said. "You've always said they're too girlie."

Swaggart kissed her again and said, "Will you think I'm too girlie if I agree to do it for them?"

Poppy smiled and reached up, running her fingers through Swaggart's soft, brown, already tousled hair.

"You couldn't be girlie if you tried, Swaggart Moretti," Poppy told him. The warm syrup of his eyes mesmerized her. Oh how wonderful he was—what a dream come true her life had become. Poppy sighed as she leaned forward and kissed Swaggart.

"I love you," he whispered.

"I love you too," Poppy told him.

At that moment, the strains of an all-too-familiar song began via the restaurant's sound system. Poppy smiled as Amore jumped from her booster seat, tugging at Poppy's sleeve.

"Mommy! I think this is it! I think it's going to happen today!" Amore squealed.

"I think so!" Poppy giggled. In the next moment, she thought her darling little girl was going to fly apart at the seams as Dean Martin began to croon "That's Amore."

Instantly, every regular customer enjoying breakfast at Good Ol' Days began to applaud.

"Daddy! Daddy!" Amore giggled. "It's happening! It's my song!"

"It sure is, sweetie!" Swaggart laughed. He stood, picking up Amore and beginning to dance around the restaurant with her.

Poppy glanced to Wally then, her emotions welling as she saw him wiping tears from his smiling eyes. Greg, Whitney, and the baby arrived at that very moment and joined in the singing.

"Mommy!" Amore squealed. "Come on, Mommy!"

Poppy laughed and stood up to join them.

As Swaggart pulled her against him, Poppy caressed her daughter's happy face with one hand.

"Who knew it would be so perfect?" Swaggart said, smiling at her.

"We did," Poppy said, gazing into Swaggart's handsome face.

Wally Dexter brushed a tear from the corner of his eye. As he watched the joy evident all around, he sighed with contentment.

As Dean Martin and the patrons of Good Ol' Days sang "That's Amore," Wally nodded. For all that could be harsh and hard in life— still the good, the beautiful, the marvel of it was wonderful.

As Wally's grandson and his beautiful young family laughed, danced, and loved before him, Wally raised his hands in the air and laughed, "That's amore!"

AUTHOR'S NOTE

I honestly do not have any idea where to begin with this Author's Note! In preparation for *Kissing Cousins* going in to print, I read the book again (of course)—making little notes as I went about things, events, or people that had inspired me in writing it. When I finished, I couldn't believe how long the list was! Thus, I truly and seriously do not know where to begin.

Maybe I'll just fiddle around a minute or two—babble on about the story (which is always at the top of the list when people name their favorites of my books and e-books) and hope that, by some miracle, my brain finds a venue of order. (Ah ha ha ha! We all know what a miracle that would actually be!) I mean, in truth, it always sort of mystified me as to why *Kissing Cousins* is so often chosen as a favorite. However, about a year ago, I finally sat down and read *Kissing Cousins* again. I loved it! I had forgotten so much about it! And how I could ever have forgotten so much about it, I'll never know—because there is a *ton* of fun stuff woven around in there. Whether I did it subconsciously, consciously, or a little of both (which is my suspicion), there are little things in *Kissing Cousins* that just delighted me to find!

I will confess to you that when I write a story, I get a little tired of it by the end. Usually about halfway through a book, my next book will start tickling the corners of my mind. That's actually a bad thing because then I want to finish up whatever I'm currently working on so I can start the next one. Therefore, it's usually literally years before

I reread a book. Consequently and as I said (because I'm nothing if not redundant), I was always kind of astonished when groovy chicks like ourselves would tell me that *Kissing Cousins* is one of their favorites—until I reread it, that is. Furthermore, during my rereading, I realized the huge, huge, gargantuan mistake I had made while writing it—forgetting to have Swaggart Moretti strip off his shirt! Ahhhhhhhhhhhhhh!

You know the story behind the shirt thing, right?—that I had promised my close friends I would always remember them and prove it by having every one of my heroes in every one of my books manage to remove his shirt somehow during the course of the romantic adventure? Well, somehow I forgot to do that in *Kissing Cousins*! I totally remember thinking about it—thinking, "Oh! I can't forget to have Swaggart take his shirt off." But then I did forget! I think it was because Swaggart can so perfectly hold his own in just a t-shirt that it slipped my goofy mind. Anyway, as you now know, that little faux pas has been corrected. Yep—we have finally seen Swaggart without his shirt. Whew! Now I can sleep at night.

Which gives me an idea as to where to start this Author's Note—Swaggart's name. Personally, I really like Swaggart's name. Swaggart Moretti—love it! Actually, his full name is Swaggart *Dean* Moretti—don't want to forget to reveal the entirety of it, now do we? (Just for fun, see the etymology on Swaggart's page in the Characters Bio section of my blog.) When I was envisioning Swaggart's character (before I even began to write the actual story *Kissing Cousins*), it was obvious that he owned a very cool manner of walking—a swagger. My husband and both of my sons have a swagger or strut—very cool—and that's how Swaggart walks. It's not an intentional thing—not contrived, but natural. As a result, a little bell went off in my brain, and I suddenly knew Swaggart's name was Swaggart.

Swaggart Moretti has not only an awesome swagger, as well as a "massive chest" and "drop-dead gorgeous" looks, but he also has Italian heritage—evident in not only his dark hair and "chocolate brown" eyes but in his surname as well. I've always loved Italian last names, and Moretti echoed through my mind as naturally as Swaggart had. Swaggart Moretti—delicious! As for his middle name, Dean—well, I think that's an obvious little pun on his parents' part—because his paternal grandmother was over the moon for Dean Martin Italian love songs.

I've received some criticism concerning Swaggart's name—not much, but a little. Of course I always wonder why anyone would criticize anyone else's name in the first place—but beyond that, I just think his name is uber cool! Swaggart—Swaggart—Swaggart. It just rolls off your tongue like sweet, rich crème brûlée—mmmm! I love it!

Now, since we've discussed the history of Swaggart's name, let's investigate Poppy's, shall we? Poppy Amore is another name that some people scoff at—but that's her name—so why scoff? Poppy—a little flower—often red. First off all, I *love* poppy seed bread and muffins! When my daughter was in kindergarten, her teacher (awesome teacher, by the way!) gave me a poppy seed bread recipe that became our family's favorite sweet bread recipe, as well as a total family tradition! Over the years, I used the recipe to make muffins too (scrumptious!). (I should include the recipe in this Author's Note, huh? I think I will! *See the end of this note.) Anyway, I not only love poppy seed breads; I have a tender spot in my heart for poppies themselves—because of the little red poppies the Disabled America Veterans fashion and sell outside store fronts on or around Veteran's Day. Plus, I think it's a perky, fun name—Poppy! It makes me feel chipper and cheerful. Thus, when I realized that Poppy's name was indeed Poppy, I thought, "Perfect!"

As far as her surname is concerned (Amore)—it means a sense of great affection or love. How perfect is that? Not to mention the whole pun thing with the song "That's Amore," right? Too fun! Poppy Emelyn Amore—so sweet and lovable—I adore it!

Okay—now my brain is working (at last). The mere mention of the song "That's Amore" certainly brings me to one of my favorite (albeit trivial) things about *Kissing Cousins*—the music in Good Ol' Days Family Restaurant! If you close your eyes and listen, can't you totally hear Dean Martin crooning "Innamorata"? Ooo! What about

"Pretend" by Nat King Cole? And Ella Fitzgerald's rendition of "Dream a Little Dream of Me"? I'm all relaxed and romantical just listening to those songs in my mind!

I *love* old 30s, 40s, and 50s music! Sure, I love an abyss full of different styles and types of music—that's true. But when I want to relax and be dreamy, it's the old stuff I turn on. There's just something easy and restful about it, not to mention romantic—vintage music is *so* romantic! But back to the *Kissing Cousins* music—this was one of the first books I wrote in which I used a specific type of music and specific song titles to help set the mood in certain scenes. I mean, can't you just see the restaurant employees and patrons enjoying a round of "That's Amore"? Seriously! Or close your eyes and imagine Swaggart's Risqué Martin groove to "Sway"! Music is a wonderful mood embellisher. In fact, I'll go as far as to say that music itself actually sets the mood in any atmosphere in which it's used. Ambiance is created by many different elements, but sometimes music trumps all the rest! Thus, I love the way songs are woven through the scenes in *Kissing Cousins*.

And—on that note—I thought I might as well include what my band back in the 80s used to call a "tune list" for *Kissing Cousins*. Why not rummage around and gather together the following songs to create your own *Kissing Cousins* tune list? I find it's especially effective in the kitchen when I'm cooking. Maybe put your *Kissing Cousins* tune list together and make some poppy seed muffins! Mmmm! So here goes—the *Kissing Cousins* tune list:

"On an Evening in Roma" (Dean Martin)
"Did You Ever See a Dream Walking?" (Bing Crosby)
"That's Amore" (Dean Martin)
"Unforgettable" (Nat King Cole)
"Dream a Little Dream of Me" (Ella Fitzgerald)
"Stardust" (Nat King Cole)
"Kiss" (Dean Martin)
"Misty," 1960 Version (Ella Fitzgerald)
"Pretend" (Nat King Cole)

"Sway" (Dean Martin)
"Innamorata" (Dean Martin)
"You Belong to Me" (Dean Martin)

Next—you know the Dreams to Do lists Poppy and Whitney had? Well, being the ding dong ducky that I am, I had never heard of an actual "bucket list" when I wrote *Kissing Cousins*. I had always secreted kind of a silent, unwritten list in my mind of things I'd "like to do someday"—I think everyone does—but I'd never put a label on it until I wrote this book. As I thought about Poppy's and Whitney's lists, I realized that many of the things on their lists would be kind of difficult to accomplish—just like many of the things on mine. Therefore, I realized they were "Dreams to Do"—things that were fun, challenging to accomplish, and, of course, romantic—basically, things that were dreamy.

Naturally, I had to draw the ideas for Poppy's and Whitney's Dreams to Do lists from *somewhere*, so I drew them from the same place I draw a lot of ideas for my stories—my real life! Thus, I thought it might be kind of interesting for us to go over Whitney's and Poppy's lists and see which things on their lists are on my "Dream to Do" list—some of which I have already accomplished. What do you think? Are you game?

We'll start with Whitney's list. Is it okay if I just type it in and then we'll go over it after we've reviewed it? Okay—here goes—Whitney's Dreams to Do list:

1.   Kiss Greg Amore.
2.   See Bon Jovi in concert.
3.   Memorize "The Highwayman" by Alfred Noyes.
4.   Ride a train coast to coast.
5.   Visit *The Goonies* house in Oregon.
6.   Read all of Dickens's and Austen's works.
7.   Learn to crochet.
8.   Win a best-of-show ribbon in something.
9.   Learn to play the piano.

10. Visit the U.S.S. Arizona Memorial in Hawaii.
11. Visit Prince Edward Island, Canada.
12. See the Statue of Liberty.
13. Learn to swing dance.
14. Learn to surf.
15. Visit Mount Rushmore.
16. Shake hands with Michael Jordan.
17. See a tornado in real life.
18. Find a starfish while wandering along the beach.
19. Hike down into the Grand Canyon.
20. Donate my hair to Locks of Love.

What a list, huh? Now—and just for meaningless fun—I'll go through and elaborate a little on each enumerated dream to do, and we'll see where the idea came from. (Do I know how to I waste your time, or what?)

1. **Kiss Greg Amore.** In truth, this one is kind of a wishy-washy answer—that being, it was simply necessary for the story.
2. **See Bon Jovi in concert.** This had been on my personal Dreams to Do list for years! *And* in 2008 I checked *this* one off my list! It was an awesome concert! Kevin, my sons, and I saw Bon Jovi perform in Denver, and I will tell you that it was fabulous!
3. **Memorize "The Highwayman" by Alfred Noyes.** This is actually on my own Dreams to Do list. Haven't done it yet—and I stress the "yet," because I will get 'er done one day!
4. **Ride a train coast to coast.** This isn't on my list, but I know it would be on my mother's!
5. **Visit *The Goonies* house in Oregon.** *Totally* had been on my list for years and years and years! I checked this one of while we were living in Washington State—and I actually checked it off twice! The first time was with my "partner-in-crime" friend, Sheri. Oh, what a trip—*wonderful!* The second time was when Kevin and I took the kids down to Astoria, Oregon, and then

down to Canon Beach. Fabulous! I loved checking this one off! It sounds silly, but it was literally a dream come true for me.

6. **Read all of Dickens's and Austen's works.** This one is something I too would eventually like to do. However, it overwhelms me to think of it, so it's not officially on my list.

7. **Learn to crochet.** This one is on my list too! I want to find the time to have my mother-in-law teach me to crochet one day. I'm afraid crocheting is one of those skills of the past that will be lost to the world in the near future.

8. **Win a best-of-show ribbon in something.** Done! Sometime in the mid 1990s, I won multiple ribbons at the New Mexico State Fair for my cherry jelly, pralines, and other candy. However, one year I entered the First Lady's Candy Box contest (judged by the governor's wife) and won best-of-show! Fun!

9. **Learn to play the piano.** I actually stole this from my daughter's list. She managed to check this one off her list while in college!

10. **Visit the U.S.S. Arizona Memorial in Hawaii.** Another one taken from my own list. I'm really not that desperate to visit Hawaii, but I so badly want to visit this monument someday!

11. **Visit Prince Edward Island, Canada.** Any *Anne of Green Gables* fan probably has this one on her list—including me! Haven't managed it yet, though.

12. **See the Statue of Liberty.** This one actually has a funny story behind it…

One year (the summer of 2006), my youngest son, Trent (who was only 12 at the time), said this to me: "Mom…there are only two things I want to accomplish this summer when I'm out of school."

"What's that, honey?" I asked.

Holding up an index finger, Trent said, "Number one, I want to see the Statue of Liberty."

I was immediately overwhelmed! Where in the world had *that* come from? We had absolutely no plans to visit New York—ever! Still, not wanting to smash his dreams on the shore of Liberty Island, I said, "Okay. And what's the second thing?"

With an expression that was entirely sincere in its earnestness, Trent held up another finger to join the first one and announced, "And number two, I want to go to PetSmart."

Naturally I burst into laughter! How random! How far apart could two summer Dreams to Do be (and I don't mean just geographically)?

Chuckling, I assured him that I knew we could most likely accomplish one of his summer daydream activities—PetSmart. However, I explained that the Statue of Liberty order was a big one to fill, and we wouldn't be able to do it. He understood, of course, and just added seeing the Statue of Liberty to his own Dreams to Do list.

But the story doesn't end there. Low and behold, that June, shortly after summer vacation began, someone in our lives at the time decided that a group of us would be taking a trip back east with him and his family. (It's a long story, actually—and it was a requirement as part of Kevin's job at the time.) The trip was to be an American Revolution history tour—and New York was one of the stops! Can you even believe that? Further incredible was the fact that the only free day we had during the entire grueling trip was in New York City! So guess what? Our family hopped on the ol' Staton Island ferry and scuttled over to Liberty Island to fulfill Trent's dream! I mean, seriously—how many parents can manage to grant both of their child's summer vacation dream getaways? Yep—little Trent checked off both of his Dreams to Do that summer—because we made sure he got to PetSmart too!

13. **Learn to swing dance.** Yep—used to be on my Dreams to Do list, but now I'm pretty content to watch other people do it.
14. **Learn to surf.** Not at all on my list! This was just something random that popped into my mind.
15. **Visit Mount Rushmore.** I would love to visit Mount Rushmore someday! We only lived eight hours away when we lived in Colorado but never could find a time to go.

16. **Shake hands with Michael Jordan.** Another random one—but I figured my oldest son would probably have this one on his.

17. **See a tornado in real life.** This wasn't really a Dream to Do of mine, of course—but I did it anyway! When I was a teenager, our family was driving back to Albuquerque from Colorado Springs, and half an hour into our trip, we saw three "sisters" in the distance! We pulled over to watch them, of course (my family has always been more interested in the event itself than in safety), and it was simultaneously terrifying and mesmerizing! The three tornadoes were side by side, and as they'd take turns touching down, dirt and debris would kick up. I remember the sound too. So scary! I also remember wishing my parents would just get us all back in the car and drive on!

18. **Find a starfish while wandering along the beach.** Not necessarily a Dreams to Do—but I've done it! Clayton Beach in Bellingham, Washington—purple starfish—beautiful!

19. **Hike down into the Grand Canyon.** Not one of mine, but growing up I watched enough rerun episodes of *The Brady Bunch* to have this one pop into my mind.

20. **Donate my hair to Locks of Love.** My hair doesn't grow anything like must be necessary to do this one, but I've always thought it would be wonderful and admired peopled who have done it.

Are you still with me? Did you make it through all that? Do you think you can make it through Poppy's list now? I'm sorry it takes me so long to blab all this out, but here goes nothin'—here is Poppy's list:

1. Kiss (make out with) Swaggart Morretti.
2. Shake the hand of the President of the United States.
3. Memorize "The Lady of Shalott" by Tennyson.
4. Ride the rollercoaster at the top of the Stratosphere in Las Vegas.
5. Visit *The Goonies* house in Oregon.
6. Read all of Dickens's and Austen's works.

7. Ride a horse along the beach in Monterrey, California.
8. Receive a stamped postcard from Scotland.
9. Eat crawfish in New Orleans.
10. Sing the National Anthem at a college football game.
11. Visit Arlington National Cemetery.
12. Own a pair of Levi's 501 button-fly jeans.
13. Learn the five Latin ballroom dances.
14. Plant a rose garden.
15. Walk the ridgepole of an old Victorian home.
16. Have a chalk-artist do your portrait.
17. Spend eight hours in a Civil War cemetery.
18. Go fishing in Idaho.
19. Serve on a jury.
20. Photograph the Albuquerque International Balloon Fiesta.

And now to detail:

1. **Kiss (make out with) Swaggart Morretti.** I could spend days going over this one with you! Sure, it's an integral part of the story, but it does have a basis as well. How many of us have ever had a crush on a boy or man that we wish or wished we could kiss? Seriously! Probably like every one of us, right? Well, that's part of the reason for Poppy's #1 Dream to Do—the other part is this little real-life happening:

Several years ago there was a sweet, beautiful girl who had a crush on my oldest son, Mitch. He had a crush on her too—at first. But as adolescence always goes—we change. We learn things and begin to know who we are and what we want—and Mitch's return of the crush began to fade. Actually, it sort of disappeared because of some of the girl's behavior toward him and things (long, long, long story).

Anywho, when the dust had settled, and I thought the sweet girl had mended her heart a bit, she was sitting with me in my kitchen one day, and she said, "The only think I want in life is to kiss Mitchel!" Her little eyes were so sad and filled with tears. It made me cry. I could see the residual pain throbbing through her—the regret for the things she had done to drive Mitch away. My empathy for her was profound! Poor thing! I knew how she was feeling—and I knew that wish, that dream would never be fulfilled and that it would haunt the corners of her tender little heart her whole life long. It was her first scar—do you know what I mean? We all have them—things that still pinch our insides or make our stomachs queasy whenever we remember them. It still bothers me—even today! Oh, the girl is more beautiful than ever and happily married—but her heartfelt, honest, pain-stricken confession that day will weigh on me forever.

So, I had to take care of it—I had to soothe myself somehow. And I did—with Poppy's realization of her #1 dream coming true! For all of those of us who still have that one "never kissed him" regret—Poppy and Swaggart's making out in the restaurant for the first time is as much closure as I can offer us! Maybe that's why it's one of my favorite scenes in any book I've ever written! Maybe that's why so many of us choose it as a favorite scene—it's a little smidgen of closer for our scarred little hearts. What do you think?

2. **Shake the hand of the President of the United States.** Moving on (I'm all super sensitive now)…I've never really had a desire to do this—not in my lifetime anyway—but I figure someone has this on their list. Right?

3. **Memorize "The Lady of Shalott" by Tennyson.** Yipee ky-yay! Done! Yep, the summer of 2009 I checked this one off my list! Hmm…I better practice it a couple of times this week—I think I'm a little rusty.

4. **Ride the rollercoaster at the top of the Stratosphere in Las Vegas.** No, thank you! Not that I don't like rollercoasters—I do! But a rollercoaster up on the top of a building—no way!

5. **Visit *The Goonies* house in Oregon.** (See previous.)

6. **Read all of Dickens's and Austen's works.** (Also see previous.)

7. **Ride a horse along the beach in Monterrey, California.** In truth, I would rather ride a horse out across the beautiful deserts

of New Mexico—but the beach sounded more winsome, so I went there with it.

8. **Receive a stamped postcard from Scotland.** As you know, I *am* a deltiologist (that is, a collector of postcards), and though I do have postcards from Scotland, I do not have one that has actually been mailed from there. So I'm still waiting to check this one off.

9. **Eat crawfish in New Orleans.** Done! And delicious! I cannot even tell you how delicious boiled crawfish are when they're prepared correctly! Mmmmm!

10. **Sing the National Anthem at a college football game.** Just a random one…

11. **Visit Arlington National Cemetery.** *Totally* on my Dreams to Do list! Totally! I hope I can check this one off in just a few years.

12. **Own a pair of Levi's 501 button-fly jeans.** Done! Every pair of jeans I owned in 1984 was a pair of Levi's 501 button-fly jeans! I love that they're back now—and although my physique has changed too much to wear them, I love that Kevin and my boys can wear them!

13. **Learn the five Latin ballroom dances.** Again—just something I like to watch now.

14. **Plant a rose garden.** I had a friend who did this in Washington, and I always thought it was an admirable accomplishment—not to mention beautiful!

15. **Walk the ridgepole of an old Victorian home.** Would love to do this! Seriously!

16. **Have a chalk-artist do your portrait.** Just an idea I had from something I saw when we were in New Orleans once.

17. **Spend eight hours in a Civil War cemetery.** Eight hours would be the short end of the dream for me! I *love* cemeteries! Still, since no one loves them as much as I do, I don't know if I'll ever be able to check this one off unless I go by myself (heavy sigh).

18. **Go fishing in Idaho.** I was just thinking of my Idaho-born friend, Barbara, while writing, and this one popped into my mind.
19. **Serve on a jury.** Done! Grand jury, however—not trial jury. I found grand jury duty wildly interesting. I'd do it again in a heartbeat! However, trial jury—not so sure about that one.
20. **Photograph the Albuquerque International Balloon Fiesta.** Done! Over and over again! *Love* it!

I think you might be getting bored now—therefore, maybe I should wind this all down and just leave you with a few trivia snippets. (Are you breathing a huge "whew!" right about now? Sorry.)

After reading *Kissing Cousins* and reflecting on where certain inspirations for the story came from, I can honestly say that it is one of my personal favorites now too. If I took the time to bore you enough with everything in this book that links to something in real life, it would take forever! So, let's just say this—"Swaggart has *finally* taken off his shirt!"—and call it good, sleeping better in knowing my personal OCD in that writing regard is at rest at last. What do you say?

Now off you go to jot down your own Dreams to Do list. I hope it includes at least one kiss wish!

Kissing Cousins Trivia Snippets

Snippet #1—Verb+plural noun. I almost didn't title this book *Kissing Cousins* because I knew that everyone would assume it meant a thing—plural noun, kissing cousins. In truth (as you now know), it's mean to be read as verb+plural noun—meaning Poppy and Whitney want to kiss each other's cousins, not their own. Still, in the end I thought it might be a funny pun and play on words. Not sure if it was a good decision or a bad one, but it's too late now, right?

Snippet #2—To begin this snippet, here's a quote from *Kissing Cousins*, "You will go out with me again," Mark said. "And that wasn't a question." When I was in college, there was a boy in one of my pop/rock dance bands (an awesome bass guitarist!) who walked up to me one day and made this statement: "Marcia…you *will* be my girlfriend! I'll pick you up Saturday, and you *will* go to the Valentine's Day dance with me, and you *will* be my girlfriend." I thought, "Hmmm…what the heck!" All my friends had been telling me I should date this guy—he was ultra, ultra uber cool, played the bass, totally handsome. So, I went to the dance with him and became his girlfriend. Guess what—it was the only time I ever got cheated on and/or dumped! So, the moral to the story is that although it may seem romantic at the moment to have a guy step up and be all aggressive and take-the-bull-by-the-horns-ish, sometimes, if your heart's not in it, it might end badly.

Snippet #3—My darling friend Sandy is the fairy angel who introduced me to Jell-O Instant Cheesecake! Again, I was in college, and Sandy and I were roommates and bosom friends, and one day she pulls out a box of Jell-O Instant Cheesecake. Mind you, up to this point I hadn't even liked cheesecake (astonishing, I know)! However, one bit later, I was hooked! And I do mean hooked! Very often after that (more often than I'd like to admit), Sandy and I would whip up a Jell-O Instant Cheesecake at three or four in the morning, pop it in the fridge, and then get up at eight or nine a.m., cut it in half, and snarf the entire thing for breakfast! Yep—there you have the real-life inspiration for Poppy's and Whitney's breakfast cheesecake!

Snippet #4—Remember when Mark and Poppy stop at the little bistro during their Saturday all-day date? Well, here's my chicken salad recipe (served in pita bread)—the very one the bistro served them!

2 cups cooked chicken (diced)
2–3 Golden Delicious apples (peeled and finely chopped)
½ cup onion (finely chopped)
2–3 teaspoons celery seed
3 teaspoons sugar
½ teaspoon salt
½–¾ cup mayonnaise
6 pocket pita bread (cut in halves)

Mix chicken, apples, onion, celery seed, sugar, salt, and mayonnaise. Chill for two hours before serving in pita bread halves. Mmmm!

Snippet #4—"Italian cream spice cake," you ask? Back in the olden days—like, you know, 1999, 2000, 2001, etc.—each year when my friends "The Groovy Chicks" and I used to get together for our annual get-together, my friend Sheri would stop by a bakery she haunted in Salem, Oregon, pick up an Italian cream spice cake, and bring it to our reunion. There we would sit down around the table one night and eat giagantor pieces of the cake. It was seriously indiscernibly delicious! The sweet cream frosting was nothing less than ambrosial! Groovy Chick Karen's quote concerning the sweet cream frosting still echoes today: "Butter! Butter! Total butter!" The cake itself?—three layers of heavenly spice (I'm salivating at the mere memory)! Anyway, that's where the Italian cream spice cake Mark brings along on his and Poppy's picnic came from. (Type in http://www.gerryfrankskonditorei.com/ and search for Italian Crème Spice Cake—read the description, darling! You'll never be the same!)

Snippet #5—You may be asking, "John Williams? John Williams? Why in the world would you choose John Williams compositions as the amphitheater concert?" Simple—because I love John Williams movie soundtracks! To choose just a very, very few: *Sabrina* (the one with Harrison Ford), the first two *Harry Potter* movie soundtracks, the

1973 *Tom Sawyer* soundtrack, *Star Wars*, *Home Alone*, *Far and Away*, *Indiana Jones*…and do I really need to go on? Love John Williams!

Snippet #6—The quarter in the garbage disposal scene in *Kissing Cousins?*—inspired by actual events. I don't remember exactly how it happened—though I think I may have been cleaning out my purse and dumping cookie crumbs or something into the sink—when, "clink!"—a quarter fell into the garbage disposal and got stuck. Now, although my darling Kevin did not yell at me, I did know he was, shall was say, more than mildly frustrated. However, in the end, after a great struggle, an Allen wrench, and more, I asked, "Are you still mad at me about the garbage disposal?" Kevin just flipped me the quarter and said, "Nope. I guess we just learned that it doesn't take quarters." Ah ha ha ha! He's so witty!

Snippet #7—I love Scooby Doo! Every Saturday morning I would leap up out of bed and run in to turn on the TV to watch Scooby Doo (the original ones with the original theme song, mind you). I even remember watching Scooby Doo the day my sister was born. Why is that significant? Well, because I was seven years old and we had to drive two hours from our home in Downey, Idaho, to the hospital in Logan, Utah, and then wait in the waiting room for eight hours while my mom struggled to deliver her. And with all that going on—my most vivid memory of my sister's birth is watching Scooby Doo in the hospital waiting room! Groovy!

Snippet #7—You know the whole thing where Poppy feeds Swaggart the pudding? Yep—dream come true for me at age fourteen! I'd had a crush on this guy for two years—he was way older than me, so it was often hard to be in the running for his attention—do you know what I mean? Anyway, we were having a big family picnic at the park in downtown Albuquerque one summer, and one of the relay games was this: One person was blindfolded and given a plastic spoon and a pudding cup (which came in metal pop-lid cans then). A second person was blindfolded as well. Then, a third person would turn the two blindfolded people toward each other and try to instruct the one with the pudding and the plastic spoon how and where to feed the pudding to the other blindfolded one! I was the one feeding the pudding to the guy I liked! It was soooooooooo romantic! And he didn't even get mad when I ended up smearing it all over his face! Ooo! I think I have a photo of the very event! Hang on…Ah, yes! Here it is! That's me with the spoon, the pudding cup, and the braces on the left. There's my friend Amy trying to tell me where to put the spoon. It's harder than it looks! I looked at the date on the photo (November 1979), and as my son Trent would say, "Everyone back then looked like Luke Skywalker"—because of the haircut on the guy I liked. Oh, and don't worry—I did eventually turn sixteen and catch this guy's eye—had some very romantic tête-à-têtes along the way too! Closure—I like it!

Snippet #8—I'd never heard the term "date rut" before—not until a friend of mine mentioned it. I'm not sure if she coined the phrase itself, but she does *not* like it! I, on the other hand, *love* it! I love dinner and a movie (or a movie and dinner); it's my favorite date! Still, my friend refers to it as "date rut." Probably because she's so much more adventurous than I am in the restaurant regard, as well as not being as easily entertained as I am by movies. I do aspire to be more like her in tons of ways, but not where "date rut" is concerned. Thus, Poppy and Swaggart's date rut dates—perfect for me! (P.S. I love double features, and Kevin and I always share a box or two of Goobers during a movie too!)

Snippet #9—One year for Valentine's Day, Kevin handed me a card sealed in a big red envelope (very appropriate). When I opened the card, I found not only a very romantic printed sentiment but a hand-written one as well. There was also something else included. On the right inside cover of the card, Kevin had drawn a little coupon. It was very detailed—complete with a rectangle made of dotted lines. It was a coupon for "One Ruby Love Ring" of my choice from Kevin! Oh sure, I loved picking out the ring and the ring itself. I lost the ruby out of the ring a few years ago, and yes, I had it replaced. But to be completely honest, it's the coupon I treasure most! So, I know exactly how Poppy felt when Swaggart gave her the coupon he'd drawn on a napkin.

Snippet #10—I have been witness to Kevin's changing many tires in my lifetime—several for perfectly competent men. It always made me feel two things: (1) proud as punch that my husband was capable, courteous, and man enough to change tires for other people and (2) dismayed and detested with the men who stood by in their pretty clothes or with their soft little hands and watched him do it. It's just a hang-up I have, and I see it as one of Mark's failings in *Kissing Cousins*.

Snippet #11—As you've guessed by now, I think it's important that boys and men are well-rounded where movie viewing is concerned. (It sounds like an oxymoron to use *well-rounded* and *movie viewing* in the same sentence, doesn't it?) When my children were little, I always tried to even out the stuff they watched. For instance, if we watched a western or military-type movie that my daughter didn't particularly enjoy, then the next time we'd watch a romantic comedy or musical that perhaps the boys didn't enjoy as much (that's putting it mildly, of course). Thus, my daughter can appreciate an occasional shoot-'em-ups, and my boys can appreciate an occasional period drama.

One year, my oldest son learned that his mother's forcing him to endure Jane Austen–based movies really did pay off—and in a big way. In 2006, sometime after the most recent movie rendition of *Pride and Prejudice* was released, a bunch of girls took to calling Mitchel "Mr. Darcy." In their naiveté, they innocently assumed that Mitch had no idea why they had nicknamed him Mr. Darcy—no idea that is until one day when he remarked, "I know what you guys are talking about, you know." All the girls giggled—certain as they were that he couldn't possible know what they were talking about. But when he stated, "You're talking about *Pride and Prejudice*..." and then proceeded to tell them the entire plot of the movie, their mouths dropped open like gasping fish. Needless to say, he was all the more their Mr. Darcy after that. These same girls took a turn at wanting to dress Mitch up as a pirate for Halloween that year—complete with eyeliner. He kindly refused.

Snippet #12—In my mind, Mr. Dexter (Swaggart's grandfather) looks just like the man who plays Mr. Dunkin of Dunkin's Toy Chest in the movie *Home Alone 2: Lost in New York*! Furthermore, his first name, Wally, is a tribute to one of the movie star crushes of my youth, Wally Cleaver from the TV series *Leave it to Beaver*!

And at last, here we are—my poppy seed bread and muffin recipe! Mmmm—enjoy!

Poppy Seed Bread

3 cups flour
1 ¼ cups sugar
3 eggs
1 ½ cups milk
1 1/8 cups oil
1 ½ teaspoons baking powder
1 ½–2 tablespoons poppy seeds
1 ½ teaspoons vanilla extract
1 ½ teaspoons almond extract

Mix ingredients. Bake in two large loaf pans at 350 for 1 hour and 10–15 minutes, in four small loaf pans for 45–55 minutes, or in muffin tins for 15–18 minutes.
Let bread cool for 10 minutes and drizzle with orange glaze.

Orange Glaze

¼ cup orange juice
½ cup sugar
½ teaspoon vanilla
½ teaspoon almond extract

Let glaze soak into bread before removing from pans.

My everlasting admiration, gratitude and love...
To my husband, Kevin...
My inspiration...
My heart's desire...
The man of my every dream!

ABOUT THE AUTHOR

Marcia Lynn McClure's intoxicating succession of novels, novellas, and e-books—including *The Visions of Ransom Lake*, *A Crimson Frost*, *The Rogue Knight*, and most recently *The Pirate Ruse*—has established her as one of the most favored and engaging authors of true romance. Her unprecedented forte in weaving captivating stories of western, medieval, regency, and contemporary amour void of brusque intimacy has earned her the title "The Queen of Kissing."

Marcia, who was born in Albuquerque, New Mexico, has spent her life intrigued with people, history, love, and romance. A wife, mother, grandmother, family historian, poet, and author, Marcia Lynn McClure spins her tales of splendor for the sake of offering respite through the beauty, mirth, and delight of a worthwhile and wonderful story.

BIBLIOGRAPHY

Beneath the Honeysuckle Vine
A Better Reason to Fall in Love
The Bewitching of Amoretta Ipswich
Born for Thorton's Sake
The Chimney Sweep Charm
A Crimson Frost
Daydreams
Desert Fire
Divine Deception
Dusty Britches
The Fragrance of her Name
The Haunting of Autumn Lake
The Heavenly Surrender
The Highwayman of Tanglewood
Kiss in the Dark
Kissing Cousins
The Light of the Lovers' Moon
Love Me
The McCall Trilogy
Midnight Masquerade
An Old-Fashioned Romance
One Classic Latin Lover, Please
The Pirate Ruse
The Prairie Prince
The Rogue Knight
Romantic Vignettes-The Anthology of Premiere Novellas
Saphyre Snow
Shackles of Honor
Sudden Storms
Sweet Cherry Ray
Take a Walk With Me
The Tide of the Mermaid Tears
The Time of Aspen Falls